To my sister, Vern
and to my beloved town of Fernie

© Copyright 2004 Pegeen Brennan. All rights reserved.

No part of this publication may be reproduced, stored in a retrieval system, or transmitted, in any form or by any means, electronic, mechanical, photocopying, recording, or otherwise, without the written prior permission of the author.

Printed in Victoria, Canada

National Library of Canada Cataloguing in Publication Data

A cataloguing record for this book that includes the U.S. Library of Congress Classification number, the Library of Congress Call number and the Dewey Decimal cataloguing code is available from the National Library of Canada. The complete cataloguing record can be obtained from the National Library's online database at: www.nlc-bnc.ca/amicus/index-e.html

ISBN 1-4120-1426-3

TRAFFORD

This book was published *on-demand* in cooperation with Trafford Publishing.
On-demand publishing is a unique process and service of making a book available for retail sale to the public taking advantage of on-demand manufacturing and Internet marketing.
On-demand publishing includes promotions, retail sales, manufacturing, order fulfilment, accounting and collecting royalties on behalf of the author.

Suite 6E, 2333 Government St., Victoria, B.C. V8T 4P4, CANADA
Phone   250-383-6864   Toll-free   1-888-232-4444 (Canada & US)
Fax   250-383-6804   E-mail   sales@trafford.com
Web site   www.trafford.com   TRAFFORD PUBLISHING IS A DIVISION OF TRAFFORD HOLDINGS LTD.
Trafford Catalogue #03-1804   www.trafford.com/robots/03-1804.html

*For my niece and nephew,
Sharon and Cec

with my love*

Big Rock Candy Town

Pegeen Brennan

Pegeen Brennan

Kilpoola Books

Acknowledgements:

I appreciate the help afforded by the Fernie Historical Association's book, *Backtracking with Fernie and District Historical Society*, which allowed me to fill in some factual information about the town.

The two pictures of Trinity Mountain (The Three Sisters) are from oil paintings done by the late Vicki Kucera, a talented artist who spent all of her life in the Fernie area.

I have used names of families who lived in Fernie in the Fifties, but in no case do those names represent the actual people. All characters are fictitious.

A special thanks to Meltem Cankaya. Her expertise and dedication made this publication possible.

Photo of author by her husband, Lee Whitehead.

Contents

BEGINNING:	Babe and Blaze	1
Chapter One	Books	2
Chapter Two	The Pass	5
Chapter Three	Coal Dust	9
Chapter Four	Lotus Flower Game	13
A	Pain	18
Chapter Five	Mountains	21
Press	Mac	26
Chapter Six	Mountains, Hotels	29
B	Lacework	35
Chapter Seven	Family	41
Press	Filler	47
Chapter Eight	Names	49
Chapter Nine	Talking Horses	53
Chapter Ten	Lotus Game II	56
Chapter Eleven	Blackie	58
Press	Big Game	62
Chapter Twelve	Expectations	64
Chapter Thirteen	Under Fernie Eyes	69
Chapter Fourteen	Christmas	73
C	Bearhunt	78
Chapter Fifteen	Dance	82
Chapter Sixteen	Italian Experience	86
Press	The Quail Block	93

MIDDLE: The Town		95
	Sun	96
	Lotus	102
	Saturn	105
	Jupiter	108
	Mercury	115
	Venus	123
	Moon	128
	Mars	132
	Diana	141
END: Blaze and Babe		143
Chapter One	Doors	144
Chapter Two	Boyfriends	148
Chapter Three	Hospital Experience	158
Chapter Four	Departure	166
A	Goddess of the North	170
Chapter Five	Abandonment	175
Press	Convergence	184
Chapter Six	Interviews	189
B	Fernie Bakery	195
Chapter Seven	By Mail	200
Press	Kissin' Cousins	205

Chapter Eight	Wedding Plans	208
Chapter Nine	Apology	214
Chapter Ten	Orillia	218
Chapter Eleven	Unwritten Letter	224
Press	The Arena	228
Chapter Twelve	Unread Story	231
Chapter Thirteen	Mine Talk	239
Chapter Fourteen	Blackie Speaks	246
C	To the Ballpark	253
Chapter Fifteen	Blaze Speaks	257
Chapter Sixteen	Winter Night	264
Press	Coming Clean	285

BEGINNING

Babe and Blaze

CHAPTER ONE

BOOKS

One of the last things Blaze did before she left for the coast was to sort through all her books. She came stumbling into my room at Arbuckles', bent over a colourful armful – red, blue, brown, green, all hardbacks — which she dumped on my bed. "Here you are," she said. She straightened up tall, squeezing a thumb into each side of her waist, her fingers edging up and down her back, I guess to ease some ache that was there. "You read all these. Every one." She jerked her head to one side, to swing her long hair away from her face, and looked at me intently. "And while you're reading them, remember everything I've told you about building a story, because you're the one who has to write it down." She looked off, out through my one little window, and let out a long breath. "Someone just has to write my story."

She sat down beside the books, and some of the top ones slid over against her. She picked up a slim volume with a blue and white cover. "Here's the one I told you about. It explains everything about style. See?" She opened the book at one of the front pages, the one that said "Contents" at the top. "See? It's all here." She moved her finger from one heading to another. "Here's a chapter on how setting works, one on character, one on point of view (that's the same as narration), and one on structure, or framework; and then it goes on to tell you about imagery and all different figures of speech. There's even a chapter on how to create suspense. And see? Here at the bottom? A section explaining all the literary terms. With examples even."

My eyes followed her finger as I bent over the book in her lap. A squarish dark block seemed to move into my head from somewhere and lodge right in the middle of my brain. "But I don't know anything about all this," I started to say in self-defence. "How can I write any..."

"Of course you do. Of course you can." Blaze flipped the book shut and handed it to me. "It's all in here." Then she turned to the other books on the bed, some with their spines up, some with their page edges toward us. "And in there. Just read, read, read. And check with those chapters as you go along. And remember everything I've told you."

"But why can't you do it? You're the one who knows everything that happened." The dark square was expanding in my head, trying to push black fingers out through my eyes.

Blaze slipped an arm around my shoulder. "It's not just a question of knowing what happened. It's that I won't be in any frame of mind to concentrate on it. And anyway, I'm too close to it. Too involved." She looked hard into my eyes. I was sure she would see those dark wet things poking out through my pupils. She squeezed my shoulder. "Come on, Babe. Don't start crying on me. You can do it. Just take your time, and when you've finished all the reading, you'll know how. At least, you'll see how these authors handle everything. You don't have to do it their way. You can set it down however it comes to you. You'll just find your own way, your own style." She jerked her thumb toward the table under the window. "And you do have my typewriter."

So that's the way it was. Blaze left with one medium-sized suitcase. She left the apartment, she left the town; she left me with that impossible job — that impossible pile of books, with only one skinny little how-to text to help me.

But that was a long time ago. Thank goodness I had lots of time and no interruptions. My office job at the Coal Company kept me busy during the daytime, but I was free most evenings and weekends. No one bothered me much in my room. Mrs. Arbuckle just muttered, if I happened to see her in the hall or on the front porch, about how much some people sleep when they should be out getting fresh air and going to dances, and a few other things I didn't catch — about boys, I think.

And thank goodness it was winter. I had never let on to anyone when I came back to town that I knew how to ski, and I managed to get myself off the bowling team. So now I have finished the reading. The great irony (I now know what irony is; that is, I can "appreciate certain reversals, when something turns out to be opposite from what is expected or people are opposite from what they appear to be") — yes, the great irony is that Blaze was the one destined to be a writer, the one with two years of evening courses at university, the one with the image of being an author and everything, the one who'd done part of a creative writing correspondence course even, whereas I, the younger sister who was just out of business college, the one with little knowledge about language and even less about literature, who never had any desire to be anything special, am now supposed to be ready to start writing *her* story. You have to admit that is irony.

CHAPTER TWO

THE PASS

Something I realized as I read through all those books, mostly novels, is that this cannot be Blaze's story only. For one thing, I have to work in the setting, and to do that I have to bring in the town and, of course, its people. In some of the books written earlier, I noticed that often the writer doesn't name the place. He will say "In the town of M___ there once lived," or "Close to the city of B___ lay the village of W___." I can't see any reason for not giving the full name, unless maybe he was afraid that the people of that town, if they knew it was their town, would start thinking the story was about them and get upset and maybe even sue him for slander, or something like that. And Blaze isn't here for me to ask, so I'll just have to do what she told me: set it down however it comes; find my own way.

Well, first of all, what I feel is that I need someone specific to talk to — an audience, as the book says. And if I make that audience the people of the town, or our own family, I won't be able to do it. There are too many things I just couldn't tell. So I am going to talk right to the people who are reading this. But I won't call you "Dear Reader" the way some of the old writers did. I'll just call you YOU (capitalized). That way YOU will know it means YOU, that it's not just some generalized use of the word.

So now I can go on and tell YOU about the town where this story takes place. Its name is Fernie. Remember, that is its real name. It is a town high (altitude: 3,305 feet) in the Rocky Mountains of southeastern British Columbia; in fact, its location — thirty miles from the U.S. border and about the same fom Alberta to the east — figures importantly in how the town feels about itself. In a couple of instances it was left off the provincial map altogether; in another, it was actually shown as being located in Alberta — somewhere between Lundbreck and Pincher Creek. For a while there was a half-hearted movement to secede from B.C. and declare that the town was, in fact, Fernie, Alberta, but nothing came of it. The three thousand and some inhabitants just continued to feel miffed, certain that their little town, hidden away in the mountains of the East Kootenays, was an intentionally neglected spot in the southeastern corner of the province.

But location isn't all that's important in a town. I need to describe Fernie so that YOU can see it, even feel it (YOU can fill in with the other senses if YOU want), and the best way is maybe to tell you how it hit me when I first came here. There is only one CPR daily passenger train that comes into Fernie from the East. And on one particular day, Blaze and I were on it. That was some years ago: September, a Labour Day weekend.

From the time we entered the Crowsnest Pass from the Alberta side, after chugging by Crowsnest Mountain itself, I kept alternating from looking out our window, to standing to see out the other side, to pushing out through the heavy doors into the space between the cars, all so I wouldn't miss any of the mountains. I was desperate to see all of each one, top to bottom, and I wanted to see how they joined one to another to make whole ranges — clear-cut and brilliant up close, misty and indistinct in the distance.

As I plunked back down on the seat, for maybe the sixteenth time, Blaze hardly looked up from the crossword she was doing but I heard her softly humming. On the way out, all across the prairies, she would look at me from time to time with a mock sad expression and start singing in a mock sad way, "Gee but I want to go, back to Ontario, Gee but I want to go home."

That was because I had never been out of Ontario before. Just because she had been born in B.C. and had this image of herself returning to her mountains, her homeland, she was okay. But I guess she knew I was already getting homesick and was trying to josh me out of it. Her singing that song made me a bit mad, but I really couldn't say much since it had been my idea that the two of us go to Fernie in the first place. Now the humming was a different tune and even though she was still doing the crossword — I saw her fill in *acer* for "maple genus" of sixteen down — she was quietly singing: "The bluebird sings where the lemonade springs, in the Big Rock Candy Mountains."

I grabbed the newspaper out of her hand then, and she didn't even try to get it back. She just shoved the pencil over her ear, threw one arm around my shoulders, pushed my face up to the window and put hers close beside it. And we stared at the mountains together as we sang:

> Oh I want to go
> Where there ain't no snow
> Where the winds don't blow
> In the Big Rock Candy Mountains.

Mountain after mountain, range after range, and everything clear and crisp all around them. You'd think the green wooded slopes and the sometimes bare, sometimes snowy, peaks had been precisely etched onto an expanse of blue marble. And it was like that all through the Pass. Nothing but trees on each side of the track, foreground for the almost vertical slopes. Once in a while an opening where a creek slashed down a draw. And, in places, the pale beginnings of fall yellowing where there were stands of poplar.

Suddenly there was a clearing — space for a small station with the sign "Hosmer" on it, but the train didn't stop. From there on, though, we were slowing down, and the trees began to give way to open spaces, straggly grass and low bushes, and a few buildings began to appear — a scrawny unpainted house, a hay shed half full of bales — and a scattering of red cattle grazing in a field.

Blaze and I gathered up our jackets, and magazines, and reached for our suitcases — let them slide off the overhead rack, felt them jolt our arms out straight as we took their weight close to the floor. None of the other passengers paid any attention. We were the only ones getting off.

CHAPTER THREE

COAL DUST

Our dad and two of the children (the boys) met us at the station, but, since I am still telling YOU about setting, I'm not going to describe them yet or give any details about our relationship. That can wait until I get to the part on character. I know that experienced authors can handle setting and character and plot all at once. But, as YOU know, I am a very inexperienced writer, so, for this first time, I'll just do them separately. Maybe later it will come together better.

Even before the train pulled out again, we walked back alongside it and, once past the last car, stepped up over the rail and made our way along the tracks. Although the air at that altitude was crisp and cool, even on such a sunny day, there was an acrid smell that I couldn't place. Then, noticing that I kept having to avoid black chunks that were scattered over the ties underfoot, I realized it was the smell of coal. I saw that the track bed itself was made of granular stuff that was black also. At every step a little cloud of black puffed up. We were walking on coal dust.

To our right was the flat open space of the railway yard. At the far side of it, in front of the line of trees at the bottom of a high hill — so high that the top of the mountain behind was barely showing above it — was a row of what looked like domes. My first thought was igloos, but it was a fleeting, laughable thought, for the domes were reddish-coloured, seemingly made of brick and, anyway, it was too warm for snow. I would have liked to ask what they had been, for I could see that they were no longer in use, many of them with their tops fallen in, some with their arched entrances crumbling, most of them with weeds and brush growing out between the bricks. But Blaze was keeping up such a chatter, if not with our father, then with one or the other of the children, that there was no opportunity.

On our left a street ran parallel to the tracks. A sign at the end of one of the blocks said "Baker Avenue." There was a row of houses but only along the far side. The near side was open, no doubt because that land was railroad property. Most of the houses were grey except where there were bits of paint still showing — pale green or pink. One set of windows still had a fine line of red on its sills. But most noticeable was the number of extra buildings — a lean-to or separate shacks — on each lot. Through some of the open doors I could see stacks of firewood, piles of coal, various tools such as rakes, shovels, axes. Most of the gates swung on one hinge. In all of the yards, weeds stood everywhere, even crowded against the squares of wire of the front fences.

But that dismal street was just the immediate scene. Looking between the houses, or over them, at least beyond them, I saw that Fernie was surrounded by mountains. (I was tempted to say it was "cradled in the mountains" but that's a term I heard some CBC reporter use about the town at a later date, so they wouldn't have been my own words.) As I said, there were mountains all around. Not up close but at a comfortable distance so that you could look at them all, one by one, by just turning your body the full three hundred and sixty degrees, without even raising your head.

So, to my right was that one wide peak that was hardly visible over the high hill. To its right, at some distance (imagine beginning to turn in a clockwise direction) was what would have been an ordinary-looking treed mountain except that on top it rose into a squarish fortresslike structure that showed, especially on its vertical sides, that it was made of reddish rock. There was a fringe of trees on its very top. Standing against the sky, it looked like a gathering of giant soldiers, armed with pikes or staves or long bows.

Next came an extended range. Mountain after mountain, one superimposed on the next, looking very much like a long line of elephants, head to flank, their massive backs curved against the sky. The right end of the range left off the elephant image to rise up into individual rock peaks far in the distance.

Right again, there loomed a mountain (I say *loomed* because it was the closest mountain to the town and therefore appeared much bigger than the others) with rather gentle green slopes and a fairly flat top. Not much rock showed on it. Although I knew the green must be trees and thick brush, it gave the appearance of being grassy and meadowlike.

The next mountains were the most impressive. They were a group of three, each distinctly different in size and shape, thus forming a dramatic configuration. Anyone seeing them, would easily guess that their name would have something to do with threeness. To the right of them was a broadfaced closer peak.

Then away in the distance, along the valley, standing alone, was an all-rock mountain, its face, with its many craggy, shadowed patterns, turned toward the town.

And that brings us full circle. Eight mountains — or groupings of mountains — in all.

I realize I have not described all of them in detail. There will be time for that later when I start relating them to some of the characters and events. For now, I want YOU to experience the feeling of being surrounded that I had when I first saw Fernie. It was a closed-in feeling, not so much of restriction as of protection and comfort.

And I must not forget to mention the river. I saw it the next day. It wound down the valley, along the highway and under it in two places. It wasn't the slow, dark-watered kind of river I was used to in Ontario; it was clear, fast water, running for the most part, shallow, over grey gravel beds. More speed, more light. I would like to say that it too surrounded the town, but it did not. Rather, it cut Fernie in two. Actually it cut it into three parts.

So the mountains enclosed the town, the river divided it. That is my beginning image.

CHAPTER FOUR

LOTUS FLOWER GAME

Before I get into the story, there are some other things (the book calls them devices) to consider. One is narration, or point of view. So far, I realize, I have been using the first-person; that is, *I am talking to YOU*. But everything I've read about first-person — and I remember Blaze telling me too - warns how limiting it is. If I stick to using "I" all the time, there are a lot of things I won't be able to tell, at least I can't tell them legitimately unless either I know them from my own experience or I can justify my knowing by saying how I found out about them. I've seen how some of the writers who use first-person get bogged down in their attempt to show how the narrator got the information. They have to resort to a second voice (someone explaining things to the narrator) or to hearsay, imaginings, conjecture, letters, overheard conversations. It becomes very awkward — and very complicated.

So, remembering Blaze's advice about finding my own way, setting it down however it comes to me, I think I've found a solution. Instead of saying how I found out stuff that I wasn't in on, I'll just have the narrator disappear. I really don't see why YOU would be interested in how I happen to know what I know; YOU just want to hear the story. If it's important YOU can fill in for YOURSELF (even if it's just conjecture) how I learned someone else's story. That way YOU will be using YOUR imagination more, and that's what reading is about anyway. This method will simplify things for me and it will be less boring for YOU.

I have heard that a lot of writers say that once they get going on a story, the characters "just take over" and "seem to write themselves." I can't understand how that works. But since this is my first story, who knows? If it does occur, all to the good. If any character wants to take over and write his or her own story, I'm all for letting it happen.

The other matter is framework, how to structure the story. Blaze explained that to me, and there's a bit about it in the little text, but mostly what I learned about it came from my reading. The first time I noticed framework was in a novel about a court case. It was a lawsuit involving a whole lot of potential inheritors in England and it went on generation after generation without getting resolved. By the end, most of the beneficiaries were either dead or insane and all the inheritance had been used up in court costs. As I got into the story, I realized that the courtroom, the case itself, was at the very centre of everything that happened. Various storylines reached out, from the centre, into the interconnecting lives of the many people, into the many parts of London, into all the information that made the story work. Before I was even halfway through the book, I had this picture of a giant web: lines going out from the centre, circular lines connecting the first lines in an everwidening network — and always, at the centre, like a watchful, relentless spider, was the court, controlling everyone. That was maybe the most noticeable example.

Some writers use the back-and-forth method: they tell you something about one person or group — get the story started — then drop that and go to another person or group and get that story going. They keep switching from one to the other, usually working up to an exciting point then dropping that to pick up the other story. Another way is to work the story around the seasons: spring is usually the beginning when everything is young, fresh, innocent; then the story moves into summer with some kind of problem or difficulty facing the characters. By fall, it's the middle of the turmoil; and then the ending, in winter, shows the outcome — sometimes resolution, sometimes death — with usually a hint, at the very end, of starting over again.

Another way is to form the story into various shapes. The triangle is popular: three people involved in something, or three places with their inhabitants interacting. The square too — with four people and/or settings as above. I can't cite examples, but it would be possible to work around a pentagon or a figure with any number of sides, even a rhomboid. It doesn't take much imagination to see how any of these shapes might form an appropriate base. Then there are the more usual patternings. The story may be worked out in parallels as in the back-and-forth method I mentioned (vertical lines), or in a layered way — one plot or set of characters subservient to the main plot and characters (horizontal lines).

But when I thought of the story I had to tell, I considered all the orderings I have observed but no matter how hard I tried I couldn't make them fit. One might work fine for the plot, another might be good for the characters, another for the setting. But when I thought of the whole in a specific way — Blaze's story set in Fernie with all the ramifications of the town, the areas surrounding the town, the stories of the people of the town, Blaze herself, the husband she ended up with, our father, the rest of the family, and even me — I saw that none of them would do.

Then I hit on just the right thing. I found it in an accidental way, or I should say it just came to me with no planning. It was sent by my friend Marie back in Orillia. She said she had found it in an import shop in Toronto. It wasn't my birthday or anything. It had simply intrigued her, and she got one for herself and one for me. It is called the Lotus Flower Game, and with it was a little slip of paper, with diagrams, explaining how it works.

It is a contraption made of a double row of seven fine wire circles, one row above the other, that are interlocking. Within each row of seven, each circle, made up of two arcs of wire, connects to a round middle wire (that acts as a horizontal diameter line for each) by forming a hook at each end. Each set of hook ends is separated by a small black bead. The top row of seven circles connects to the bottom row of seven by a little wrap of wire at the circumference — at the bottom for the top row, at the top for the bottom row. Each connecting wire with its seven wraps looks like a miniature metal spring. Thus there are seven beads on each row of circles (a total of fourteen) and there are seven wraps of wire joining the upper and lower sets of circles. All this elaborate connectedness allows the circles a maximum of movement and, therefore, a maximum of shaping of the whole figure; for each circle can remain flat, in one place, or it may capsize on itself completely in one direction into a half circle, in one plane, and, to a limited degree, in the other direction to form a half circle in three dimensions.

YOU can imagine how excited I was as I played with the contraption. It was almost limitless in the way I could manipulate it into various shapes, designs, configurations.

On the instruction paper there are eight diagrams in a row — eight shapes you can push the wire framework into; and there is a name beneath each diagram: The Sun, Mercury, Venus, The Moon, Mars, Jupiter, Saturn, and Lotus Flower. Below that, the explanation:

> LOTUS FLOWER is a game which was founded in India more than 2000 years ago. The ancient Indian people believed that the figures made by them give the human organism the energy of space, that was necessary for their

being. At the same time playing the game, one makes a massage of the tops of his fingers, that are rich of nerves. That leads to an improvement of blood running and throws away the stress and nervous pressure.

Already I can see its possibilities as a pattern and, to tell the truth, I've discovered there are more configurations possible than those the eight diagrams suggest. For, as I kept playing with it, more patterns gradually popped into being; the range of possibilities kept expanding. Now I have doubled the original number: eight new ones (so far); sixteen in all.

It's going to be tricky, but this model is flexible enough to give me lots of ideas for the framework of Blaze's story. Maybe I'll just end up going in circles, but my aim is to have those circles interconnect. What I like is the way they expand and contract, bend and flex, stretch out, collapse: the patterns are everchanging.

A

PAIN

Life is pain. It starts with pain. The first sound a new-born baby makes is a cry. That cry never stops even though he learns to keep it hidden inside. It's pain to grow up, to want a girl, to marry, to leave the ripening grain fields of home for a foreign country, and to watch your own newborn come into life with a cry.

It's pain to watch a son grow up. To sit with loose hands at the table and know — even without the grating of forced dresser drawers and the crumpling, folding, stacking sounds of the throwing off of school, and this town, and this house – know that he is putting all of himself into one suitcase that he will carry in one hand out through this door.

It's pain to watch a wife grow old. To know the skin is no longer strong enough to keep sorrow from creeping out of the flesh to lie exposed, like the bare roots of an old cabbage plant, on the face, the neck, the bend of the elbow. Skin so thin it cannot much longer keep the swelling veins from bursting their blueish flow out over the backs of the hands, the lumps of knuckles of the fingers. Fingers that over and over have bound this flowered cloth — a piece torn from a sugar sack — around the pain that makes the head swell and expand, with bulges of bone and stretching skin, to contain it. Life is pain. One long night of pain.

Old man Chmielewski felt in front of him for the table but it was not there. His spread fingers moved to the left, to the right, and discovered nothing but darkness. He dropped his hands to the chair beneath him but the chair was not there. It was the edge of the bed. The slanting mountain of pain sagged his shoulders and sent spasms of pressure down to weigh his feet to the icy linoleum. He heard his wife breathing. The sounds wrapped him and the darkness — a long breath drawn in, a short sigh puffed out through closed lips. Wrapped him and held him like a warm river curving in and around the mountain of pain and cold.

One hand on each side pushed him up from the rough flannelette of the sheet and the hard edge of the mattress. The breathing sounds followed his hands and wrapped their groping along the side of the bed until his foot struck something into noise and they stopped. When they resumed, they were back in place on the pillow and he stooped to touch what he could not see. A shoe. He pushed one foot into it but it was the wrong one. He pulled it off and put the other foot in. Hands groping again, under the bed, along the corner at the bottom. The pain rising and plummeting, screaming out that shoes make no difference, whether one or two. He stepped carefully with his left foot so the shoe would not scrape. Then the door, to the right and down, the knob hard and cold in his hand. A strong pull to ease the door over the buckled edge of the linoleum, then a pause. The breathing was still at the pillow as he squeezed the width of the pain through the narrow doorway and pulled the door almost closed again with only a slight rattle of the knob as he let go.

Hands sliding slowly along the wall, feeling the raised leaves and flowers and buds of the wallpaper, almost all the way to the light switch by the back door. The pain straining at every point on the inside wall of his skull, straining and screaming out that light makes no difference. Pain is enough. It fills life, fills it completely. There's no room for light. Feeling beyond the switch where his greatcoat hung on a nail. Pain is enough. Nothing else is necessary.

At the bottom of the porch steps, his shoe crunched noisily against the hard snow. Another step and he stopped. The pain edged higher up its mountain for the sudden moment of surprise that the snow was no colder than the linoleum, then dropped back to throb into every corner of its old place. He walked out of his back yard into the lane. As he turned left, he felt no need to look for the three great shapes of Trinity Mountain. They had already crowded into his head with the other one. And then the warm river of his wife's breathing caught up with him and wrapped itself beneath the pain, curving in and around the base of the mountains.

There was no more town of Fernie. He was walking the sunny streets of Mielec. He could see the Tatra Range to the south, flannel clouds wrapped loosely around the peaks. Then the murmuring of water. It was the familiar grassy bank of the Wisloka that helped him down its warm slope.

The stars were dimming in the winter sky. The street lights — the electrical crew, after long and heated deliberation by council, had installed automatic control late in the fall — had already shut off. The town was asleep. No one saw Andrei Chmielewski's towering pain out for its early morning walk, although afterwards, when he wasn't over at CPR Bill's place where Mrs. Chmielewski figured he must be when she woke up and found him gone, Gino Caravetta reported that he had seen footprints in the lane behind Baker Avenue, but only those of a left shoe, although it was difficult to be sure, the snow was so hard in such cold weather.

It was almost two months before they found him. He was wedged behind a log in the clay below a high point of the river bank. It took the town engineer and several of the volunteer firemen a good part of the morning to work the body free and get nets around it so they could haul it up.

20

He lay before them on the trampled, melting snow. A fragment of flannel still wrapped one arm. There was a shoe on one foot, the laces still tight and tied in a bow. Some little blue flowers showed through the mud on the rag around his head.

CHAPTER FIVE

MOUNTAINS

YOU remember I described the mountains surrounding Fernie. But did you note that there were eight of them? That is, eight either separate mountains, or ranges, or groupings. I will take YOU around the three hundred and sixty degrees again, this time giving the names, positions, and anything else connected.

The broad-topped one barely in view over the high hill to the northeast is Coal Creek Mountain. Fernie is a coal-mining town but, apart from the visible use of mine tailings along the railroad tracks and the accompanying discernible smell of coal and, unlike the blackened towns of Michel and Natal further along in The Pass, it shows no sign of mining. That is because the mine is not in Fernie. It is located up a creek called Coal Creek, at a place called Coal Creek, about ten miles to the south. The three daily shifts of miners travel from Fernie to the mine site on the mine's own railroad, the M. F. and M. – named for Michel, Fernie and Morrisey, the two M places being communities near Fernie: Michel to the north, Morrisey to the south. Thus Coal Creek is the name of the creek, of the mine, of the townsite near the mine, and of the mountain.

The next mountain I mentioned, the one with the fortress-like top of reddish rock, is called, fittingly, Castle Mountain. It lies far beyond Coal Creek (the creek). There are ranges along both sides of the creek, in behind Coal Creek Mountain on one side and Castle Mountain on the other, but they are not predominant on the town's skyline.

The long range of mountains was not named after the elephant shapes as I would have guessed (or as YOU might have guessed). Someone long ago must have had a different fancy, because it is called the Lizard Range. It runs in a northwesterly direction. And to tell the truth, I've never heard the names (if there are any) of the individual rocky peaks at the northern end of it. Once I rode on horseback with my dad up the Cedar Valley Road out of West Fernie, all the way to Island Lake — a small conifer-surrounded body of water with, yes, a scraggly island in the middle. It lay at the foot of one of those mountains. Ever since, I have thought of them simply as the Island Lake Peaks.

The looming green mountain to the west of town — well, a little northwest — is Fernie Mountain. It, and the town, were named after William Fernie, an English explorer who came to the region around the 1880's. There is a story about him and an Indian princess he met. Fascinated by the black chunky beads she was wearing, Fernie promised that if she would reveal their source, he would marry her. She did; he didn't. Because of his broken promise, the princess' mother climbed all the way up the broad green mountain and from its flat top laid a three-way curse on the whole valley below: Fire, Flood, and the third is somewhat controversial, some say Pestilence, some say Strife.

And the curse? Well, any long-time resident of Fernie will give you proof of its impact: 1) The big fire of 1908. According to an account that was published at the time, it "raced through the Old Town razing the timber east of the tracks and on into the new townsite, thus completely surrounding the entire city with a ring of destruction." YOU will notice the use of the term, city. That is what it was called then, when the population was five thousand, and that is what it is still called now, at three thousand. After the fire, only stone, brick, or concrete were allowed for any permanent building. That is why Fernie's business section looks the way it does today.   2) The big flood of '48. The Elk River swelled up over its banks, covering not only the adjacent area but flooding over the highway and up into the main part of town. It swept away houses and bridges; it cut the town off from the world. 3a) Pestilence. There is a long ramshackle building on the ridge at the foot of the high hill to the south that still bears the name of "Pest House." That was where victims of the great 'flu epidemic of 1918 were isolated from the rest of the town. A few survived; most died. And weren't the many mine disasters over the years, cave-ins, blow-outs – with their entrapment, injury, death – another kind of pestilence? 3b) Strife. Some said the third curse wasn't pestilence but strife. Well, for strife. . . Just take the mine alone. There have always been hostilities and quarrels related to the mine: between management and labour, between the super and the pit boss, the pit boss and the fire bosses, the fire bosses and the miners, among the miners themselves — stories about who did what he was supposed to do as a good miner, who did nothing but sluff off his whole time underground; who was a good partner, who couldn't be counted on even in good times never mind bad; who was conscientious, who took mine property home in his pockets or his lunch bucket after every shift. But not only the mine. Just look at the mayor and the town council right today. Oh, there has been strife all right. So, Pestilence or Strife, YOU can take YOUR pick. Without a doubt, the old Indian lady's curse looms over the town, and this part of the Elk Valley, just as does Fernie Mountain itself.

      Then, set back in the distance to the right, a group of three mountains that was immediately my favourite – Trinity Mountain or The Three Sisters. For one thing, I liked the fact that it had two names, and that the two seemed to be in contrast. "Trinity" made it serious, even holy, whereas "The Three Sisters" was very down-to-earth, something more connected to me; because, YOU see, there is another sister. There are three of us: Blaze and me and Pearl Anne. Later I will explain how we came to have the names we have. Right now I just want to make this connection between us and the Three Sisters. Sometime, to me, Pearl Anne is the highest peak, just because she's the oldest, Blaze is the one to the left, and I'm on the right. At other times, Blaze is the one in the middle because she is the middle one in age; then Pearl Anne is the one on the left, as the oldest. In either case, I am the third — the one on the right, the one furthest east. All three, of grey granite, rise high above the tree-line.

The first peak has a dramatic shape. Against the sky, it slants up to the right at about forty-five degrees then drops almost straight down to give the impression of having a sharp craggy shoulder. That part nestles into the beginning slant of the middle peak. The middle one is hard to describe. It is higher and broader, but its shape. . . well, the salt and pepper shakers at the Diamond Grill have that look only YOU have to imagine a shaker that has a kind of bulky asymmetrical mass with its top at an angle so that one side is lower than the other and there's kind of a flat ovoid surface slanting toward YOU. That isn't very good, I know, but it will help YOU to imagine it. The third peak is ordinary. It's just a plain little corner of a triangle sticking up into the sky. If it weren't part of the Trinity configuration, no one would notice it particularly.

The next mountain, to the north, is called Proctor. L.M.Proctor was one of the owners of the first sawmill in the area, set up near the present golf course. It's a kind of returning mountain; I mean, Fernie Mountain is up close, Trinity takes the eye away to the northwest, then Proctor draws in the perimeter of vision, bending it back towards town. It doesn't have the flair of the Three Sisters; it gives the sense, somehow, of a brooding masculine presence. This year they've been trying to get a ski hill going on its near slopes but it's so treed, right up to the top, that it'll take an awful lot of clearing to make even one run. And it's not accessible enough. They'd have to put a bridge across Fairy Creek for one thing. The creek starts somewhere high up the Trinity slopes, is caught for a while at the town's reservoir, then makes its way into the Elk River not far from the north highway bridge. There's a town joke about why Fernie beer is so potent. On the bottles it says, "Beer from the Mountains," but everyone knows it's the water that makes the difference: water that comes from the bottom of the Three Sisters. Some people even want to change the brand name to "Three Sisters Beer." Anyway, the Proctor ski slope is across from Fairy Creek and there isn't even a road to it. The enthusiasts have to hike in every time, along their trail, newly blazed with axes and machetes and things.

   Last in the circle is the distant, standing-alone, craggy, all-rock mountain that's called Hosmer Mountain. All the adjectives I've just used tell YOU it's a very spectacular mountain, but it has another remarkable feature. When the setting sun is on its face, people in town — those who know about the phenomenon — look for the shapes of shadow that the jutting crags cast back onto the flatter surfaces. For novices, the pattern is hard to make out. It is a horse and rider. The horse is coming straight toward the town, the rider sitting tall on its back. Maybe it is William Fernie. And off to the side of the horse's head is the figure of a man, walking too, and seemingly holding onto the bridle. Some say he is the Indian guide. Once a person has managed to make it out, it will never again be lost to him.

   I hope YOU will forgive me for taking so much time over the mountains. My excuse is that they are a very important part of what the town is. It's not really my fault that Fernie has such a complicated setting.

PRESS

MAC

Our town has a weekly newspaper but everyone says we really don't need it as long as we have Mac. And it's true. He's not only more efficient and up-to-date than *The Fernie Free Press*, we get the news through him much sooner.

Mac is the night guard/janitor at the jail, a two-cell place that doesn't get much use. It's in the back of the big bare RCMP office at the bottom of a flight of cement steps that are under the entrance to City Hall. Mac shuffles across the street every morning, as soon as he gets off work, to the varnished swinging doors of the post office in plenty of time to meet the earliest of the uptown workers and in time, too, for the miners coming off night shift — and he stands there, missing nobody, doing his important business of supplying the latest items of interest, news that's hotter off the press, so to speak, than anything that gets into the paper.

He's a bit of a weather forecaster too, not that he ever uses up precious time to pass a word about it, for the people move pretty fast into our post office since most of them are already five or ten minutes late for work; in fact, he's often used as an excuse: "I would have been here on time but Mac stopped me. . ." No, he just stands there inclining his head (he's quite a tall clothesline-pole of a man) over the people as they pass through. If his black and grey tweed cap is on his head, it means variable cloudiness with chances of rain (or snow); if it's in his hands, we can be sure of sunny periods for a start, although it may cloud over or even get windy once he's gone home to sleep. If there is no cap in sight at all – that is, if his balding head is bare and his two hands clutch rhythmically at the metal clasps of his braces – chances are he's left it in the jail, in the front cell where he keeps his comic books. On such a day, we have to make our own predictions or listen to the forecast on the radio, because Mac will never waste precious time talking about anything as mundane as the weather.

Yes, he's much more efficient and up-to-date than the newspaper. *The Fernie Free Press* comes out every Thursday but, by then, because of Mac, all the news is stale. YOU see, there's no place like an RCMP office for news. The cops are called to all the accidents — and there are quite a few on our mountainous roads, on the curve out by the tunnel, for instance, where there's a straight drop to the river. It gets quite a few prairie drivers every summer. And the police are informed straight away by the hospital or the doctor when anyone dies. Even if they are not officially informed, there's always one of them seeing one of the nurses (especially Frances Ptucha or Rosa Caravetta). That's how they hear about the new babies too, and how long the labour was, and whether or not the father was drunk when he got to the hospital. Failing that, there are always the girls at B.C. Tel. We all know that Vera and Marion, and even Carrie who has just started at the phone job, dream of becoming Mounties' wives — a Mrs. Sandy or a Mrs. Angelo — even if it would mean some northerly post among the Eskimos; and there's nothing like a telephone girl for a news source when all she has to do is not quite take off the headpiece. However it happens, the whole communication system somehow feeds back to Mac, sitting there in the first cell, right behind the big desk with the phone on it, seemingly immersed in his horror comics or Bugs Bunny.

So, he's more efficient (for one thing, no one can ever detect any spelling mistakes or type-set errors — like the time the column on the church's fundraising actually said, in print for the whole town to see, that the Sisters of the Holy Family Church "had a very successful, fifty-five-dollar profit from their *panty* sale"), and he's more up-to-date (the obituaries, depending on the time of week of death, often don't appear in print until well after the funeral) and, what's more, he's cheaper. Sure, he's likely to ask for a loan now and then, but it's never more than fifty cents or a dollar and, at that, he's careful not to hit up the same person more than once or twice a year. That's a lot less than a subscription to the *Free Press*.

The main advantage of Mac's circulation is that he supplies items that never get mentioned at all in the paper. There was a real teeth-and-claws fight, for instance, that Ellie and Rita got into at the Castle over Squinty, the bartender. And the time young Billie Ferguson ran all the way to the hospital when they phoned that Gracie had her baby (it was their first and it came early) — ran all the way from the North End and didn't even think once, until he was home again three hours later, about the '45 pickup he had just bought that was parked right in front of the house.

Of course, Mac doesn't set himself up as infallible. One morning he retailed the news of old Mr. Neidig's passing. Some had flowers already sent to the funeral parlour, and sympathy cards mailed to Mary and the family, before they discovered that he was still alive. Mac just bowed his head, even lower, and admitted that his source had been unreliable. After all, a light on in the morgue the middle of the night didn't always mean someone had died. It seems that Violet Rossi had gone in there looking for the mop and pail. And, as everyone knew, the old man had been pretty low for a long time.

Anyway, our town doesn't really need the newspaper; in fact, we would be better off if we didn't have one. It just causes confusion. When anyone mentions the Free Press, we're never quite sure if they mean the newspaper or Mac unless we happen to catch them saying, "I read it in. . ." or "I heard it from. . ." Still, sometimes, they make it perfectly clear from the start by crediting the news, directly, to "Mac's Free Press."

CHAPTER SIX

MOUNTAINS, HOTELS

As YOU can see, I've been putting off attending to characters. I've talked a bit about Blaze and myself, and I've mentioned our father and a couple of children and our sister, Pearl Anne, but I know I've avoided coming to grips with any of them (or us); that is because I'm not terribly comfortable with people. I like to leave them alone; I want them to leave me alone. Still, I have this story Blaze says I must tell.

I think I need to ease into it. And it has just occurred to me I can do that by introducing, for a start, a few people by connecting them to the setting. That way, because it is easier for me to talk about places than people, I can practise a bit on some minor characters. Then maybe I'll do better when I get to the main ones.

Fernie is a town of eight hotels. And in case YOU think, "What a coincidence. That's the same as the number of mountains," well, that's *why* there are eight. It's a well-known story around town. It started with the Scotsman, Ian Robertson, who built the first hotel. "The Fernie" was a natural choice since it was the name of the town, just as Hosmer has the Hosmer Hotel and Michel has the Michel Hotel (only they were built later), and it was just an extra that it was the name of one of the mountains too. The way the hotel faces, originally there was a good view of Fernie Mountain from the front tables. That was before MacDonald's Transfer went in across the street.

The Fernie set the precedent. The next hotel builders were a father and two sons by the name of Elsted. They were a religious family: the grandfather had been an Anglican minister, and they felt the name "Trinity" was fitting for an establishment run by the three of them, especially when they intended to provide a quiet place for teetotal customers, ones who wanted to avoid the raucous and foul-smelling bar-room atmosphere that permeated The Fernie. Once it was obvious they just couldn't compete, the Elsteds sold out to a man by the name of Ursual, a young man from the south coast of Yugoslavia. His first step was to turn the quiet dining room on the main floor into a twenty-five-table beer parlour. As soon as it was just as loud and just as smelly as the one at the Fernie, he was on his way to having a successful business.

For a long time, there were only the two hotels — the one run by the Scots family, the other by the Yugoslav. Then came a sudden growth in population. The Coal Company brought in a bunch of immigrant workers from Europe, mostly Slavs and Italians, to work in the mine, so quite a bit of building started up. There was a need to accommodate the new drinkers, for one thing. That's when "The Castle" went up, and "The Proctor." YOU see, the new owners were keeping up the idea of giving their hotels the names of the mountains. Both of the new establishments were on Victoria Avenue (Fernie's main street) but, since it's quite a long street, none of the four were very close together. I had a hard time finding out the names of the owners but, finally, came across some old issues of *The Fernie Free Press* that had a historical section about the beginnings of the town. It was a Mr. Abe Britney who built The Castle — he even put up a false front with crenellations on top and a bit of a tower. And the other one was a Zuffa. He hadn't just come over with the last bunch of Czechs; he'd been in Fernie from before. His descendants still live in town, but they don't own The Proctor now.

The fifth hotel was one built, intentionally, without a beer parlour. Like the Elsteds, A.E. Greenbank came from a refined and religious family. He wanted his hotel to be quiet and refined too, and he looked for his clientele in quiet and refined people. Gradually, because there weren't as many of that bent as he had thought, he began enlarging the rooms, taking out walls to make flats, or apartments. So today, it's an apartment block, but it's still called a hotel: The Grange Hotel. Greenbank had considered the mountains that were left; there was already a Hosmer Hotel (at Hosmer); he wouldn't use Coal Creek as a name because of its association with the mine (the miners were the ones who frequented the beer parlours), so, all that was left was the Island Lake Mountains (an awkward name) and the Lizard Range (a name that might make residents squeamish). Thus he settled for just "The Range." It wasn't long before people were calling it "The Grange" instead, because they thought that name was suitably pretentious and, after all, the building was grey. He finally gave in and changed the sign.

One of the men of that wave of Italian miners was Carolei Ciriani. Having put in his obligatory time in the mine, and having lived frugally by eating plain spaghetti and putting off getting married (he met Yolanda soon after he arrived), he saved enough money to buy, cheap, an unsavoury lot at the very south end of Victoria Avenue, and there he started building. Friends, townspeople, even the councillors and the mayor, were loud in their warnings. A sixth hotel in a town the size of Fernie was not a good business venture, they said. But Ciriani worked steadily to make his dream of owning a hotel in his new country come true. He built little by little, making enough to live on as he used up his savings, by working part time at Fernie Meats. He had been apprenticing as a butcher in a little side-street shop in the outskirts of Rome when the chance arose for him to go to Canada and work in the mines. The question of a name for his hotel was the least worry he had. He agreed to take one of the mountains that was left — and he decided on Coal Creek Mountain because there was a better view of it from his site than from any of the other hotels — but he said there was no point in naming a hotel after a mountain that already shared its name with a creek, a mine, and a townsite, so the name was going to be "The Roma." No one could change his mind and, since there was no actual ordinance in place to enforce the namesake trend, The Roma it was.

With its cedar-strip trellises and plaster-of-Paris bunches of purple grapes, and its live Italian music (various friends and acquaintances took turns playing the accordion or the guitar, or singing snatches of opera), and, maybe most important, the strong amber-coloured wine made by Ciriani himself that he could have on the table at a moment's notice (just one quick trip to the cellar, as long as he was certain there were no Mounties in the vicinity), the Roma soon became the most popular bar in town. It didn't much matter if not many people stayed in the rooms. There was always a good time, with lots of money flowing, at the Roma. There is still a song known about town — by the old-timers at least — the lyrics of which are sung to the tune of "The Beer Barrel Polka." It goes:

> In the Roma, in the Roma
> That's where you'll find my father
> Without any bother
> You'll find him drinking beer.
> Every day when Papa gets his pay
> To the Roma he goes right away
> And all the bums they hang around
> Until poor Papa's broken down.

Then back to the chorus again: "In the Roma, in the Roma," etc.

They say, too, that the reason the area became more or less the town centre is that businesses quickly vied for space close to the action at the Roma. In later years, Old Ciriani turned the running of the hotel over to his two sons and one daughter. He himself lived for making wine and hunting bear.

Only a couple of years after that, a man by the name of Crabbe — Chester Crabbe — came to Fernie from Vancouver Island to build a hotel. He had made his money speculating in various mines in the north. One of them, a copper mine, enjoyed a remarkable success. I'm not totally clear about it. Some said he had a background in geology and that's how he knew where to invest. Some said he chose Fernie as a new area so he could do a little prospecting on the side. Anyway, he built a "cute" little hotel. Its bar was like a tearoom, similar to something you might see in Victoria. He even started out wanting to call the place "The Victoria"; appropriate, he thought, since it was the name of his home city and also the name of Fernie's main street. But when he heard about the town's tradition, he decided to go along with it. He picked the Island Lake Mountains, and called his hotel "The Islander." Strangers are always asking how come the town can be on an island, and the townspeople joke that it's because Fernie, so forgotten by the rest of the province, is an "Island of Remoteness".

Hosmer Mountain was then the only mountain without a hotel (in Fernie) named after (or connected to) it. That the name was already taken was the problem. As far as I know, there has never been more than one Greek who ever lived in Fernie. His name was Nikos Moustakakis. He came to Canada with the express intention of opening a restaurant. And, after cooking at the "Kriti Village" in Vancouver for nearly seven years, he took himself and his savings, along with a sum that he had recently acquired through selling the family hectares on Crete, to Fernie, where he built a hotel right next door to The Proctor. He wasn't afraid of the competition offered by the other establishments because the reason he built the hotel was so that he could put in not only a taverna-type bar but, more important, a first-rate Greek kitchen. In no time, his place was as popular as the Roma; in fact, many drinkers who left the Roma bar to get a bite to eat — Nick's specialties were souvlaki and moussaka — found it more comfortable just to stay on after the meal and continue their drinking.

The Greek loved that last unclaimed mountain, the one with the horse and rider. To him it was Bellerophon astride Pegasus in his attempt to ascend Olympos. Nick even said that, like the soul of Odysseus, when choosing lots for reincarnation, he gladly chose the one neglected by all the rest, claiming that it would have been his first choice even if all the mountains had still been available. He simply changed the mountain's name to that of the Greek mountain of the gods and called his hotel after it: "The Olympos."

So that is the story of the hotels. Some were built early, at the beginning of the town; a few were even rebuilt after burning down in one of the big fires of either 1904 or 1908. Some went up during the Twenties and Thirties. The Olympos is the latest, the newest. Mainly, what I want YOU to see is how closely the eight of them are connected to the setting, to the mountains that encircle Fernie.

B

LACEWORK

When I first saw Fernie I was a tourist. I was on holiday from my restaurant business in Vancouver. I wanted to see the mountains. There was something about the town that touched a memory: maybe it was the clear sky, the freshness of the air, the mountains. Well, of course it was the mountains. It was a town swung in a high valley with mountains rising up on all sides. Not too close, so you felt crowded, but just the right distance, so you could see how different, how individual, each one was. They gave the town character. I knew I'd have to come back.

I sold out at the coast and built a hotel here. It seemed fitting to call it the Olympos because I am Greek. Who here knows, or cares, how far Mt. Olympos is from where I grew up?

Now that I am settled in Fernie, I can look back and trace what gave me the dream of leaving Crete, the dream of coming to this faraway country of freedom and business opportunity. Here I am known as Nick from Greece. My story is of Nikos from the little village of Aghia Galini on the southern shore of Crete, and it all has to do with my early attitude toward being a tourist.

I often used to wonder what it would be like for tourists to arrive in our village at the foot of the mountains. After a long, winding, hot and dusty road high up under the sky, they would catch their first glimpse of the bright sea to the south at one turning, then lose it again until the gorge opened and showed them all the houses, white-walled and red-roofed, and the curve of golden beach with its grey fringe of low olive trees. Still ahead of them would lie the reddish switchbacks cut into the steep slopes of the rough hills. Once at the bottom, they would lose sight of sea, beach, houses and all as they entered the upper end of our main street with its great eucalyptus trees that always looked to me like two long rows of high marble pillars, grey and peeling with age but drooping with nervous silvered leaves that gave our village a deceptively grand and cool effect. Then, as they emerged from that shaded extension of archway, they would see before them a rather untidy (in places, even grubby), ordinary village street, one lined with tavernas (or restaurants, cafés, bars, pizzerias — depending on which name the owner thought most likely to draw customers). And they would find themselves moving between two lines of people, a strange mixture of villagers and tourists (the percentage of which depended on the time of day), all seated at the many tables arranged in rows (or no longer arranged in rows because they had constantly been moved since morning to keep them in the shade of whatever was overhead — tamarisks or olives, or arbours covered with grape vine).

    To me it was all very familiar because every summer since I was small (after my grandmother died), it was my daily task to drive our few goats, sometimes as many as six, sometimes only two, along the whole length of that street, up the hills, and even into the gorge beyond, wherever there was something for them to eat.

    At first I was lonely with only the goats around me, even though I knew them very well and felt happy in their company and important in knowing that my father had given me a great responsibility. But I came to enjoy watching them feed as they clambered through thorny brush to nip off green, or partially green, leaves, their heads nodding up and down as they quickly chewed and swallowed, their tails short and erect as though they were always tense with expectation. The way they rummaged out every edible piece of growing thing left me awed at their thoroughness. And I came to so delight in controlling them, keeping them on the move to new "patches" that I found for them that, soon, when I took them back down in the late afternoons, I sensed a personal triumph in their sleekness and in the full swing of their udders as I drove them through the eucalyptus colonnade and into the hot openness of the street where the tourists and the villagers sat at the tables — the tourists sipping soft drinks or beer (some of them even eating supper already), the villagers drinking coffee or raki and playing backgammon.

Some of the men might call to me. "Hey, Nikos. You make your father's goats fat." Or, "Hey, Nikos. Lots of milk for the little ones tonight, eh? And lots of cheese for winter." The tourists wouldn't understand but they would smile and sometimes one or two, usually girls, would lean into the street and stretch out slim brown arms (or slim white ones, depending on how long they had been around the village) to pet the goats or give them crusts of bread. And then someone, usually a tall young man in shorts and bare feet, would stand up and take a picture of the girl feeding the goat. This I had come to expect and I would let the goats slow down ahead of time and I would stand back a while before I drove them on.

But one day, just as I was about to urge them forward, a fair girl in one of the long, flowing, lowcut dresses that our shops hang out for tourists (hers was pink with white lace at the top) jumped up, calling out something so shrilly that the goats started back and had to be coaxed forward again with more food. I didn't understand what she had said and I didn't understand why she was moving toward me with a piece of bread in her hand. But with everyone smiling and pointing, and a young man with a camera positioning himself, I realized that she wanted her picture taken with me as well as the goats.

As she approached, she bent forward and offered the crust to Arketá, the lead goat (the one with the bell, although hers had lost its clapper and no longer made any noise) and, as she did so, the lace at the top of her dress poked forward and I was looking down into — between — two soft curves of brown, with a golden curve of belly below and a fair fringe of hair. She had nothing on underneath.

She straightened abruptly and I was aware that Arketá was tugging at the crust just at the moment I felt an arm move around my shoulder and heard the click of the camera. Then she was holding out her hand and saying something to me. I realized that she wanted to give me a coin, but I couldn't see that I had done anything to earn it. When I didn't take it, she tried to push it into my hand. I closed my fist but one of the men (Old Filippos I think it was, the one with all the tomato glass houses along the beach west of the village) hollered at me, "Take it, take it. They've got lots of money." And someone else yelled, "You bet. They're Americans." Another said, "You might as well have it, Nikos. She thinks you are picturesque." It was in Greek, *graficos*, but it was a word I did not know. All I knew was the sweet pleading face in front of me.

My hand sprang open, I snatched the coin, then struck out at the goats with my stick to hurry them away. Not used to such treatment (at least not since the death of my grandmother), they leapt in different directions, one of the younger ones pushing between two tables and knocking over a chair. Even after I got them together enough to herd them along, there was still a lot of laughter — from villagers and tourists alike.

I turned the goats off at the very first lane rather than going to ours at the end of the street as I usually did, and I made them run fast through the hard-rutted back streets all the way to our small enclosed yard. When I had pulled the gate to and twisted the wire around the post, I slipped behind the big olive tree and stood very still. I opened my hand and looked at the coin. It was a five-drachma piece, the one with the winged horse. There was a deep mark in my left palm where its edge had dug in. I held it a moment, then climbed up and wedged it into the crevice of a high branch, the place where I kept things safe from my young brothers and sisters.

My mother was sitting by the open window at the back. Without looking up from her crocheting (when she was not in the fields she made various things — lace purses, tablecloths, and, I realized with a start, lace tops for dresses — to be sold in one of the tourist shops), she said, "What's the matter with you, Nikos? You shouldn't be running the goats when they are full. You know it will sour the milk." I said I didn't feel very well. She looked at me then and, for the first time, I saw how old and work-worn she was. Her face was dark and lined from years in the sun. The way her shoulders sagged over her lacework, I could not imagine that she had any breasts at all. She told me to go lie down until it was time to see to the chickens. Then she went back to her crocheting.

In the dusk of the loft, I thought about my lie. But I hadn't really lied. I did feel sick, somewhere in the middle of my belly — in the middle of my self. I couldn't tell whether it was because I felt wrong for having accepted the money or because I had such a longing. It was a strange, mysterious pang. I couldn't even tell what it was I longed for.

Gradually, as I lay there, the pain went away. I kept my eyes closed and pictures came into my head, pictures that showed me what it was I wanted. I longed to buy a new bell for Arketá, and coloured ribbons and pompoms for all the goats. Or even straw hats like the ones the donkeys wore on the Kriti postcards for the tourists. And I longed to have a seaman's cap for myself, and shiny black boots. They were on the postcards too.

As I stretched out on the narrow bed, I thought of the many tourists forever coming out of the mountains and down into our village. Whatever *graficos* meant, I could make them all want to take pictures of me and the goats.

I would accept their money. Then some day I would have enough saved to go away from Crete. I would go to where the tourists came from, where there is lots of money. I had enough already for the ribbons. That would be a start. Later the boots and the cap and the pompoms. I opened my eyes and got up. . . . And all the ribbons would be pink with white lace.

CHAPTER SEVEN

FAMILY

As I told YOU near the beginning, Blaze and I walked along the track beside Baker Street with our dad and the two boys. Their names were Sydney and Jackie. We knew about them but he had never sent us any pictures. They were both sandy-haired and freckled. They both wore pants that were too big for them. They both wore shirts, partly tucked in, with sleeves that were too short. They both had greyish underwear showing at their necks and wrists. The older one, who seemed about my age, had a bad limp, or at least a definite shuffle that made him very unsteady on that uneven footing. Even so, Dad took my suitcase from me and pushed it at him. When I objected, he said, "Don't worry, he can handle it. It'll help make a man out of you, won't it, Old Timer?" And he grabbed Blaze's case himself.

As Sydney and I fell behind, I tried to take the suitcase back from him, but he swung it out of my reach, almost unbalancing himself as he shifted it to his other hand. His eyes danced and his pale face broke into a wide grin. He said some words but they were so garbled I couldn't make out what they were. I asked him twice to repeat them. Each time he did his grin became even wider. What I finally made out was, "I can handle it."

Dad had hugged us both as we got down from the train and kissed Blaze on the cheek. Now they walked ahead together, his arm around her shoulders. With the crunching of the cinder-like gravel, I couldn't hear much of what they said, just a few snatches that let me know he was explaining something about the mine. Jackie kept close to Dad's left leg, trying to match his stride. Every few yards he had to take three or four extra steps to catch up.

After we had walked a little way, about the time I saw the sign, "Baker Avenue," Dad let his arm drop from Blaze's shoulder and he tugged at something he had tucked into his belt. When he flipped it free, I saw it was a piece of hemp — a gunny sack. "Here you go, Jackanapes," he said, pushing it into the boy's hands. "Might as well make yourself useful. There's a big chunk right there for a start." And he pointed at a hunk of coal just on the outside of the left rail. He put his arm back around Blaze and as they walked on I heard his low laugh. "They're not bad little buggers, either one of them." Jackie scooped up the piece of coal, dropped it into the bag, then darted on ahead to pick up another.

Have YOU ever noticed that there is always a discrepancy between what you expect and how things actually are? Sometimes you expect something to be terrible and it turns out to be okay. Sometimes you expect something to be pretty good and it turns out just the opposite. Well now I can't quite remember just what I expected our dad's "home and family" in Fernie to be like. Over the years, he had sent us pictures from Mountain Park where he worked — a mining town up in the mountains south of Edson, Alberta. Mostly they were of his horses, Des and Tex. Des was short for Desert Gold and Tex for Texas Storm. But sometimes his house, a square trim little wooden building, would appear in the background; and when he built his barn, he sent a separate picture of that. It was small and neat too.

The house on the last lot on Baker Avenue, where that avenue ran into the last street at Fernie's North End, sat pretty much alone. To the side toward Coal Creek Mountain: Baker Avenue, a wire fence, the railway tracks, and the sawmill; to the front: a stand of towering cottonwoods that separated the last street from the edge of the golf course; on the Fernie Mountain side, a few vacant lots, one of which our dad had use of as a garden plot; to the back, the Baker Avenue line-up of houses we had just walked by.

His house, the one he had felt lucky to find for his new family when they moved to Fernie after the closing of the Mountain Park mine, was Baker Avenue's last word, the final touch, *la pièce*. . . for ugliness. It won out over the whole long straggle of sagging, peeling houses with their weathered outbuildings and lean-to's. The one feature it had over its neighbours was its colour. Not that much of it was left. Calf-shit yellow, our uncle in Ontario would have called it.

Set into a bit of a hillside — no more than a mound, really — it was higher at the front than at the back and, since there were no steps going down to the lower ground, the little square front porch stuck out in midair: unused, sealed off, no way out or in.

As we approached from the back, Jackie veered off across the yard, made up of bare, packed earth and patches of weeds, to the huddle of wooden shacks, seemingly leaning into each other to keep from falling. He dropped the partly filled bag of coal at one of the open doorways and was beside us again by the time we had set everything we were carrying — the two cases, Blaze's portable typewriter, our jackets and over-the-shoulder bags, and a cardboard box tied with string — on the square of planking at the back door. Sydney stumbled against my case as he let go of it. Its far corner hit the side of a tall metal can, tipping it over and spilling out the contents. Vegetable peelings, mostly potato and carrot, interspersed with eggshells, coffee grounds, cabbage leaves, soggy bread, spread out over the boards. Dad, his hand on the doorknob, swivelled around at the sound. "You clumsy ox! Now you get all this mess cleaned up, every scrap, do you hear? And when you're done, take it down to the garden the way you were supposed to do in the first place." The low laugh again.

"God, these kids." And he swung the door open saying, "Here we are home, Bertie. Bring that little Stormy over here so he can meet his big sisters."

He closed the door behind us. It was one big room – bare wooden floor, a cook stove to the left, cabinets to the right, a sink under a small window. Bertie was sitting on the far side of the kitchen table, one arm resting on its patterned oilcloth cover, the other around a bundle of white and blue flannelette. She smiled across at us. The wide grin, the light skin and freckles, reddish hair, a pale kind of red. As she pushed back her chair, she hoisted the bundle away from her breast and quickly closed the top of her dress. "I thought you'd be longer," she said. Her voice was light, highpitched, with a kind of singsong whine to it. "I just wanted to make sure he was settled down before you got here."

She and Blaze were hugging. They had met two years before when Blaze spent her two-week holiday with Dad at Mountain Park. Blaze hadn't been pleased about Bertie then. It was to have been a trip for just Blaze and Dad, the two of them, riding out from the town into the mountains all around the Cardinal River Valley. But he had to bring *her* along. It wasn't just having the extra person — Blaze wouldn't have minded that because Bertie did most of the cooking, something Blaze wasn't at all crazy about herself, and she was a good rider, and she did most of the looking after the pack stuff on the mules — it was that she was a married woman with four kids and she left the kids at home to go on this trip with her and Dad, her sleeping robe beside his in the tent and all. Blaze didn't know who was looking after the kids; the husband worked in the mine too. She guessed he had no trouble getting evidence, because it didn't take long for the divorce and then Dad and Bertie were married immediately; and that's how he got a whole new instant family. When Dad wrote us that Texas Desmond had arrived, we didn't even have to count the months.

Anyway, they were hugging now as though they were best of friends; and Blaze was taking the baby, and Bertie was folding the flannelette back so we could all see his face. It was smooth and full and white. He looked out from the blanket, blue eyes wide, no trace of a smile.

Blaze said, "And of course you know this is Babe. Babe, this is Bertie." Bertie moved toward me and we gave each other a slight hug and she tried to kiss my cheek but I guess I didn't bend down quite far enough. I felt her lips kind of brush along the side of my neck.

"He's really cute," I said.

"Yeah, he's real cute, all right." Dad's laugh again. "Right now anyway. But you should hear him when he gets screwed up for a howl." He grabbed him from Blaze, blanket and all, and hoisted him over his head. "Isn't that right, Old Stormy? Isn't that right?" His head was back and, as he looked up, he bounced the baby from side to side. Tex opened his mouth in a crooked smile and held it that way. A long thread of saliva stretched down from one side. "Hey you little bugger, don't do that to your old man." He swung him over to the end of the table and plunked him into the high chair. He took out his handkerchief to wipe his cheek. "You sit there young fellah. Now you can drool all you like."

A movement caught my eye. I looked past the high chair to where a door was opening a little, closing, then opening again. Dad noticed where I was looking and made a jump in that direction. "Come on in here you little shyster," he yelled and, next we knew, he had hold of something and was dragging it into the room. "Come on, you might as well get it over with. You can't go hiding away in the bedroom." He turned the child toward us.

"Here she is. This is Old Granny. Say hello to Blaze and Babe." And he pushed her forward. "She looks backward right now but in no time you'll be wishing she'd stay this shy."

She was a female version of the two boys. All that made her different was the length of her hair and the fact that she was the middle size. The shirt maybe fit a little better, not showing quite so much of the underwear and instead of the baggy pants, she wore a too-long printed skirt, the hem hanging loose in several places.

Blaze put a hand on her shoulder. "Your name isn't really Granny, is it?"

"That's what *he* calls me." She shot a look in Dad's direction, then twisted her body toward Blaze, one shoe moving back and forth along a crack in the floor. "But it's really Randy. It's short for Miranda. That's what my real dad wanted me to be called."

Dad made a grab for her. "Randy Granny, Granny Randy. What's the difference? You're like an old grandma anyway." She sprang aside, nearly bumping into my legs. Then she put her arms around Jackie, holding him in front of her. They were both giggling. "Come on now you two. Get out there and bring in your new sisters' stuff. We'll get them settled and then have some supper."

Just then the door opened. Sydney shuffled in with the big can. "Well, here's the old-timer. That makes everything complete. Here we are, Bertie, all together. One big happy family."

PRESS

FILLER

Sometimes nothing happens at all during a whole night shift but that doesn't bother Mac. He goes to the post office as usual, always ready with some filler. One such morning he greeted each person at the door with, "I guess you haven't heard that the Matron got drowned last night?"

The responses varied. "No! You don't mean Miss Schilling!" or "What? Roseanne?" or "Does Doctor Martin know about it?" to all of which Mac, holding the eye of the speaker for a moment, answered "Yep."

Then, "How would she ever get drowned?" "What on earth was she doing near the river?" or "Oh, no. She's so young," and always, "How did it happen?"

"Don't know." Mac bowed his head low and held his cap in both hands in front of his chest, his accustomed stance when someone was dead. "All I know is they found her under the dock."

And one by one, their post box keys ready in their hands, the people heard and passed through the doors smiling. Nothing like a little harmless confirmation of gossip to start the day. Everyone knew about Roseanne and Doc Martin.

Except for Patsy Rossi, just off the train from Coal Creek, his eyes still black-edged with coal dust. When he heard the announcement, he stuffed his key back into his pocket, hoisted his lunch bucket under his arm and hurried away. His wife did sewing and alterations for Roseanne Schilling and she wouldn't know yet. Everyone he met coming up the hill he shouted at, "Miss

Schilling's drowned," not waiting to answer any questions that their surprised mouths might ask.

It wasn't until he got to the Salvation Army house, almost to the highway, that he stopped. "Goddammit. We don't have no dock in Fernie."

Then he turned and walked slowly back. Maria would be real mad if he came home without checking the mail. By the time he reached the post office again, Mac had already gone home to sleep.

CHAPTER EIGHT

NAMES

    Her name wasn't really Bertie. It was Florence. He met her when he moved out from Ontario. Actually, he met her husband first; they were on the same shift in the mine. Even Blaze doesn't know the details about how anything happened. By the time of her visit to Mountain Park, things were well on the way. Bertie laughs about the name. "I didn't know his name was Terrence. I really thought Tare was short for Ontario, where he was from, so that's what I called him. And he sure was something different, like he was from another planet, not just another province. You know, when I first knew him he was so all closed in; talk about tall dark and silent; he just seemed to be mumbling to himself. When Frank first brought him home to dinner, I couldn't make out half of what he said. And he was so straightlaced then. Do you know, he wouldn't say one swear word in front of a woman? Look at him now! We're in B.C. but he still talks and teases and gets mad like an Albertan. But he sure wasn't like that at first. So that's what I called him, but he soon got even with me. He just started calling me Alberta. I hated it, I really did. But then he shortened it to Bertie and I got so I didn't mind."

    So that explained why she's Bertie and he's Tare. Maybe it's just as well. Terrence and Florence would sound pretty funny together. Terrence was his grandmother's family name. We had never heard him called anything else.

    But it's funny about names, isn't it? Blaze and I found out real soon, since people here in Fernie don't mind being frank, especially if it's a kind of joke, we found out that everyone called him Hopalong. Even at the beginning, when we were still okay about him, we didn't blame them. After all, it's natural with the name Cassidy, but on top of that, he always wore that goddam awful black ten-gallon hat. Blaze said, "You think that's out of place here? You can imagine how I felt when he wore it in Orillia and I was in high school, and I had to walk along Main Street with him." And I said yes I remembered because, of course, she had complained enough about it at the time. Nobody ever said it in our hearing but I always wondered if Fernie people called us Hopalong's daughters.

There are lots of nicknames in Fernie; it's a real breeding place for them. I wonder why people feel the need to pick on one particular thing about a person and turn that into a name. Most of them are pretty obvious: Blackie, Curly, Baldy, Shorty — words to do with how that person looks. But sometimes they're just the reverse: Curly for a bald guy, Baldy for someone with bushy hair, Tiny for a huge man, and so on. That sort of ironic thing, sarcastic even. Smiley is another.

Then there are names that are short for, or a twist on, the person's real name. When we came to Fernie I couldn't get over hearing about two guys — they were partners even — who were called Tango and Polka. I imagined they were both great dancers, each with his own specialty. But it turned out that Tango was short for Orlando (an Italian first name) and Polka was short for Pokadamski (a Ukrainian surname). Some other Fernie names in that category are Carny, for Carnsworth, Mitch for Mitchell, Brownie, Smitty, the usual. Maybe the best was one of the high school teachers, Mr. Creamer. We all called him Cream Puff. Another one I couldn't get over was a Mr. Hector Dick who happened to have red hair. Of course he went by Red.

Then some names spring out of a person's job, or habits even. In town there's a CPR Bill, a Telephone Mike, a Bullseye Pete; a miner called Moke, because he started as a four-year-old bumming cigarettes, saying "Gimme a 'moke"; an ardent fisherman called Trout, a man called Fish (because his last name was Sturgeon), and one who still goes by Dolly because he liked to dress up like a girl when he was a kid. And there's Gentleman Jim, called that because of his habit of saying, "You're a real gentleman" to everyone.

YOU notice most of these names belong to males. The only woman I can think of in Fernie who had that kind of name (I mean other than a short form of her own name like one of the nurses, Miss Jordan, who got Jordie all the time) was Boxcar Mary. She was the town prostitute. She worked out of the Roma but the story was that she'd never deny a customer even if she had to take him to one of the boxcars on the CPR siding. There was another one, an out-of-towner called Smokey. I don't know how she got that name but the fact of her existence sure cut down on the number of men who would dare go around singing, "On Top of Old Smokey."

Nicknames are one thing Dad was always big on. So his wife was Bertie, Sydney was Old Timer, Randy was Granny, Jackie was Jackanapes, and Tex was Stormy. I really hated all those names.

He didn't have nicknames for Blaze or me, except for "Girl" once in a while. I guess there was no need. The names themselves — and they are our legal, full names — are bad enough. He named us after a team of horses he used to work with up in the Cariboo. Once when I complained about mine, Blaze said, "Well, don't forget Pearl Anne. Her name comes from that team he had earlier. One of us could have been Blaze-Babe or Baby-Blaze even."

And then I said, "It would have been you. You came first."

And she said, "At least you two were named after fully-sexed horses — mares. How do you think I feel being named after a gelding?" Then I reminded her about Paul Bunyan's blue ox, Babe, and how even she sometimes calls me Blue.

Well, even though I was born in Ontario, we both have B.C. for our initials. Names are funny. I wonder how much they affect a person's life.

CHAPTER NINE

TALKING HORSES

Obviously they didn't have very much in the way of bedding. Although it was early September and still very warm, our bed had a set of flannelette sheets, not quite long enough and the blue stitching at the edges was coming undone. Over them was a heavy canvas-covered sleeping robe, a fairly new one; Dad said it was one of the best, that he'd ordered it from McLeod's in Winnipeg the year before to take hunting.

The room they gave us was next to the kitchen at the back. Well, both bedrooms were next to the kitchen since, except for the small bathroom just inside the front porch, there were only the three rooms. There was an upstairs — a long triangular-shaped space under the slope of the two sides of roof. The three children went up by way of a steep stairway out of our room. The baby's crib was in with Dad and Bertie.

There was a scratched-up brown dresser with a drawer each for Blaze and me. The bottom drawer was for the kids' clothes since there was no room for furniture upstairs except for the two beds: a narrow one for Randy alongside the railing of the stairwell and one a little wider for Syd and Jackie at the other end, under the one dusty window. I think the boys used to sleep in our room. But they didn't really use the bottom drawer. Their clothes were always in heaps, small ones since they didn't have much to wear, beside their beds.

Blaze squeezed what there was in the drawer far enough over to give her room for her make-up: Nivea cream and pancake stuff, mascara and lipstick, eyelash curlers, and a little bottle of Bluegrass perfume. I'm sure she'd bought that because of the miniature prancing horse on the side. All those cosmetic things were important to her. She'd done some part-time modelling in Toronto, along with her dental office job. That was something that made me feel kind of guilty about getting her to come to Fernie. She might have made it as a full-time model. But she said it was okay; what she really wanted was to become a writer, so it would be good to get some different experience. She let me put my curlers and hairbrush in with her stuff and there was still room for her journal, and a copy of *Vogue* that she'd brought to read on the train. There was no closet.

The morning after we arrived, we had just finished putting our clothes away, having hung what dresses and skirts and things we could on the four hooks on the back of the door, and were trying to push our suitcases under the bed, when we heard someone on the porch outside our window, and then a knock. Footsteps across the kitchen, the door opening, and we caught bits of Dad's side of the conversation. "Oh, hello there. How's it going?" and "No, it's okay. I'm on afternoon shift. Aren't you too?" and "Oh, sure, I've got a bit of time. What's it you want to know?" By then he had stepped out on the porch and closed the door. The window was shut so we couldn't hear any more. Whoever it was must have been standing on the far side, over by where Syd had spilled the garbage.

When Blaze and I went out into the kitchen, Bertie was sitting at the kitchen table, the baby asleep in his buggy beside her. She smiled up at us, a paring knife held against the length of a red peel of an apple. "A visitor," she said. "It's young Herbie Weiss. He and his dad often go hunting with Tare. Probably wanting to arrange a time." She offered Blaze a cigarette from her package of Exports and they both lit up; she asked me to pour us all some coffee. She had a fresh potful on the stove.

The door opened again. Dad came in. "Hey, how about some of that coffee for me and Herbikins? I'm just going to take out a couple of chairs so we can sit in the yard. No point in wasting the sunshine. He says he's thinking about buying a horse and wants to know all about Appaloosas. Says there's a guy down by Elko has a couple to sell." He scooped up two of the wooden chairs and headed back through the open door. Bertie got up and, adding a splash of milk to two of the mugs I had just filled, went after him.

When she came in and closed the door, she leaned against it a minute, laughing. In a kind of whispering voice she said, "That dad of yours," shaking her head. She crossed to the table and sat down. "He really believes Herbie wants to find out about Appaloosas."

I guess we both looked surprised. I even said, "What do you mean? What'd he come for then?"

She picked up her cigarette from the ashtray, took a long drag. She said it to me, but she was looking sideways at Blaze. "Can't you guess? You're the newcomers in town. Your dad has probably been bragging. Now he'll keep him sitting out there talking horses the rest of the morning, boring him to death."

That was the very first inkling we had of the effect a couple of new girls in a town like Fernie could have. Well, I shouldn't really say "a couple" because I was barely thirteen and not very developed yet. But Blaze — she was a different story.

She puffed at her cigarette, sipped her black coffee, keeping her eyes steady on the serene face of the sleeping baby. But I could see her feet under the chair. And the top one, resting on the instep of the other, was moving back and forth really fast. I could just imagine what was going on in her head. A young hunter, someone interested in horses, that would give her some different experience. The very stuff she needed to become a writer.

CHAPTER TEN

LOTUS GAME II

When it gets difficult to get on with writing this story, I sit at my table and play with that Lotus Game contraption. But the more I pay attention to it, the less I can relate it to its name. We don't have any lotus flowers in Fernie, but if it has any power to it at all, it should work for any part of the world. And that is starting to happen. For me, it has become this town.

The two main wires that hold it together, the only two that are parallel, make me think of the two ways in and out of Fernie: Highway Number Three and the CPR. Blaze came in from the East on those straight, shiny tracks — with me. These many years later, she went out to the West on the winding strip of asphalt on a Greyhound bus — without me. So that's my reality.

And all the other lines curving, intersecting, folding back on themselves? Well, the river, of course, cutting under the highway in two places. (I say that even though I know the river was there first and the bridges were built over it.) Cutting and dividing. The people held within that long curvature of the river, between the two bridges, are Fernie. The part beyond the river, West Fernie, is just that — what lies beyond, what is apart. The differences between the two lie in obvious things: in Fernie the taxes go to city hall; the Fernie council and mayor do the managing; the Fernie Public Works maintain the streets; the Fernie Electrical Crew look after all the lighting. In West Fernie, taxes go to the B.C. Government; some official of rural districts in Victoria is responsible for management; B.C. Highways crews look after the roads and streets. It's true, the Fernie crew sees to lighting in West Fernie and even sends the town's meter reader over to read the meters. But only in the matter of police are the two the same. Both are under the jurisdiction of the RCMP. But even there, there is a difference. When they're not commenting on how "the cops have wooden legs," councillors have been heard joking with the constables about tickets for speeding. "When you chase a speeder," they say, "make sure you catch him this side of the bridge so the fine goes to the town, not to the government." It's only a pleasantry but it shows the difference.

  No, it's not the Lotus Flower Game. It's this town, Fernie.

  So the wires lead in and the wires bend out. They arc into mountains. There's inclusion and exclusion; cutting and dividing; joining and intersection.

  And, of course, to accent the pattern, there are the black beads...

CHAPTER ELEVEN

BLACKIE

Blackie touched the brake just enough to swing the three-quarter-ton around the corner into the alley, then hit the gas as he swerved into the parking space behind the grocery store. I bet Bogey wouldn't know how to drive a truck like this. Key off. Emergency on. A quick look in the rearview. Head a little to one side. That's the right look.

As he jumped down slamming the truck door behind him, he saw that Cash was at the back door. Oh here we go again.

"How many times do I have to tell you to take it easy with that truck?" He was a small man, a small dark man, with a head that seemed too little even for him, and his slim hands were constantly in motion. In the store they were always stacking cans, or ringing up cash, or stamping on prices. When they weren't doing any of those things they kept up their activity by underlining a point here, expanding one there, driving home this fact or that. They were certainly expressive hands. Right now one was hanging on to the middle post of the wide doorway, allowing the slight body to lean far out over the loading ramp so that the other could translate, out into the parking area, each important word as it was uttered.

"That's a brand new vehicle." The forefinger indicated the red truck, seeming to point directly to the driver's door where "Cash Grocery/ Fernie, B.C." stood out in bold black letters, with "Free Delivery" below in gold. "But the way you abuse it you'd think it was a year old already." That was accompanied by an open hand in an upward movement. "If you don't ease up on her, you can stay right here," fingers and thumb all pressed together and pointing downward, jerking several times toward the platform he was standing on. "You can stay right here and do the loading."

Blackie stood solid, balanced evenly on his two feet, looking up at him. He was dark too — even darker. His hair, slicked with Brylcreem so it swept up into a shiny flourish in the middle, looked even blacker than it was. It and the heavy curve of the black brows set up a striking contrast with the pale eyes, narrowed now to river-green slits as he opened his mouth wide in a loud laugh. "Goddammit, Cash. You know I'm the best goddam driver in town. Who'd you put on instead? You want all your customers complaining about your slow delivery?" He raised his foot so that the toe of his boot scraped along under the gold letters on the door.

"Watch that paint!" The hand, doubling to a fist, poked out at him. "And before you go, I want to see that vehicle washed and shining." The hand expressed the circular rubbing motion of the cleanup.

"Aw forget it." Blackie swung around and with his shoulders rotating to one side then the other as he stepped, he moved to the back of the truck and flung the doors open. "I'll just dump these empties and I'm on my way. I'll take it by the Esso in the morning for a wash."

Cash stepped back, the hand let go the pole, as the cardboard cartons landed around him. "Yeah? And they'll just put it on my bill. There's no need to pay that kind of money. . ."

"No," Blackie shouted as he heaved the last box and slammed the door shut. "No need at all when you got me to do it for nothing. Is that what you mean? Well, I'm out of here. Got to see a man about a dog."

As he turned his back on the spread-open hands, now both raised to the clear blue of the mountain air, he reached for his pack of cigarettes and moved off along the alley. That's about how Bogey would have done it. Strike the match with his thumbnail, look up at an angle as he raised the flame, take a long drag.

"Hey there, Blackie!" The voice came from the shed at the back of the firehall. A ragged figure moved out of the shadows toward him. "Can I come with you?"

"Oh, it's you old Siddy Boy. Sure, come along. But I'm just going to the Proctor and you know they won't let you in there. Not for a few years anyway."

"The Proctor?" Syd shuffled into step beside him. "I thought you liked the Roma best. I could go that far with you."

Blackie stopped and looked at him. It was still a bit hard to figure out the speech. Sometimes took a minute. Then he walked on. "Well, the Roma's one of my favourites. But I like them all. Any one of them will do." He grinned sideways and winked. "It's just that right now the Proctor's the closest." Another drag or two and he could chuck the smoke. Bogey'd never smoke it down to the butt. And that way, he could be just lighting up as he went into the bar. "What's up with you anyway?"

Syd looked behind him to make sure there was no one to overhear. "I got two sisters."

"What do you mean? All you got is Randy. She hasn't split in two or something, has she?"

"No. I mean I got two *new* sisters. They just come to live with us. He's their dad."

"You mean they're the old man's? You mean Hopalong's?"

Syd was grinning wide. "Yeah, and they're real nice."

"How old are they?"

"One's younger'n me, a little bit. The other's more like you. No, younger'n you."

Blackie had stopped again. He ground the butt into the gravel of the lane, put one hand on Syd's shoulder. "What's her name?"

"The young one's Babe. The other one's Blaze."

"Blaze eh? What's she look like?"

"She's like you."

"What do you mean?"

"She's tall like you, and her hair's like yours, and her eyes. That's why I came up here to wait for you. I says to myself she looks like she could be Blackie's sister, not mine."

"Like me, eh? You mean she's beautiful!" A loud laugh. He slapped Syd on the back. "Good for you, Siddy Boy. Blaze eh? Well you take a message from Blackie to Blaze. Okay?" He removed his hand and walked on.

Syd kept beside him. "Sure."

"You tell Blaze that Blackie will be calling around real soon. You tell her Blackie will be coming by. Coming by to have a real good look at her fire. You got that?"

Syd looked surprised. "Fire?"

"Yeah, to have a look at her fire. Don't forget that. You got it?" Syd nodded. "Okay kid, here's my watering place. You go home now and tell her. Tell her what Blackie says."

He closed the door on Syd and the alley and moved forward along the darkened hallway toward the sound of drinking men and the double – fresh and stale – smell of Fernie beer. He carefully touched the upward curve of his hair. Blaze, eh? Well, well. I wonder if she can whistle. Then he was at the door that opened into the bar. Time to get out the cigarette and the match.

PRESS

BIG GAME

Hunting starts the first day of September with sheep and goat season, then opens up for deer, elk, and moose two weeks later. And it closes for everything, except bear, the end of December.

Every year, it seems, there are amusing incidents to do with hunters around Fernie that, once they've been told and re-told, get built into the great fund of hunting legends that everybody knows about.

These stories don't appear in the *Fernie Free Press*; they're not that kind of news. No, they start with the participants themselves, sometimes told as a joke on one of the others of the party, sometimes admitted shamefacedly by the very one who is (or instantly becomes) the butt of the joke. Always, they find their immediate way to Mac. Here's the one he told this fall.

"I guess you won't have heard about the big one Patsy and Salvadore and Joey got on the weekend?"

The responses varied. "No. What was it? A moose?" And "Are those three still hunting together? I thought Sal and Joey had a fight down the Flathead last year." And "Good thing Patsy has those two to hunt with. He turns around once in the bush, he's lost."

"Well, they were down in the South Country. Joey just pulled off the road there by old Anselmo's place and you know how cold it turned Saturday morning? And that bit of new snow? Well, they headed off into the bush, following some fresh elk tracks they said. After about five minutes they heard something big crashing through the brush ahead so they fanned out, figuring to circle around it. They kept hearing it and they kept circling. Then first thing they knew they all met up. They all came together in some thick pines. You know how they grow down there in the South Country. And just off to one side, there was a big clear spot. That's where they figured whatever it was had gone. So they let off their safeties and rushed out, all three of them, shooting straight at the big black furry thing that suddenly showed up in the clearing."

"Was it a moose?" "Don't tell me they got that old black bear that's been giving everybody the slip!"

"No, it wasn't a moose. No, it wasn't a bear. It was Joey's pickup. Seems they'd wrapped it up in an old buffalo robe, one the family'd brought from the prairies. To keep it from freezing. When they took it off, there she was. Just riddled. You can see it for yourself, over at the Esso if you want. Curly towed it in last night. Yep, they got a big one, all right."

CHAPTER TWELVE

EXPECTATIONS

One big happy family. That is what he called us that first day. Well, it was big all right. Eight people in one family is quite a size, especially in that house. But happy? Maybe for a while.

Something I can say, Bertie was nice. She wasn't the stereotyped stepmother at all. For one thing, she was quite young, a lot younger than our dad. Too young to have five children already. (I guess I forgot to mention there was another boy — between Syd and Randy. He was with the father over at Britannia Beach.) Of course, she had started off early; Syd was born when she was sixteen.

She was lively. She liked nothing better than lots of people around, especially if they liked to eat and enjoyed talking. She was a great cook. Lots of times when I couldn't sleep I'd slip out to the kitchen in the middle of the night, without turning any lights on, just to have one more of her sausage rolls or dumplings. Everything she made was good, even as left-overs.

And she was generous. We were there for a month or so before Blaze found a job — and, of course, I was going to school — but Bertie kept Blaze in cigarettes, bought Sportsman for her especially, even though her own brand was Export, and she saw to it that there was enough other stuff we needed, like Tampax and Kleenex and writing paper and stamps. Blaze and I had both used up all our money just to get the train tickets.

And she didn't seem to be at all jealous the way stepmothers are supposed to be. Dad was a bit stand-offish with me, I guess because he'd never been around me much. I was just over a year old when our mother died, and he had gone west soon after. He left the three of us with family; we kept getting moved from one set of aunts and uncles to another. One aunt lived in Barrie, the others were all on farms up around Orillia. He had been back for a visit maybe three times in all. So it was no wonder we didn't feel comfortable.

But Dad and Blaze, that was different. He was always poking at her, teasing, putting an arm around her, squeezing, tickling, even giving her a whisker rub the way men do with young children. It made me sick. I thought he was plain silly, and it made Blaze so different, all giggly and foolish. They would look at each other, both of them with their eyes all twinkling, and then one would make a lunge and it would all start up. It didn't seem to bother Bertie at all. She'd just say, "Your dad is so happy to have the two of you here." I know I couldn't have stood it if I were either of them, her *or* Blaze.

Then I found out one day that he was disappointed in me. Remember how I mentioned there always seems to be a discrepancy between what you expect and how things actually are? Well, I knew that was true for me because Dad, and his house, and the new family weren't anything like what I thought they'd be. I don't think they were for Blaze either. At least, I remember how she kept saying while we were on the train, especially as we got near to Fernie, that the one thing she was really looking forward to was a good hot bath. I knew that after she left the farm and started working in Toronto she got into the habit of having a bath every day. She said it was really important to be super clean when you were "going to business." She was very fussy like that. She wouldn't eat anything with onions in it either. Anyway, after we'd arrived and got to the house and had supper and done the dishes and everyone was sitting around the kitchen table, Blaze said suddenly, "I think I'd just like to have a hot bath."

Bertie looked up from the baby's suckling sounds, shot a glance at Dad and said, "It's kind of late, isn't it?"

Then Blaze looked surprised, looking at her watch, "It's only 9:30. I usually have it much later, just some time before I go to bed."

Well, it turned out there was no hot water set-up in the house — no hot water at the kitchen sink or in the bathroom. The taps had only cold. No hot water tank at all. Bertie used water from the kettle for washing dishes. It was always singing its quiet song on the stove. But it was too soon for us to have noticed.

Dad said, "You want a bath? Okay. Granny will fix it up for you. Come on Granny. Get the boiler in here and fill it up." He motioned her away from the table and pointed to the back door. Blaze tried to say no, not to bother, but he wouldn't hear of anything different. "And Syd, you hop to it and bring in some more coal. You were supposed to do that before now anyway. Get a good hot fire going."

So we both sat there feeling bad. He wouldn't let us help. Said it was good for them to be useful. Blaze was embarrassed because she'd asked; I was embarrassed for her. We tried to make some kind of conversation with Dad and Bertie but we were too aware of the awkward efforts of the children: Randy running water into a pail in the sink then swinging it over the edge to pour into the copper boiler on the floor, part of each pailful slopping down the front of her skirt; and Syd staggering in with the bucket full of coal which he then loaded onto a narrow shovel. Chunks kept spilling onto the floor. Those he picked up with his hands and dropped, one by one, into the holes where he'd removed the stove lids. Black smoke billowed up and sent the smell like that along the railroad track throughout the room. Over an hour later the water in the boiler was hot and Dad emptied it into the tub in the bathroom. That's roundabout, I know, but I wanted to show YOU that things were different from what Blaze expected too.

But I had never thought that Dad would have had certain expectations as well. That first Saturday, just after we arrived, he and Blaze came back after an all-day trip up under the first of the Three Sisters. It wasn't to go hunting although Dad did take his rifle along. It was just for us to get the feel of the mountains, he said: the climbing , the difference. He had wanted both of us to go, but I couldn't because I'd set up a time to study with Gordie who lived not far from Dad's place, at the very end of Main Street alongside the golf course. He was in my class, the only one who was friendly so far, and he thought I could help him with French. Blaze and Dad had a great day. At least, they came in laughing and Dad kept teasing her about the DP guy, as he called him, they'd run into — the only person they saw up there all day. Apparently he was just finishing his lunch when they came across him sitting on a rock in the shade of some small alders. It was somewhere up where Fairy Creek begins. And, as Dad said, he took an orange out of his pack, looked as though he was ready to offer it to Blaze, then, changing his mind, said "Sorry Miss, last one." Dad kept poking Blaze and saying that to her: "Sorry Miss, last one." And she was teasing him about splitting open the back seam of his pants. She told Bertie and me, "I said you should be going home in a barrel, and you know what he said?" And she jabbed him in the ribs. "He said, 'Well, I certainly won't be backing into town'." That was what they were like. And Bertie just laughed, even added a little joke of her own: "It's like the bear that went over the mountain," she said. Then, after a pause, "with the little bear behind."

      Anyway, what came out of that day that showed me that Dad had expectations of me was that he told Blaze on the mountain, and she told me after when we were in bed, that he had thought I would be out "running all over the mountains with a twenty-two." That's what he said. "Running all over the mountains with a twenty-two, shooting coyotes and cutting off their ears to collect the bounty. Not sitting around talking a bloody foreign language with boys."

Well, I did know how to use a twenty-two; I used to shoot groundhogs for my uncle on the farm, but only because they were doing a lot of damage to his crops. But I'd never seen a coyote in my life. I couldn't see what harm they could be doing up on the mountainsides so why would I want to shoot them?

And the bounty bit just made me feel that maybe he wasn't so happy that I was there, costing him money, when he had a big enough family already.

CHAPTER THIRTEEN

UNDER FERNIE EYES

It was hard for me to do homework in that house. I was used to having my own room at the farm. I had even fixed up a little table with some boards for shelves to make it into a desk. There wasn't anything similar that I could do in Blaze's and my room. There wasn't even a chair. I could lie on the bed but there wasn't enough light, just the bulb on the ceiling, even for reading. So I'd end up at the kitchen table. It was light enough by the window but it was tempting to just stare out across Baker Avenue to the planer mill, and watch the smoke puffing up from the burning sawdust pile. Mostly, I couldn't even see the high hill beyond it. Bertie didn't like to put Stormy out in his carriage for a morning sleep, but she said it wasn't nearly as bad as in Michel and Natal, where the babies and all their covers got black all over after ten minutes. And the women couldn't hang out their washing. The coal dust would stick right to it while it was still wet. She didn't like living so close to the sawmill but she was glad Fernie's mine was six miles away in Coal Creek instead of right in town.

That one particular afternoon there was only Bertie and Jackie and me in the house. Dad was on day shift, and Syd seemed to roam around uptown a lot after school (Bertie had told us about all the various guys he'd go to visit, mostly at wherever they worked. They all liked him, she said; seemed to take an interest in him). Randy was looking after the little girl next door, and Blaze was uptown with Tex. She liked to take him when she went to the post office to check the mail. She got a lot of letters from friends in Ontario. One time there were seven letters for her all in one day. She liked the image of herself pushing the baby in the stroller.

She liked to think people would assume he was hers — the young mother with the beautiful baby boy. She laughed a bit at herself about it to me; said she even turned her high school ring around so the plain side showed and looked like a wedding ring.

She should have known better, though. She should have realized that everyone in town knew immediately who we were. Just because they were all strangers to us didn't mean that we were strangers to them. After all, they all knew everybody in town and we were the only two newcomers. For instance, it was only about a week after our arrival that Sydney came sidling up to Blaze at the sink where she was filling the boiler for her bath and punched her gently on the arm and said, "I know someone who's going to come over and see you."

Her hand resting on the tap, she said, "Who? Who even knows me?"

His mouth was in its usual wide grin. "It's Blackie. My friend Blackie. It's something about a fire."

Blaze looked to Bertie questioningly. Bertie laughed. "Oh, that's Blackie. He drives the delivery truck for Cash Grocery. And he *is* pretty black, in quite a few ways."

"What do you mean?"

"Well, for one thing, he's real dark. Black hair. Part Indian. And for another, he's a terrible drinker. When he's sober, he's the nicest person, but when he's drunk he's a real rangatang. Always in fights or some kind of trouble." She turned to Sydney then. "You shouldn't even be telling him about these girls being here. You know better than that."

She reached out to slap at him but he swayed out of her reach, laughing. "He's going to come to see you."

And it wasn't more than a week later when she got a ride home with Kenny Ferguson. She had been uptown checking at Trites Woods Department Store to see if she could get a clerking job and this young blond guy pulled up beside her in a blue Studebaker. All he said was, "Can I give you a lift anywhere?"

She said, "Okay, thanks. I'm just going home," and was about to give him directions, but he said, "Yeah, I know where that is." He didn't say anything else as they drove along Victoria Avenue except to tell her his name when she asked, and the place he worked — East Kootenay Power. He just turned over to Baker Avenue and stopped by the back door.

So she must have realized that everybody knew Tex wasn't her baby, that they all knew he was her half brother. Still, that's what she was like.

But I was talking about sitting at the table looking out the window that one particular day. Suddenly there was a rush of footsteps down the stairs, the back door banged shut and, next thing, I saw Jackie running out across the road and climbing through the wire fence. I called to Bertie who was at the ironing board by the door to the front porch. "Is it okay for Jackie to go across the road? He's over on the tracks."

"Oh yes." She set down the iron and came to the window beside me. "That just means that Lee Choy is coming. He must have spotted him from upstairs. All the kids love to see him. He gives them candy, that hard kind with the stripes. Lee Choy, the Chinaman."

And sure enough, there was a figure in drab clothing coming into view from behind the cottonwoods, heading toward uptown. And Jackie was running along the tracks to meet him. When they came together they both stopped. The man reached into his pocket and extended his hand to the boy. They walked along together, the boy's head tilted up to the man, until they were even with the house. Then Jackie turned off into the ditch, ducked through the fence, and came smiling into the house, one cheek enlarged and one hand clutched tight.

"He works at the mill," Bertie was saying. "On the green chain. And he's the watchman too, because he lives so close. He's got a shack on the far side of the mill property, along the tracks.

It's a flat place, so he's got quite a good-sized garden. Sells stuff to anyone who wants to go down there and get it."

Lee Choy, I thought. A nice Chinese name. And I still had the image of the lined cheeks, the slanted eyes, the straight-across smile, that had just passed by. For one moment he had looked directly across at the window. He knows we're here, I thought. Just like everyone else in town, he knows who we are.

CHAPTER FOURTEEN

CHRISTMAS

I can't remember clearly just how Dad's estrangement started, I guess because it wasn't very definite in the beginning. I do know that by December he had totally removed himself from us. I remember that because of the way Blaze was so definite about making it a good Christmas for the kids, in spite of him.

Afterwards, we tried to backtrack to figure out what had happened to change things. First there was the fact that I didn't go running all over the mountains shooting coyotes. Then there was that day that Blaze told him about some self defence holds she'd learned at the modelling school in Toronto, and he said "Why don't you show me?" in a tone that meant it was some womanish thing that wouldn't work. Somehow she managed to flip him right off the bed onto the floor. There was no one more surprised than she was. She had never tried it on anyone so big before, just on the other would-be models. Certainly not on anyone over six feet and about a hundred and eighty pounds. She laughed at first, but when he didn't say anything, just got up and sat on a chair, she tried really hard to apologize. He finally said, "Don't worry, Girl. It didn't hurt nothing." But he just sat there. She told me after that she felt kind of good in a way. If she could flip him like that, it meant she could protect herself from. . .well, whatever. It must have occurred to her, just then, that there wouldn't be much need for self defence techniques in an out-of-the-way little town like Fernie.

Another time, when he'd got over the indignity, or whatever it was, of the surprising flip, he was back doing his usual tease routine when he spotted a hole in the knee of her jeans. He stuck his finger in it and said, tugging, "You know, if anybody showed up in the mine with this kind of thing, the guys would just grab hold, give it a jerk and rip the pant leg wide open." There was something about that low laugh and the pulling at her jeans that made her slap his hand away and step back. He went after her, poking her in the ribs and trying to make her laugh. She stood stock still and said, very forcefully, "You know, Dad, I don't really like that."

He pulled back. "What do you mean?"

"Well, I really don't like you tickling and fooling around all the time."

That was it. The end. He never touched her again. No more poking or tickling. Not even a hug. All that was over.

And the time the Schianni brothers picked us up outside the post office and insisted on driving us home. Instead, they took us all the way out to Hosmer, just to show us the country, they said. They were both quite nice and even talked Blaze into going to the Hosmer Hotel with them for a beer. She took a minute first to flip her hair up and put a few pins in it, so she didn't look under-age. I sat in the car and watched the sun as it sank slowly behind the Lizard Range, colouring the backs of the elephants pink and mauve as it went into the sparse clouds. We were late getting home. Bertie and the kids had already done the dishes and the chores. We told Dad how we hadn't wanted to go and that it was just a drive out toward Michel. He didn't say anything, just went out. Afterwards, he told Bertie, and she passed it on, that he couldn't stand the way we ran around with those wild Schianni boys and then lied about it. I guess somebody told him about the Hosmer bar. She said he was real disappointed in us.

Even by Christmas we didn't have any money ahead, but, as I said, Blaze was determined to make it a good day for the kids, to make up for the bad feeling around the house. She was working as cashier in the grocery part of Trites Woods by then and I did some waitressing at the Diamond Grill after school and on weekends but we still didn't have much to spend on presents. Nevertheless, she found an old used toboggan somewhere, probably at Ed's Second Hand, for only a few dollars. She worked on it when the kids weren't around — sanded it endlessly, repaired the rope, put on several coats of varnish. That was the big secret, the big present, for them all. I think we had some little gifts besides. And I don't remember what we gave Bertie or what she gave us. Blaze and I went partway up to the Saddle and cut a nice bushy little balsam, and we got the kids to help make the decorations.

By Christmas morning the tree was all ready. It had to go in the kitchen, of course, squeezed in between the window and the side of the cupboard, but it looked jaunty, and even defiant, with its paper garlands and foil baubles. Both Bertie and Blaze had been saving the silver paper from their cigarette packs for weeks. And the house was filled with the smell of roasting turkey.

We all helped Bertie. It was Syd's job to keep just the right amount of coal on the fire for a steady temperature. I peeled the potatoes and carrots and put them on. Blaze did the apples for the pie. Bertie was the only one who could make good pastry or gravy. Jackie opened the tin of cranberry sauce and wiped the glasses. Randy put a checked tablecloth over the oil cloth, and Blaze pulled nearly everything out of the cupboard looking for plates that matched. She had even bought some paper serviettes with poinsettias on them.

When everything was on the table, Bertie went over to push open the bedroom door. It was locked. She turned for a moment, her hand still on the knob, and we saw the way her jaw was set tight. Then she faced the door again, knocked softly, head bent, saying, "Dinner is ready, Tare." She returned to the table, motioned for all of us to sit down. Jackie reached toward the bowl full of stuffing. She slapped his hand away. "You wait," she whispered.

He sat up straight, his hands in his lap, his mouth set in a straight line. Right before, I had teased him that I was going to scrub off his freckles with the face cloth, and I had run the damp towel over his hair and then slicked it back with the comb. With his skin so shiny, even red in spots, he looked like a sad-faced celluloid doll with a bit of a fever. Blaze leaned over toward him. "Jackie, you look handsome as can be." She was whispering too. His face relaxed. He almost smiled. And we all waited.

There was the thump of a book hitting the floor. Usually he read paperbacks — Zane Grey, Louis L'amour, anything Western he could find — but lately he'd gone back to some of his old hardcovers. There was one on Billy the Kid, one about the history of the West, and a set on horse training. I'd seen them the day before when I was making their bed and cleaning up in there.

The door opened and he came out. Dark woollen pants over longjohns, sock feet, and the wrinkled black silk neckerchief that he always wore, its silver-dollar keeper pushed up tight against his neck. He hadn't shaved or anything. His hair stuck up at the back. He took his place at the head of the table without so much as looking at any one of us.

It would have been a dinner eaten in total silence if it hadn't been for Blaze. She praised Bertie for the turkey that was "done just perfectly, and so brown" and for the gravy and the dressing; and me for the vegetables "cooked just right." She made the kids have seconds of everything, all the time telling them they had to be nice and full so they could enjoy opening the presents. That was going to happen right after the pie, *with ice cream,* and before we did the dishes or even cleared the table. Then afterwards, we would all go out and play in the snow. Wasn't it a nice sunshiny day? and maybe even go up the little hill by the Pest House. Bertie cut the pie and passed the plates along, Blaze flourishing a spoonful of ice cream over each, then plopping it down on top of the flaky crust. Dad had pressed his fork sideways into the pointy end and was raising the first mouthful by the time she got to his place. She flicked the ice cream onto his plate anyway, then went on to Syd who was waiting with plate raised. Dad finished eating the pie only, looking intently all the time at some point on the tablecloth in the shadow of the teapot. Then he got up, scraping his chair legs on the floor, and next thing we knew the door closed and there was the click of the lock.

    We tried not to look at each other. But I could see Randy and Syd were smiling a bit, uncertain just how to be. Bertie was shaking her head. Blaze reached for a cigarette, offered one to Bertie. "Couldn't even put on a shirt," she said, striking her match on the package, right across the head of the man with the fish.

    And Jackie leaned sideways, looking up into her face as she held the match. "Can I have his ice cream?"

C

BEARHUNT

He shifted the rifle from his right shoulder to his left but the ache was still there. His rubber boots crunched through the dry leaves and the sprinkling of snow. His right foot felt sore, must be rubbing. Maybe a hole in the sock. At least there was a trail up to the Saddle. Before long it would open up. Once he was on the spine of the ridge he would be able to see down along both sides. He knew the spot where Tango said he'd seen the tracks that morning. If the bear was still around it would be visible from there, at least with the glasses.

How long had he been hunting bear anyway? He hadn't started until long after the boys and Helen were grown up. Probably when they took over running the hotel. The changing of the sign, that was what stood for the changing of his life. Winkie sitting on top of the ladder, with a bucket of paint and a skinny, long-handled brush. The old greyed letters: *1908 Roma Hotel Prop. C. Ciriani*. The new ones were black and glossy: an "s" added to *Prop*; "and family" added to his name. And he had called up, "You'd better go over the old part too."

But Winkie had hollered back, "No, it's better to leave it like this. Then everyone will remember you, that you were the one who built the Roma, back in '08."

And it was right after that he had the dream. He still remembered it clearly. Until then he hadn't realized that the hunt had always been part of him, even back in Italy. He hadn't been born in Rome like everyone thought. That was just easier because no one here knew anything about the places in Italy — only Rome, and maybe Florence, Naples or Venice, just the big cities. And the leaning tower of Pisa (which they always pronounced "pizza"). One thing they did know was that Italy was shaped like a boot;

some even joked about how Sicily got kicked out into the sea because it was an island separated from the mainland at the toe.

Well, he could have told them about Peschici, he realized now. He could have said how it was on the Gargano Peninsula and explained that the Gargano itself was actually the spur, just above the heel of the boot.

The hillsides there weren't like this, not all a tangle of alders and huckleberry bushes. No, the slopes were covered with pines and oak, and underneath it was all clear, like a smooth, quiet carpet. Oak and pine woods and, in places, ridges of chalky rock, looking like white-washed walls running along the curve of the hill. And he walked up in there, listening to the sea off to the east. What was the hunt then? Nothing he'd been clearly aware of. Had he thought about bears then?

There were herds of greyish cows, with long tails that were especially hairy and black at the ends. They wore massive rounded brass bells at their throats. And there were herds of goats — black goats, with shaggy hair and erect tails.

How had he first thought of bear? Or was it just the hunt for a new place, a new country even? He remembered looking out from the window of the bedroom he shared with three brothers. Far below were the two little sculpted bays with the stone jetty between. The rocky walkway curved out into the translucent pale blue of the water; arcs of foam came pushing in to shore. He could remember the exact shape of the white, crested waves because they seemed like a message in that new strange language, the one that edged into one small corner of his brain. The message coming in from the sea. Sea after sea, or Cee after Cee — his initials, waters moving westward, pushing at the sand of the shore.

And when he stood down there on the sand looking up to the two headlands — the one to the north tree-covered, slanting down to end in a sheer rock cliff drop to the water; the one to the south solidly covered with the tiers of white houses of his village (an ancient town on an ancient hill) — was the urgency of the hunt with him then? Before him the noisy sea, behind him the quiet valley filled with olive groves and vineyards. All to be left behind.

But he had brought with him the ideas of both, and they stayed always with him: the plastic grapes, some green, some purple, hanging in the bar; the yellow raisins ordered every year from Australia for making wine; the olives, briny and tart, a full barrel of them to dip into, bought at Martinelli's store.

The dream was always with him too. Even after all the bears over the years. He had long ago lost count. The dream had formed into words; it could recite itself to him at any moment. It had been with him since the beginning, before he'd found Yolanda; long before the children were grown. Not in Italian. Not in English. It was simply thought without language.

> I knew I'd find my bear at that place. But I was in no hurry. I wanted to put off the actual confrontation. So I stayed on the higher ridge, lying among the yellow lilies, knowing. But before long, he came up that ridge and I knew then that he knew too. So there was no putting it off any longer. When I took up my rifle he turned, sadly moving down again. I followed, thinking: the further down he goes before I get him, the easier it will be. It should be easier, too, shooting from behind. But he turned, and I had to shoot him full in the face. After he fell, I still felt the danger and went to him. But he just opened his mouth weakly, and we both knew it was finally done, after that long awful hunt.

He lowered his head and shook it from side to side to dispel the dream. He would soon be in the open. Just another five minutes along the trail. As he brought his head up, he stopped suddenly. There, just where the trail curved to the right, was the bear. A young black. It must have just rounded the curve. It sat on its haunches looking at him.

He took the rifle down slowly from his shoulder. He raised the barrel, releasing the safety catch as he brought it up level. He could see glints of light in the amber eyes that looked at him steadily. Light eyes. More the colour of goats' eyes. Bears were supposed to have dark brown. These were the colour of ripened grapes, or half-ripe olives. A gust of wind whipped a tamarack branch against the tree trunk just beside him. It made a swishing sound, like waves on sand. He lowered the barrel, rested the wooden butt on the ground. The bear stood up, turned and loped off, disappearing around the bend of the trail.

The old man turned then too. He knew that he and the bear would hear each other's retreating footsteps for a long time.

Mother of God, he thought. Why do I tell them I'm from Rome? He slipped the rifle strap over his shoulder again. From now on everyone's going to know the truth. His step was quiet and quick on his own tracks in the snow. Yes sir. Everyone's going to know I'm a Peschici man.

CHAPTER FIFTEEN

DANCE

Dad and Bertie didn't have a radio so the only way to keep up on what music was current out in the rest of the world was to play the juke box or, in my case, since I worked at the Diamond Grill, to listen to what other people played on it. The selections were mostly Country; that's what everyone in town seemed to like, and that suited me okay because I had been brought up listening to Western stuff on the radio, and on old records. When I was a little kid I took a real shine to Gene Autry.

But Blaze was different. She had danced to a lot of Big Bands in Toronto — Duke Ellington, the Dorseys, Artie Shaw, Glen Miller. She used to go with a guy from Ottawa who worked for the National Film Board. Whenever he was in Toronto (and it seems he was there a lot) he'd take her out to things like that, and to fancy restaurants. That's how she came to know about menus and wine lists and foreign movies and, of course, music. One night, she said, she actually bumped right into Stan Kenton. She was hurrying along a hallway to go to a washroom; he was in a hurry going the other way.

So she had expectations of Fernie that weren't very real. The first time I noticed — well, the first was the hot bath incident, but the one *after* that — was the first time she went to a local dance. It was not long after Herbie Weiss was over that day talking about Appaloosas. He got in touch with her soon after that (I don't know how, because Dad and Bertie didn't have a phone), and he asked her to go to the dance with him; it happened to be down in the South Country, at Roosville. She told me all about it the next morning.

They drove down through Phillips Canyon; that part really impressed her. After you go through the tunnel and past Elko, you turn south off Highway Three and what you're doing is following the Elk River on its way to join the Kootenay just above Dorr. You start off on the flat — that's what the South Country is like: all flat and pines and hardly any underbrush — but then you begin going down, and down. It's all switchbacks, and there are lots of trees so you feel awful closed in. And you keep going down like that, back and forth, around sharp corners, until you get right even with the river. There's an old wooden bridge. Then you start going up again and it's the same thing: switchback after switchback, dense trees, and steady climbing. Then suddenly you're up on the flat again. I didn't have to get all this description from Blaze because I've been there, myself, since then, quite a few times. It was still fairly light when they left so she saw most of the canyon going the one way. Coming back she said it was scary, all in the dark, but mostly because she thought Herbie was driving it too fast.

Roosville is right on the U.S. border so YOU can tell how far they had to go, about thirty miles. You have to go past Grasmere, and across Tobacco Plains. That's the Indian Reserve. Anyway, she said that by the time they got there it was too dark to see anything much. She didn't think it was a town, just a few houses, a church, and this dance hall that was off by itself with some trees around it.

YOU can imagine her going in there with all those Big Band experiences behind her. I have to imagine even them: fancy dresses and tables with candles, and waiters on the go with drinks, sparkling glasses with olives and maraschino cherries and swizzle sticks in them. (I knew about them because Blaze had a collection of swizzle sticks, with the names of the nightclubs on them, that she kept in our top drawer). And the stage with the Big Band players and all their instruments, and the big square of shiny hardwood dance floor.

The Roosville hall was more like an arena. There were chairs all along the walls, at both sides and one end. The wall at the other end was covered, at least up to reaching height, with double-wire pegs where people hung their coats and jackets. And there was a little stand there too where they sold pop and hot chocolate.

It was already crowded when they arrived. The first thing that surprised Blaze was a little boy, about eight, out dancing on the floor with a rather fat woman. Then she saw that there were lots of children, mostly on the sidelines, and old ladies and old men, in fact there were people of all ages from babies wrapped in blankets to white-haired and hunchbacked persons barely able to shuffle from one chair to another.

And the music. It was a live band of three: guitar, fiddle, accordion. That was the first time she'd ever heard pieces such as "Bonaparte's Retreat," or "Oh My Sholilah," not to mention all the strange new ones whose names she couldn't remember or maybe didn't even hear announced.

But she was excited about the new dances she learned and she even showed me the steps. Dad and Bertie did have an old gramophone and, along with all the Wilf Carter (Dad's favourites were "Swiss Moonlight Lullaby" and "Old Shep"), Hank Snow (he liked "Movin' On"), and his most favourite of all, Kitty Wells (especially "Dust on the Bible"), there were some polkas and schottishes. We did the step-step-kick and the twirling around until we were half sick with dizziness and giggling.

So that evening at Roosville was a success. It was partly the unexpectedness of it, I think, not so much her time with Herbie. She said too that there were two good looking young guys there. She said "*really* good looking." She asked somebody about them; they were two brothers, from the Reserve.

The other thing she said was, "Remember the guy who sent the message with Syd? about coming over? Blackie?"

I looked up expectantly. "Was he there?"

"Yeah, he was."

"Did you dance with him?"

"No. He wasn't inside much. Herbie says he doesn't know why he goes to dances. He mostly just sits out in his truck and drinks beer."

She looked away quickly, then hoisted Tex out of his high chair and said, "Come on old baby. It's time to do 'Call of the Pipes' again." She stood him on the floor in front of her, his back against her knees. Then, bending over him, with one hand grasping each of his ankles from behind, she started the tune: "Dah dah, d'dah dah dah" as she made his little cracked leather shoes step in time. Forward four steps: right, left, right, left; then a four-beat pattern with the right foot: forward, side, back, stand; and the same with the left; then four steps forward again. He seemed to enjoy it. At least he was laughing out loud. But, at the same time, his wide eyes had kind of a surprised look.

CHAPTER SIXTEEN

ITALIAN EXPERIENCE

As YOU can see, there were many things that were very different for us. One that I haven't mentioned specifically so far was the variety of the people's backgrounds in Fernie. During our public school days in Ontario, everyone in the community was of English or Scots or Irish descent — and mostly Protestant. When I went to high school in town, there was one Jewish girl, Goldie, and one Italian family, Pincivero, and there were two or three Roman Catholics in every class who, every morning, left the room and stood in the hallways so they wouldn't have to listen to our version of the Lord's prayer.

Blaze came in contact with more ethnic types when she went to Toronto. She modelled for some Jewish wholesalers and she lived not far from an Italian open market and she even went to a Catholic church once, for midnight mass, just for the experience, she said. She told me many times how important it was to keep open-minded and learn all you could about other people and their ways. She seemed particularly interested in "the Italian experience."

So Blaze liked working at the grocery in Trites Wood Department Store; it gave her the chance to learn about many different people. It was a quick way to get to know the town, she said. She was the cashier. It was the first time she had ever run a machine like that, but it was real simple for her and she liked packing the various items into the big brown paper bags, keeping the light stuff and the fragile stuff on the top, and making everything fit just right.

Not that everyone in town got their groceries at Trites Wood. A lot of people, Bertie for instance, swore by Cash Grocery.

Mr. Cash had a solid reputation for giving the best buys, the best service (he would take your list and get everything on it for you himself), and the fastest delivery. Also, everyone knew how well he treated his staff. He gave them regular raises and always a big bonus at Christmas. They knew ahead of time how much it would be because it was figured out as a certain percentage of their salary. Blaze's bonus that year at Trites was a pair of nylons — taupe, at that, a colour she didn't even like. Some people said Cash set up the bonus scheme because he'd rather give the money to his workers than to the government. But even that added to his reputation. Everyone approved wholeheartedly.

There were a couple of small stores in town too; one down by the hospital, one on the other side of the highway in the Annex, and one in the North End, not far from Dad and Bertie's place. It was on Victoria Avenue (YOU will remember that was Main Street), just a few blocks from the golf course. The kids went there for candy whenever they had a few cents to spend. I had seen the sign "Martinelli's Grocery" over the door.

Even though not everyone went to Trites Wood for groceries, most people went there fairly often for something or other because it was a department store. The grocery was in the middle, with the hardware and then the ladies' wear on one side, and men's wear and dry goods on the other. Upstairs, along with the office complex and the washrooms, was the furniture department.

So Blaze got to know the people of the town much sooner than I did. Or, at least, they knew who she was. An old man she had never seen before, coming through the check-out with a pipe in his mouth and a tobacco pouch in his hand, said to her in a very broad Scots accent, "And are you missing the city life? Must be a real change for you." It turned out that his daughter lived in Don Mills; he and his wife went to Ontario nearly every year to visit her.

And a middle-aged man with a thick Polish accent said, over a sack of potatoes and a cartful of cabbages (on special that day), "You're the girl that's good with guns? Your dad said I could come over sometime and you sight in my new rifle. It's a two-seventy. That okay?"

Then there were the younger ones who came by just to look her over, the new girl in town. Reginald from Menswear told her about one who kept asking him to introduce them. He was shy and wanted to do things right. His father was the mayor.

Blaze liked the people she worked with too. That was part of the reason she enjoyed the job. For one thing, they were all male. She told me once she got along a lot better with men than with women. For another, they were of different backgrounds. Besides the manager, Salvador (Italian), there was Johnny (Slavic), who ran the meat counter at the back, and Joe (Czech), who looked after the fruit and vegetables, and there were two young ones — Eddy (Italian) and another Johnny (Ukrainian). They were teenagers who came in after school and on Saturdays. They were her favourites. They teased her and joked with her, quarrelled over whose turn it was to help her with the bagging, brought her chocolate bars from the basement storeroom, and told her stories and bits of gossip about everyone in town, but especially about Salvador whom they disliked intensely although, since he spent most of his time upstairs bothering the secretaries, Blaze wasn't clear just what their problem with him was. She liked Eddy in particular and every time he came to work she got him to teach her a few new words in Italian.

I remember it was Eddy who gave Blaze the spaghetti recipe. She brought it home one day after work and was showing it to Bertie. Bertie had never made Italian spaghetti in her life and she was real anxious to try it. "Let's make it right now," she said. "For supper." When they checked the cupboards, I was the one who got sent to Martinelli's store for the missing ingredients, since Cash Grocery was already closed.

The bell tinkled over the door as I went in. A strange mixture of smells came to me out of the darkened interior. As my eyes adjusted to the dimness, I made out rows of wooden barrels along one side and open bins — a set of large ones and a set of small ones — along the other. The back wall was pretty well all shelves, right to the ceiling — shelves with various coloured pickles or preserves in jars, and rows of tinned goods and bright boxes, some of metal, some of cardboard. At the front, low beneath the small oval of window, was a long counter with a glass-fronted case displaying cheeses of all shapes and sizes: some squat and round, some in rectangular slabs; some with waxy coverings, some crusted with a web-like fibre, some dark and orangey, others almost white; some cut into so that they showed their solid shiny interiors or their gaping holes, others whole with their thick rinds ranging from pale yellow to bright red. There were sausages in there too, of different lengths and colours and sizes. All the cheeses and the sausages had little paper flags, stuck in on pins, with printing on them in black letters giving the name and the price per pound.

I didn't take it all in at one glance the way it sounds; I've been back there many times. That first time, I just darted my eyes about the place for a general sense and, as I finished with a sweep up above the counter, a broad calm face moved out from behind the red pointy peppers and white bulging garlics that hung in long strings from the ceiling. He didn't say anything. He just looked at me, his eyes like small peepholes in a pale expanse of face, and twisted his mouth from side to side.

"Could I have some spaghetti?"

I thought I heard a sigh as the bulky body emerged from behind the counter. He moved toward the row of large tins. "What kind?"

"I don't know. They just said spaghetti."

He raised his eyes to the ceiling. "I have vermicelli, spaghettini, fettucini, linguini..." As he said each name, he rested a forefinger on a different tin.

"Do you have any just plain spaghetti?"

The sigh came again. "How much?"

"Oh, they didn't say. Enough for one dinner?"

"How many people?"

"Seven," I said, then added, "But three of them are just kids." I thought after I said it that it was kind of strange because after all, Syd was nearly my age and Randy wasn't much younger.

He took out two handfuls of the long skinny sticks that looked like stiff lengths of yellowish string, then pressing it all together, as much as both hands could hold, moved back to the counter where he set it on a sheet of brown paper, using one hand to keep the lengths all parallel while he wrapped the paper around with the other and tied it with white string. His head turned slowly to look at me again.

I said, "And some cheese. Do you have Parmesan?"

He slid a door open at the back of the glass case and reached for a small hard looking slab. "How much?"

"I don't know... Well, enough for that much spaghetti?"

He brought out a wide-bladed knife from somewhere below and deftly cut off a chunk. I thought I could detect a little flick of amusement about his mouth. When he wrapped it, this time in brown paper with a waxy surface that went next to the cheese, he raised his eyes to my face again.

"Tomato paste," I said.

Without a further question, he shuffled to the far end and took one small tin from a lower shelf. On his way back he stopped at the row of small tins and looked at me questioningly. I was at a loss but I shot a quick look at Blaze's scribblings on my piece of paper and said, "Allspice?"

"Oh." And he scooped out some reddish powdery stuff. "You got Mrs. Megale's recipe, have you?"

"I don't know. My sister got it from Eddy. Eddy at Trites?"

"Yeah, that's Eddy Megale." He was back at the counter, setting the tiny paper bag on top of the packet of cheese.

"And that's all," I said, crumpling the paper and shoving it into a rear pocket.

"No, you need some of these." He reached up and pulled off two of the wizened red peppers. "And one of these." He plucked a fat white garlic and plopped it on the counter.

"But the recipe doesn't call for..."

"Never mind. You add some of *my* recipe. Mrs. Megale is okay but when you use allspice you need lots of garlic. Cut it up real small." He held the garlic between the thumb and forefinger of his left hand and made little chopping motions with his right. "Fry it in with your onions." Now that he was smiling, his eyes didn't seem so small. They weren't lost in his face any more. "And when you get it all together, when it's cooked and mixed on the platter, with the Parmesan grated on top, then you do this." He picked up a pepper, crunched it between his fingers and thumb, letting the little red bits sprinkle onto the package of spaghetti. "Not too much. It's hot. You gotta get used to it." He swept the garlic, and the peppers with all the little loose bits, into another bag. "There you go." He punched in the prices on the till and showed me the white slip.

"Thanks," I said. "Thank you very much," and held out a bill.

He took it, and gave me the change. "Get your stepmother to help you with it. She's a good cook. But be sure to tell her about the garlic."

I hadn't seen him move but just as I was going out — the bell was still tinkling — I felt a sharp pinch on my right buttock. I closed the door fast but still I heard his voice coming through.

"You come back again. And next time, bring that big sister of yours."

I hurried home with the parcels. Blaze was the one who should have done that shopping. I wasn't the one who was so keen on having "the Italian experience."

PRESS

THE QUAIL BLOCK

The temperature had risen during the night. What had been a white, smooth covering the evening before was now a layer of greyish slush, especially where boot prints had chequered it on all the routes leading to the post office.

Hornquist hadn't come around that way yet with the plough.

Despite the wetness and drabness, Mac stood outside on the wide cement landing, up to his boot tops in slush, his cap in his hands. As each arrival stomped up the steps in front of him he made sure to sound very serious. He kept his eyes lowered.

"I guess you haven't heard about the rebuilding they're gonna have to do in the Quail Block?" That was the name of the building that contained Quail's Hardware and several small stores and businesses, ones that changed hands fairly often.

He waited for some response. "No, what happened?" or "Which one is it this time?" or "Do you mean the new laundry? I'd be surprised if there wasn't some damage with all those Chinese living in back."

"No, it's in the old drugstore place. Stairs completely collapsed."

"You mean where Ekaterina just opened up her gift shop?"

"Yep, that's it. Ekaterina's new place. Stairs to the basement have to be completely rebuilt."

At that, an anticipatory smile appeared on the listener's face. Everyone knew Ekaterina, daughter of the Dalmatian couple who ran the bakery. Too many bakery sweets, all her life, the town had always murmured. At fifteen it was public knowledge that she weighed an even two hundred pounds. In the last nine years she and her parents had been careful never to divulge her weight, but everyone agreed the figure certainly had not gone down at all. And they laughed at their own play on words. No, the figure certainly had not diminished. If anything, it had grown. It had grown alarmingly.

But now, "What happened?"

"She was goin' down to the washroom." Mac held his cap by the peak in one hand, pushed the fist of the other into it to make a fat bulge. "And she went right through them steps, just like that. Lucky it was near the bottom."

"What'd she do?" and "Was there anyone around?"

"Well, it happened just after quittin' time. Lucky Bert was late closin' up. Said he was showin' some American every darn fishin' rod in the store. If he hadn't heard her, she'd a been there all night. Caught — wedged – right in between them steps. He said he had to go and phone Wilf for help. It took them over half an hour to get her out."

"Was she hurt bad?" or "Is she in the hospital?"

"No, she's fine. No more'n a scratch or two. Runnin' her business same as usual, even with Jock there puttin' in the new stairs. But Wilf and Bert, that's another story. Neither one of them'll be at work today. Both on their way to Cranbrook."

"Cranbrook? What's in Cranbrook that's got anything to do with it?"

The fist squirming inside the cap. "They both had to get appointments with the chiropractor. Wilf pulled the muscles in his shoulder and Bert put his back out."

MIDDLE

The Town

SUN

Punishment. What good is punishment? It doesn't really change anybody's ideas, especially when it's old world punishment here in Canada. He shifted his weight to his left knee to try to ease the pain, but he already knew it wouldn't help. Every time he was punished, he tried to work it out logically and always ended up with the same answer: even distribution of weight minimizes the pressure at any one point on the skin. The skin of his knees caught and pinched between his kneecaps and the kernels of wheat on the floor. Why punish his skin for his insistence on his rights? He sat back on his heels but that only shifted the pain to the balls of his feet. No, he couldn't let me keep my shoes on. He has it all figured out in that old world mind of his. He straightened his feet out behind him, even though he already knew the consequences of that move too. Why was the skin on the top of his foot (now on the bottom, next to the floor) more sensitive? Probably because of all the metacarpal bones — yes, that was it. It wasn't only the skin that hurt but the bones too. Now the wheat dug in the whole length from his knee to his foot, all along the tibia. Or was it fibula?

Wheat, of course, because it was harder than oats. It's a wonder he doesn't make me kneel on corn. Or would it be less painful because the kernels are bigger? He brought his toes under again and the wheat dug in at once. In the same old grooves? or in new ones? He raised his eyes to the small opening cut into the boards of the wall where dust motes moved leisurely in the light. No, if corn hurt more, then it would be corn. He let himself float with the specks of dust, felt himself bumping softly among them, nothing but air all around. He tried to discern the ones that were floating in the shadow. Bump the wrong way during the romp in the sunlight and get banished to the shades? Are there rules for them too?

No moving of the knees. No leaning to the side. No scraping away of the wheat from the floor. No moment to cheat, with her sitting in the doorway, the rhythmic click of the needles knitting up the hardness of wheat, the pain of his very sinews.

Back to the pressure points, on the skin and the bone. When he grew up and contracted some strange disintegration of the knees, the specialist city doctor would show him the x-rays and shake his head. Nothing the medical profession can do for the capella once it's been pitted by wheat. A common ailment among men of your age, especially ones of Slavic origin like yourself.

Slavic origin. How he hated that phrase. In this country where he was born, where he was born a citizen with the right to free speech. Just because they want to hang onto their old language. Well, they can destroy these knees all they want, they won't force this mouth to speak it. They don't get away with pretending not to know English.

The shaft of sunlight had changed its angle gradually so that his body was partly in shadow now. He knew that he was at least fifteen minutes over the time but there was still no hesitation in the clicking sounds behind him. He would not turn around. He would not utter any plea in that language. And if one English word came out? The decision was hers. Those were the rules, made clear before *he* left.

The sun fell on only his left knee now. He strained to feel the last of the heat, to catch the last of the light. Out there on the mountainside, the early September yellow of dried leaves, the crisp yellow of holiday sun. In here, the kneeling on wheat, the last day before the beginning of school. At least, from tomorrow on, not so much time in the house. He could get the coal in and do the garden work after school. That would keep him outside. Then his homework. And this was the year he was starting Physics. A fly settled on the narrow sill, working its front legs and turning jerkily one way and then the other in the full sunshine. Turning and knocking its legs together so that the sound filled the shed . . .

The clicking noises stopped. The knocking again, at the back door of the house. Not the fly. Its legs were motionless now as though it, too, were waiting for the word of release. Movement behind him and the scraping of her chair on the wood. He heard her steps on the boards of the walkway. Then a voice. In the old language. "Oh, there you are. Didn't you say to come by about ten?" A familiar voice. An old world neighbour. Her voice sounded closer now. "You punishing that boy again?"

Then his mother. "It's just finished. Let's go in now."

When he heard the back door close behind them, he pushed himself upward slowly and stepped, with bent legs, out of the pile of golden wheat. Some of the kernels stuck firmly in the deep holes they had made in the skin of his knees and his feet. He picked them off one by one, then rolled down his pantlegs.

* * *

He was a dark figure, stepping unevenly but fast, along the tracks that edged the valley just east of town. Dark without, for he had grabbed up his black wool jacket in his hurry to get away from the house. And now it was too hot on him out here in the sun, with the heat reflecting up from the rails and grey cinders, mixed with the smell of the baking creosote of the railroad ties and the languid drifting of yellow leaves. But he would not take it off. That would mean he'd have to slow down to unshoulder the old thirty-thirty and hold it first in one hand and then the other to get at the sleeves, a thing that the darkness of anger within him would not allow.

The ties weren't the right distance apart for an even stride. Two at a time made it too long; one at a time, too short. He had long ago solved the problem by compromise — covering two with his left foot and one with his right. The loping but hesitant gait, along with the dark woolly jacket and his long arms, made him look all the world like a rather skinny, small-headed bear ambling awkwardly along between the two shiny metal tracks.

And his anger rode awkwardly inside him. That boy. Mikel. He had failed to be strict enough with him. He wasn't like the others. Quicker, better at school. Wanted to be a doctor. All the more reason to have the two languages. No reason not to have the best of both ways of life. What made him so defiant? Maybe he'd been too strict with him. No, a child should listen to his elders — his own father, one who had experience of other countries, other ways. What did he know at that age with no experience of anything except this mountain town? If only his mother would help and make him mind. Instead of treating him like some child prodigy. Janko and Olga were no better — him bringing gadgets and new books whenever he came home, and her still treating him like a baby even when she was carrying one of her own, and ready to have it any day now.

The bridge over the creek was just ahead. Suddenly, he stepped over the rail on his right, shifting his rifle to the other shoulder as he started down the bank through the goldenrod and the fireweed. His change of direction was so quick that his feet seemed still to be walking the ties, so that even when he reached the higher growth of alders on the upward slope, his left foot continued to cover more of the uneven ground than his right. He kept several hundred yards to the west of the creek but he could hear its narrow gurgling from time to time in the still air.

His anger was riding lower now. It had moved from a tight sharpening in the chest down to a dull ache in the abdomen. His thoughts were still with the boy and shifted back and forth from somewhere under the pushing energy of his weathered cap to a definite pressure in both his knees. At the same time they hovered over ripening fields of wheat and the figure of his own father resting his weight on his scythe and narrowing his eyes on the brightness of the sun.

The trail was one he had blazed himself and used so often there was no need to pay it any attention. His feet found the way over the low-lying alder trunks spread out, octopus-like, from each centre, and then up the needle-covered hardness of the higher ground. Through the flat of the meadow, the long grasses, and he was already at the darkness of the cedars, at the salt lick.

Now he was glad of the jacket. On the familiar rock, not actually worn from its years of use but smooth and free of moss on both sides, he felt the cool of the cedar shade. It was damp and musky. The smell of skunk cabbage even though the limp leaves showed no memory of spring and its yellow flowers. He eased the thirty-thirty from his shoulder and, laying it across his knees, took the clip from his pocket and slipped it into the magazine. One action of the bolt and the clicking of the shell slotting into the chamber. He raised the rifle, sighting between the low huckleberry bushes into the space above the wetness of mud, sharply cut at the edges with the slim triangles of deer tracks. He released the safety. It wouldn't take long. It was the right time of day, there was no wind, and he had made no noise.

Holding the rifle ready, his elbows braced one on each knee, he did not even have to think of this day — Labour Day, the start of hunting season — or of the waiting freezer (still holding a little of last year's game), or of the past sureness of waiting at the salt lick. Instead, he thought of wheat on the board floor of a shed, of a wife who, by now, would have been defiant enough, in spite of his instructions, his rules, his threats, to gather up her wool, wrap it around the skein, stick the needles into it, and . . .

There was a slight sound behind him, the sound of brush being parted. He knew the sound — an urgency for salt. He swung around, his finger on the trigger. He'd get the boy to come help him with the skinning . . .

He heard only part of the bigger sound. By the time it finished reverberating up and down the mountainside, he had pitched backward, down, down into a golden haze of broiling wheat. His bent knees caught on the hump of the rock. The spreading red patch hardly showed on the front of the dark woolly jacket.

LOTUS

She snuggled against him in the dark. So nice to be held. So nice to be kissed. She could hear the way the water made its little gurgling sound over the stones; she could hear it even over his loud breathing. It wasn't sinful just to be kissing, even if it was in the dark, even if her mother had said all that about how men — even boys . . .

"This is a nice spot," he said.

She could see just a hint of the outline of Fernie Mountain above them against the dark of the sky. "Yes, I like it by the river."

"No, I mean this spot," and he moved his lips across her neck, flicked his tongue lightly over her earlobe.

She shivered. "Oh, don't do that. It makes me feel funny." She shifted her weight in his lap. "Are you comfortable? Am I too heavy?"

"I like you being heavy," he said. "I like you sitting on me like this. But my leg is getting a bit stiff." He dropped his arms. "Here, why don't you use my jacket?"

She shifted over as he struggled to get his arms out of the sleeves. She saw the movement of the jacket, a light shape across the darkness. Then he was pushing it under her hips. "Pretty gravelly here. Is that better?" He crouched facing her, his arms around her shoulders and back, pulling her to him. "Here, let me get my legs under you too. It really is rocky."

She felt the need to unbend her knees but his pressure against them kept her in a cross-legged position. She pulled her mouth away from his. "Rico, I don't think we should . . . Can't we just . . . Let's stop for a while and have a cigarette. You know what Father Morley will say . . ."

"You don't have to tell him."

"Of course I do. If anything happens, I have to confess. And so do you."

"Well, nothing'll happen. I don't want to have to tell him anything either. But couldn't we just, you know, get closer?"

She heard the fumbling and felt something different pushing. It was that part of him, pushing up along the inside of her thigh. "Don't do that." She tried to pull back.

"It's okay, Lottie. I'm not going to go in. Let's just feel what it's like. See? Isn't that nice? We don't have to do it or anything."

"Okay, just a little. As long as we don't really do it. Remember, we promised we'd be virgins for each other. It does feel nice. Is that really what you're like all the time?"

"You mean him? No, not all the time. You do that to me. It happens because we love each other so much. I wish your parents had let us set the date for June like we wanted. Oh God."

"No, no more. Let's stop. Rico, please stop. We don't want to be sinful. We'll just have to wait till after."

They stood up, arms locked around each other. She suddenly let go and pulled up her skirt. "Oh my goodness."

"What is it?"

"I don't know. Light a match, will you?"

As the light flared, lit up her fingertips, he said, "That's blood."

As it flickered off she said, "I just can't understand that."

"What's the matter, Lottie? Why are you bleeding? Did I hurt you?"

"I don't know. It isn't nearly time for my period." She wiped her hand on a kleenex, then dabbed the kleenex up under her skirt.

He put his arms around her. They stood leaning together. "I'm sorry," he said. "But at least we didn't do it."

The next morning as Enrico came down the stairs he met the fiery gaze of his mother. Her voice was high-pitched. It made

104

him think of the sound of the donkey engine in the mine, when it was winding up to full power. "What were you up to last night?"

"Why, what's the matter?"

"This is what's the matter. Your new white jacket." She grabbed it off the peg by the door. "And you hang it up as though it's nothing. Look at that, it's got blood on the back, and right through to the lining. You said you were going over to Lottie's."

"But I did. We went . . ."

"Now don't go denying everything. You were out getting drunk again and got into another fight. And then you come sneaking in here in the dark." She threw the jacket at him, turned away in disgust. "You'd better see if you can clean that up before your dad sees it."

He caught it in mid-air, held it close. He didn't say anything, not out loud. But silently he was mouthing the words. Okay Ma. Okay. Have it your way. I won't deny it.

SATURN

Blackie liked to listen to his grandmother's stories about her people. They were his people too. He had heard the stories ever since he was a young child.

Time is an old, old man. We used to call him Tunaxa. That is the oldest word in our language. He was the father of the Kootenai and the Peigan. He lived in the East. That was before our people came over the mountains from Alberta.

And when they came to this valley it was teeming with animals. All kinds of animals — buffalo and elk and deer and moose and bear. And there were mountain goats and sheep, cougars and wolves, and all the smaller animals. And the river was full of fish and the air was full of birds. Our people had many horses. They were better horses than the ones belonging to the other tribes. Mostly my people hunted the buffalo. But when the buffalo became scarce, they learned to catch the fish. It was not called the Elk River in the beginning but the Stag River because an old, old bull elk watched over it. Some people thought he was the reincarnation of Tunaxa.

Our people lived all through the valley. They had a big camp here, right where Fernie is now, and one up at Fort Steele. But the main camp, called Big Village, was at Tobacco Plains. They called it the place of the flying head. They travelled back and forth on trails. There were no roads then. The main trails went along beside the rivers. There were trails along beside the Wigwam River and up the Lodgepole as well as the main ones by the Kootenay and the Elk. It was all called East Bank Country, and we were the East Bank Band. They used those names because we were on the east side of the Kootenay River. The Kootenay itself was named after our people — the Kootenai. That means water people.

But what I wanted to tell you was about the horse and rider that I showed you on Hosmer Mountain. The man on the horse is Yau Ke'Kam. He was a kind of wonder boy to his people — something like a super boy. When he was still young, no one could go up into the valley from Tobacco Plains because a big squirrel (then squirrels were as big and powerful as grizzly bears) closed off the entrance and wouldn't let any creature pass through. With the help of a friend, a Bighorn Ram, he guarded the western entrance of the valley — right at that narrow part by Elko — and he sent his wife to guard the eastern entrance at Crowsnest Mountain. She had the help of Raven. Whenever another creature tried to enter the valley, Ram killed it by pushing rocks down the mountainside onto it. If any tried to enter from the east, Squirrel's wife and Raven made them get tangled in the thick underbrush and dense trees so they starved to death.

Yau Ke'Kam, who was a kind of super boy as I said, decided to end Squirrel's bad ways. He tricked Ram by getting up in a cave high above him — you know the one in Broadwood Mountain we see across the river when we drive to Elko? From that cave he rolled rocks down on Ram and killed him, and when Squirrel came to see what happened he did the same to him. Then he forced his way through all the dense woods to the other entrance of the valley. He didn't have any trouble overcoming Squirrel's wife and Raven because they never gave a thought to expecting anyone coming from that direction.

Well, that's the main story that everyone knows. Yau Ke'Kam had to work at keeping the Valley open for all the creatures. He cut out the tangle of underbrush every year. As time went by and he got older, he took his son, Tur Ke'Kam, along to help him. One time when they were on their way back to Tobacco Plains from Crowsnest, Tur Ke'Kam's horse got scared by a snake.

It jumped straight up so fast that it dumped the boy off. He fell down the side of a cliff. Yau Ke'Kam left the horses standing on the trail and crawled down to help. Just as he reached him and saw that he was dead already, a big rock rolled down after him and pinned his legs. It was too heavy for him to move and there was no one to help him. He just had to stay there, day after day, night after night, beside his son's body. And every day he got hungrier and hungrier. Finally, although he didn't want to, he had to start eating the flesh of the boy — his own son.

He was there for a very long time with that big rock still across his legs. He was there so long that everything became dark all around him. I don't mean it was night. It was a darkness that never turned into day. He closed his eyes and didn't open them any more. He didn't know anything until there was a big flash of light that made him open them again. It was a flash of lightning and it had split the rock in two. When he got to his feet, he saw the spirit of Tur Ke'Kam coming out of the split rock. It put its hand out to him and led him up the cliffside to the trail. It helped the father onto his horse and then began leading the horse along the trail. So that is what you see there on Hosmer Mountain. The son leading the father out.

Blackie said then, "What about the other horse? Did it wait there too? or run away?"

"It's there too. Except that it's following the first horse. So you can't see it."

"Where is he leading him?"

"They are on the road to Time. He's leading him straight back to the beginning — to Tunaxa. That's why they are always on the mountain. The trip will take a very long time. The trip to Tunaxa is forever."

JUPITER

When anyone new arrives in a small town, everyone in that town knows about him or her right away, long before that person can sort out who's who or even start to see any difference in faces. That's how it was when the tall stranger arrived in Fernie just at the end of August.

First off, he had a big long car that stood out right away — because it was a Cadillac (there wasn't one single Cadillac in the whole of Fernie) and it was a bright yellow. On top of that, it had foreign plates.

There were people who noticed it crossing the West Fernie bridge as it came into town. There were more people who saw it turn off the highway and head up the Cox Street hill toward Main street. There were many more who saw it drive past the various businesses – the court house, the post office, the hardware, the hairdresser's, the two grocery stores, the one department store, the Diamond Grill, and Mabel's Café; even patients in the doctor's waiting room remarked on it. And they all had a chance for a good look because it drove the length of Main Street, down and back, twice. Finally, it pulled into a parking space just north of Quail's Hardware.

He came in by himself so, to start with, Wilf and Paddy and the other clerks took him to be a single man, although they knew immediately after that he wasn't because Ekaterina told them about the woman sitting alone in the yellow "limousine" with Nebraska plates, right in front of her gift shop next door. He wanted to buy a hunting licence so that's how they found out all about him. His name was Carlyle Logan, he was a United States citizen residing in Nebraska, he was a self-employed contractor, he was forty-one years old, and he planned on hunting in the area for goat, sheep, deer, elk, moose — the works; at least those were the ones he bought tags for. He made a point, too, of asking if for sure there was open season on bear.

Then they found out where he'd be staying in town because he asked them about a motel — not a *hotel*, he didn't want to be holed up in one room — and when they explained there were two: the Red and White (the original one) and the Snow Valley (started up, and named after, the new ski hill on the Lizard Range), he wanted to know how much they cost per night and when they told him, he wanted directions to the Snow Valley.

They could see he was in good shape. He was tall, about six-foot-four, wouldn't weight more than maybe one eighty-five, and looked energetic, at least he didn't move slow. And they could surmise that he was well-off, being a contractor for one thing, and travelling in that vehicle that far to hunt, which meant having to pay for the expensive out-of-province, out-of-country licence, and choosing the Snow Valley over the Red and White when the rates were nearly double; he didn't wear the usual GWG jean stuff and corks like the guys in town, but light corduroys and yellow leather boots. Another definite thing about him, although it was not immediately obvious because he wore a hat — the felt Aussie kind, swept up on one side — was that he was totally bald. Wilf and Paddy wouldn't have known that first day except that just as he got out on the sidewalk, he whipped the hat off to swat at a black hornet that came right for him.

Nobody, except maybe Jake and Agnes who ran the Snow Valley, could say anything about Mrs. Logan. If ever you saw her out on the street somewhere, you'd have a hard time placing her; one of those people you know you've seen somewhere but can't remember where. So when the town heard about the episode, most people hadn't even been sure that the American — you know, that tall skinny bald guy with the yellow Cadillac? — even had a wife. But after the episode, no one could ever forget her.

It happened right in front of the Proctor Hotel. No one could say afterwards where Logan had gone, although most were sure he was in the Proctor having a beer. But the yellow car was parked there, the left front tire up over the curb, and Mrs. Logan was sitting in the front seat, the passenger seat — knitting, they said after.

It was some boys, coming out of the pool hall — Hank Phillips and young Miller — who first realized something was amiss. They stood there at the rear of the Cadillac for a few minutes, then rushed back into the pool hall and phoned Connor. He's the game warden. Well, he happened to be having a coffee in Mabel's Café but the office knew where he was so as soon as they called him there he was able to get right down. Mabel's is only a block up the street. He pulled in with his pickup right behind Logan's car. He was on the wrong side of the street so the two vehicles were back to back. And then he stood there with the young guys and, sure enough, they'd been right to call because there were definite noises coming from the trunk. Connor may have talked to Mrs. Logan, but it seemed all he could do was wait until Logan came back.

And when he did, that's when the row started and a lot of people gathered around. The stories vary, of course, about how the conversation went. But Connor was telling Logan to open the trunk, Logan was saying he had nothing in there, that Connor had no power to make him open the trunk. What everyone did agree on was that their voices kept getting louder — Connor shouting that he knew damn well what was in there; Logan yelling that he wasn't doing anything illegal, that he knew his rights as a United States citizen. And Connor pulling out his revolver and saying, "You'll damn well open that trunk or I'll blow it open." Well, Logan didn't back down even then. He bellowed out that he'd better not damage his car, and he put in that part again about his rights as a United States citizen.

The crowd was already backing away. There was a shot, then a couple more. Connor pried up the trunk door. There, crouching on a scrunched up plaid blanket, blinking in the sudden bright light, were two bear cubs, one black, one cinnamon. They had metal chains around their necks, joined together.

In all the commotion — Connor grabbing the chain, shouting out orders to some of the young guys to set down the crate in the back of the pickup, hands helping to hold the cubs, to ease them out into the crate, to close it securely, to raise the crate from the ground to the tail gate — in all that commotion, well, who would have thought to look in the front seat? Connor's last shout to Logan was, "You follow me over to the police station." And then Logan moved from where he'd been standing at the edge of the sidewalk, to open the door on the driver's side.

Well, he didn't follow Connor to the police station. He yelled out at him, "You've shot my wife!" and drove straight to the hospital. But, by the time Dr. Martin got to her — he rushed right out to the car — she was already dead. No, she hadn't been shot. It was a heart attack.

There were charges and counter charges and, quite a while later, a couple of days in court. Logan ended up paying a stiff fine for capturing the cubs; Connor was cleared of any legal responsibility in the case — the court deeming that, if anything, Logan himself was the cause of his wife's death; as to the cubs, as soon as the magistrate had enough evidence about them, he cleared them for release. Connor had made Logan tell him exactly what part of the South Country he'd taken them from.

You'd think the man would have stayed away from Fernie forever after that.

But two summers later, in the middle of August, the big Caddy showed up in town again; however, it wasn't yellow any more. This time it was red, but, according to Mort and Bob at the Texaco, you could still see the original yellow around the inside of the doors and in a few other spots at the edges of the new paint job. The paint on the trunk, though, was flawless. Replaced, for sure. And this time the driver was a slim, pale-haired woman in her late twenties, with a baby. He was with her, but mostly he rode in the passenger seat. They stayed at the Snow Valley, as before; since it wasn't yet hunting season, everyone wondered why he was back. They just drove around on all the back roads. Lots of people saw them. They sometimes went swimming at Baynes Lake. They took the baby right in with them, bare naked.

Lots of times the woman, Betsy was her name, drove around without him. There was the story of her driving down through Phillips Canyon doing about sixty all the way on those twisty roads, the baby sucking at her breast, and her steering with her knees. That was after Logan's daughter joined them. Yes, there was a daughter. She was a tall girl, quite a bit bigger than the stepmother. The reason she hadn't come with her parents the first time, two years before, was that she was away at some ballet school in the East. She didn't strike you as being a ballerina — she was so tall — but apparently she had just finished a tour, doing *Swan Lake*, across the southern states. Actually, she was graceful, the way she moved. Especially in her tight jeans. She was twenty or so, about the same age as Blaze Cassidy, Hopalong's daughter. Blaze was a model in Toronto before she came to Fernie, so I guess that's why she and this Eleanor got on so well. She was the one who told about that ride down the canyon. She'd been sure the baby was going to fly out through the open window on any one of Betsy's wild hairpin turns.

Well, nothing happened while they were in town. He must have just brought them up here for a holiday, or to show them the place where the first Mrs. Logan died. However, everyone was on the look-out. The youngsters (and the men and women as well) never passed the car, wherever it was parked, without stopping for a moment to listen at the trunk. Some even speculated that Logan had painted it red in case there were any trickles of blood, which would show up right away on any other colour.

Just before Labour Day, a couple of the young Kennedy boys, who had been shooting gophers up by the Fairy Creek reservoir north of town, ran breathless into the first house on the upper road over the river – the Pointers' place – and told Mrs. Pointer they needed to phone the game warden. It seems the red Cadillac was parked up by the falls and there was no sign of anyone around. She looked up the number for them. Connor was in the office at the time and said he'd be up there right away.

Mrs. Pointer walked with the boys back to the Fairy Creek road. She was as curious as they were to see what was happening. About a half mile above the crossroad they saw the familiar pickup coming up behind them. Connor waved as he went by. They told about it in town later, how Mrs. Pointer said, "Isn't that Constable Sandy with him?" and the boys assured her it was. He must be suspecting something real serious if he had to get the R.C.M.P. in on it.

But then the red Cadillac appeared over the hill. It didn't slow down on the narrow road as it approached the pickup, so Connor had to swerve off into the low shrubbery to let it pass. It sped on by, kicking up bits of gravel as it went past the boys and Mrs. Pointer. It moved fast all right, they said, but not so fast that they missed seeing that Logan was at the wheel and that the passenger was his daughter, Eleanor. Not so fast either that they missed seeing that she was covering her face with a white handkerchief. They turned back then.

It wasn't until the boys were crossing the bridge back over the river into town that the pickup overtook them again. Connor slowed beside them. "I don't want to see you boys out with those twenty-two's again, do you hear? Not until you're old enough to get a licence."

It was the year after, later in the fall, that we heard the rest of it. Logan had been shot dead, with a high-powered rifle. The wife Betsy was arrested for murder, but she got off. It seems she convinced the court that she shot him, not in *self* defence, but in defence of Eleanor, her stepdaughter.

The *Fernie Free Press* had picked up the story from a Nebraska newspaper. They didn't show a picture of him, but there were Betsy and Eleanor, their faces side by side. The headline was: WIFE SHOOTS HUSBAND IN DEFENCE OF STEPDAUGHTER. At the end of the write-up there was an editor's note, saying that the Logan family had spent some time in the Fernie area over the past few years and that, thus, the deceased was well-known to the residents of the town.

MERCURY

He knew it was a good plan. He had been working out the details over the whole month, to be ready for this day. The two main requirements were that it be in hunting season and that it be when the mill was shut down. So he had waited for Labour Day.

Just as he was cutting over from Baker Avenue, the Cassidy girl (her old man, the one they called Hopalong, lived in the yellow house right across from the mill), Blaze, came running out of the house. "Hey, Steve," she yelled. She crawled through the fence and crossed the tracks.

His first impulse was to ignore her, just go on ahead through the gate, but then he thought, "She's seen me already, anyway. Maybe I can turn it into some help for my alibi." So he swung around and waved for her to come over. He didn't move to meet her, just stood and waited as she strode toward him through the long dry grass and weeds.

She was tall and slim. Her dark hair swung from side to side as she walked. She was smiling at him, calling out something but he couldn't hear the words. How he wished he'd been able to get somewhere with her. But she'd never been interested. And now it was too late. But what she saw in that damn Blackie he couldn't figure out — the bloody drinker and braggart that he was.

She came up to him, a little out of breath. "I don't want to hold you up, Steve, when you're going hunting." A jerk of her head indicated the rifle on his shoulder. "But I was wondering if you could just tell me fast how to make those cabbage rolls you said your dad was so good at?"

He said, "Sure. Do you have something to write on?"

She took a small pad out of her hip pocket. She already had a pencil in her hand. "I want to make them for supper and

Bertie doesn't have a recipe. Blackie's coming over to help us celebrate. You know, it's a year today since Babe and I came to Fernie." Babe was her younger sister, about fourteen he figured. Bertie was the stepmother.

"Yeah, that's right." He took the pad and pencil. "Syd was telling everybody for weeks before you came, 'I got two sisters coming from Ontario. They're going to live with us.'" His take-off on her stepbrother's slurred speech was exact. They both laughed.

He was thinking, how nice the way those pale-coloured eyes crinkle up almost into crescent shapes when she laughs, when he caught a movement behind her, along the tracks. A dark lumbering figure. "Hey," he said, "this thing is too damn small to write anything on." He pushed the pad back into her hand. "Come on in the yard and I'll find something better." He hurried through the mill gate and she followed. When they were in by the wall of the lunch shack he stopped, pointed down past the piles of lumber to the big yellow forklift parked at the end of the row. "That baby's my partner on the job," he said. "She's brand new. Funny to see her sitting there when we're both off for the holiday."

Blaze nodded, murmured. "Yeah, Blackie told me you get to drive it. I think he's jealous they didn't give it to him." She was bending down, pulling one burr after another off the cuffs of her cord pants.

He tried to keep his voice low and even. "I'm the senior driver, you know. And, anyway, he's pretty new on the job. He'll have to put in some time on the green chain . . . you know." He moved on ahead. Making sure he kept the shack between himself and the tracks, Steve found what he was looking for — a short length of two-by-six. "This should do," he said and, pressing the pencil into the soft wood, started writing down the list of ingredients, telling her directions as he went along. When he finished, he handed it to her. "And don't forget. They're good with sour cream on top."

She smiled and thanked him, the eyes crinkling again. "I hope I didn't hold you up too long?"

"Oh no," he said. "I'm not in a hurry. I'm just going up the hill here. Past the cemetery. I might run into something up the ridge. It's nice to get out right away when the season starts." He patted the butt of his rifle. "This is another nice partner," he said.

"Yeah, a two-seventy, isn't it? Like my dad's. Well, good luck. I'll let you know how the cabbage rolls turn out. Thanks again. Thanks a lot." And she turned toward the gate.

But he did not go up the hill to the cemetery. He walked down the row between the piles of lumber until he came to the forklift. He took the rifle from his shoulder, leaned it against the front wheel. Then he sat down beside it and took out his cigarettes.

As Blaze crossed back over the open space she saw the back of a dark figure moving along the tracks. "Oh," she thought. "There goes Lee Choy. Off to the Diamond Grill to gamble." Babe had told her about the secret room in the basement, under the restaurant. "I wonder if Jackie missed seeing him go by."

***

Steve had passed the bridge over the creek. He was almost to where the trail took off from the tracks to lead across a flat meadow and into the cedars before he realized where he was. Then he thought of the salt lick. Perfect, especially if he did jump a deer. Just a day out hunting.

It had all gone as planned. He had waited a while by the forklift to make sure that Lee Choy had time to get engrossed in his gambling, so there was no danger he'd be coming right home again. Every five minutes he had climbed up on the side of the last stack of lumber to check that there was nobody walking along the tracks. When the time felt right, he had crawled carefully through the fence into Lee Choy's garden, scuffing his feet as he went to make sure he didn't leave any definite footprints. He was careful, too, not to disturb the two highly visible prints that were already there — made by boots slightly smaller than his own, ones with a distinctive latticed tread. When he had been stacking two-by-fours at that end on the Friday, he had seen Blackie drop over the fence to help himself to a couple of Lee Choy's carrots. Made to order. He could hear himself saying, "If he'd steal the Chinaman's carrots...."

The door had been unlocked as he knew it would be. In all the times he had gone there with the old man, whether for a quick drink during lunch break, or for a longer session after they'd come from the Roma or the Olympos, he had never seen Lee Choy use a key. Probably didn't even have one. The room was dark even on that bright day, but Steve did not need to see. Two steps to the bed, a hand slid under the mattress over on the wall side, and he felt the worn leather pouch, exactly where it had always been. All the mill crew knew it was there. All of them had borrowed money from Lee Choy many times over the years. He would take them through the unlocked door, step across to the bed, slide his hand under the mattress, and bring out the old leather bag.

Steve dropped the pouch down the front of his shirt. At the door he stopped a moment to see if anyone was in sight. Then he was back beside the forklift, breathing heavily, more from the excitement of it than the effort. It was a bit slow counting. Most of the bills were small — fives and tens. Over eight hundred dollars. He reached up beside the seat for the oily rag he kept there, wrapped it bulkily around the pouch and stuffed the bundle in between the two-by-fours, in an angled space he had been careful to leave when he made the stack.

He had cut across the open field at the end of the mill opposite from where he and Blaze had entered. The way he angled toward the tracks he was able to keep the stand of cottonwoods at the edge of the golf course between him and the yellow house.

No one had seen him and now he was away from town, far down the tracks, heading for the salt lick. Yes, if he could get a deer, there would be no suspicion whatsoever.

He stood a long time at the big cedar at the north side; his eyes had grown accustomed to the darkness in there, his heartbeat had settled to a slow, even pulse. But the feeling of excitement and elation still buzzed in his head and through his body and limbs. He held the rifle and waited.

Then what happened was so fast that afterwards he could not recall the exact sequence. A crackling in the underbrush the other side of the lick. Something coming down the hillside. He just had time to swing the barrel in that direction when he saw a movement through the low-hanging branches. Definitely a set of horns, a four-spike at least, thrust outward beyond the hump of rock. He fired, but the image had already moved sideways out of the scope.

He sprang to the rock, following the noises crashing up the hillside. No use even trying to go in there, or to fire again, it was so thick with alder and huckleberry. He lowered the rifle, rested the butt on the rock, on the soft bulge of the rock . . . the soft mound . . . . His breath caught in his throat. He whipped the rifle aside, pushed through the shrubs to the far side, searched past the woolly jacket for the face. My God. The buzzing in his head was deafening. His stomach churned. Old Man Pozniak.

The last flash in that fast sequence, the one he made sure he impressed on Corporal Pine when he got to the RCMP office, was the dozen or so blowflies. Blowflies, big and black, settled in a bunch on the front of the jacket. As he told the officer, several times over, he might not have noticed them on the dark material except for the fact that in among them he could see, very clearly, a cluster of yellowish eggs. If there had been time for blowflies to lay eggs how could he possibly be the one who shot the old man?

* * *

Next morning, when Blackie slammed on the brakes and jumped out of his grey Chev coupe, there was a bunch of the crew standing around the open door of the lunch shack. He knew they'd all be talking about Old Man Pozniak, and about Steve. The news had swept all over town as soon as the corporal and two of his men had gone down the tracks to bring out the body. Nearly always, the first response to the news was something like: "Well, it's a wonder Old Pozniak didn't get it long before this. I don't know how many times I've come across him in the bush and thought he was a goddam bear." And everyone thought of the widow, and of the three children — the grown son, and the daughter who was soon to have a baby. The first grandchild and he'd never see it. And of the young Mikey, still in school — the one who wanted to be a doctor.

A double sadness lay over the town. One man was dead. The other wouldn't be let free until they could figure out just how the accident happened. He'd lose his hunting licence for sure, and his rifle. And, in all likelihood, he'd be charged with manslaughter.

One of the older men moved out of the group and took a few steps toward the gate. "There you are, Blackie. I'm gonna do something I'll probably regret. You think you could give that forklift a try? Seeing as how Stefano will be taking a longer holiday? Or do you think you can drive it?"

Blackie came through the gate, his upper body swinging from side to side as he walked. "You know goddam well, Joe, there isn't a goddam thing I can't drive."

There were a few calls from the group. "This isn't one of Cash's Mickey Mouse trucks, you know," and "Yeah, you'd better treat her good or Steve'll clean yer clock when he gets back," and "We've all seen the way you drive, Blackie."

"Don't you worry, you bastards. You better get your trucks lined up. You're gonna see some boxcars bulging today." He swung over to the doorway, reached in to throw his jacket on the bench. "Hey, you in here, Choy-boy? I thought you'd be on your way back to China by now. How much did you add to your stash playin' mahjongg? I bet you were rakin' it in all weekend."

The eyes looked at him mildly out of the lined face. "No, it was fantan. And I don't add nothing," he said with a kind of melancholy in his voice. "This time I lose everything I go in with."

"Oh yeah, I've heard that before. I bet you're the richest guy in the crew. At least your gamblin' pays off sometime. Not like me. With drinkin' you never get any payoff, except a colossal headache and sick in the gut." He laughed as he turned away, repositioned his cap on his head. At the corner of the lunch shack, he glanced across at the yellow house. Blaze would have gone uptown by now, but she'd be over with his lunch at noon. Of course she'd already know.

But by noon he had something else to tell her. All morning he had worked along the one row. They were loading two boxcars with two-by-fours. The last pile to be picked up looked kind of crooked. Mister Steve isn't all that hot at running this machine. He'd have to slip the forks in just as far as that part where it was out of line, then lift slowly so the rest didn't slide off. That was when he saw it. At first he thought it was just an old oily rag. But when it fell to the ground, it kind of flopped open — enough for him to see the leather, to recognize what it was.

"But how did you know it was Steve put it there?" Blaze was sitting beside him in the car, a salmon sandwich partway to her mouth. "Couldn't it have been someone else?"

"No, it was him all right. He always talked about someone stealing that pouch. Anyway, I saw where he went through the fence. You know, he's got boots just like mine." He forced one foot up between the gear shift and the seat. "See this tread? Exactly the same. Only his are bigger."

"So you just put the money back?"

"Yeah. It's right back in its little nest under his mattress. Old Choy's never going to know. And nobody else either."

She reached over and patted his shoulder.

"I figure," he said, "dumb Steve's got enough trouble right now without having to tangle with a frantic Chinaman. But he's so stupid it would've served him right. You'd think he'd have had enough sense just to take the money and leave the goddam pouch."

Then, reaching down to the floorboard, he winked at her and smiled. "Here, do you want a couple of nice fresh carrots?"

VENUS

How many love stories are there in a town this size? The list is unending. Fulfilled love, unfulfilled love; love gone right, love gone wrong; love lost, love gained — even regained; violent love, mundane love; first love, second, third love, and so on. Love as joy, love as burden. The endless tally. It's all here. Her hand spread wide over her upper chest. Right here. Even though there has never been anyone but Victor. There has been only him . . .

Her body was rigid, absolutely still. She let her breath out, tried to breathe naturally.

Myrtle was standing at the sink. From the small kitchen window she could look straight out over the houses of West Fernie, across to the Lizard Range. The great white backs of the elephant shapes merged one into the other; hardly any outline at all — snow against snow. Just down the hill from the back yard she could see the river or, rather, she could see where she knew the river was. It lay somewhere under the ice; the ice lay under the snow. She knew there would be an open space next to the near bank where the water moved fast over the rocks. But she couldn't see that part from the house. The water keeps moving, she thought. Whether in the open, whether sealed under the ice. It keeps moving. Passing by, passing by. Who was it who said, "Everything passes"? Who said, "All this too shall pass"? Someone who knew.

And now, what is passing in this house? My mother has died upstairs. Found dead after breakfast. The doctor has come. The ambulance will take her away, to the morgue. And my love is on his way to comfort me. And I will comfort him. Our mother.

She turned unsteadily from the sink. It should have been the two of us who found her. She should have let us face it together. But whether she knew it or not, she has never wanted us to be together. It was just like her to delay, to hang on, until we were apart. She knew this was the day Victor would be away, the day for the trip to Golden. She had waited to die until he was inaccessible, in places where he couldn't be phoned. But the message had got through to Golden; now he was on his way back....

A movement above her stopped her in front of the fridge. The ginger cat had stretched a paw out, straight and long, over the rim of the wicker basket. It yawned wide, two rows of sharp teeth tilted to the ceiling, then closed its mouth and flipped the paw back in. Myrtle reached up, scratched the ear closest to her, then moved her fingers to feel under the chin. The steady tremor of the throat seemed to transfer to her body. She felt suddenly calm, as if the warmth of the purring were entering her veins. Like water, warm water, coursing lightly under the ice.

It had always been ice. There had never been open places, and now — too late for a complete melt; there could never be a full springtime. She folded her arms tight across her chest, watching the flick of the rusty ears above the basket.

She found herself at the front room window. The move had not been conscious; she must have come to see if there was any sign of the ambulance. Nothing in the street, just patches of bare pavement between the side ridges of ploughed snow. At the O'Rourkes' house across the road the two little boys, steadying themselves with hockey sticks, were passing a puck back and forth on the rough surface of a small square of ice. They were too young to be in school.

Her hand stroked the head of the black and white cat perched on the back of the chesterfield. Automatically, her fingers moved to check the tremor of the throat. Again she felt the purring enter her body, move out through every fibre to the extremities of her limbs. A warming flow. She pulled her old grey cardigan tight so the one side crossed over the other, flattening her breasts in toward the warmth.

Then she moved more quickly. She went from room to room. She'd find them all. She'd set them all purring. The grey and white one was on a chair in the dining room; the all black one was stretched full length on a side windowsill; the other black and white one was sitting on the mat looking expectantly at the back door. That was five. All purring. The old tabby, too decrepit to walk any more, was in the grocery cart in the hall, beside the outlet for plugging in her heating pad. Myrtle wasn't sure but she had a feeling that the old thing purred continuously, never let up. The tortoise shell and the grey tom — both from the grey and white's last litter — were curled up together on the couch in the sun porch. And that was it then. She had all of them purring. The vibrations were pervasive; they filled her body, filled the house. So loud. She didn't hear the ambulance when it stopped at the front door, just the doorbell, cutting through the buzz.

* * *

Now she could open the door at the foot of the stairs. She could leave it open. She could take it off its hinges altogether. The cats could spread out all over the house, fill the upstairs even.

She watched each scuffed brown slipper place itself on each worn place in the middle of each carpeted step, all the way up. Up the stairs to emptiness. The body removed.

She stood at the foot of the bed. The thin cotton spread was strung off to one side, the flannelette sheets seeming to flow in the same direction. They had slid her over that way then, from right to left. The pillows, one on top of the other, were set at an angle too, pulled slightly to the left. A depression still in the middle.

Myrtle yanked the spread off. Threw it on the floor. Folded the two grey blankets. Tugged at the sheets. As she freed the corners at the top, the pillows bounced to the middle of the bed. She stripped them, stuffing their cases in with the sheets as she rolled them up from the bottom. She threw them on top of the spread. Then, scooping them all up together, she went into the hall and flung the whole bundle down the stairs.

In the linen closet there was a cardboard box with a few bottles and jars in it — old shampoo, aspirin, eye drops. She took it to the bedside table and dropped into it the medicines, the hair brush, the box of tissues, the copy of *Silas Marner* with its bookmark about two thirds of the way through. She used the doily to wipe the table top.

She reached to the top shelf of the closet and took down new sheets. She ran her hand over the smooth, stiff cotton. It was covered with blue and white sprigs of flowers. There were pillow cases to match. The bottom one had fitted corners. And the new blanket. Blue and white too. She flipped the new spread expertly so that it fell almost perfectly into place. It was a heavy chenille, of generous size. The creamy white fringe swept out from the edges where they touched the floor. There was extra at the top to cover the pillows and tuck in under them at the front.

She heard the phone. The ringing penetrated, became part of the flow. She moved from the far side of the bed, running her hand along the nubby texture at the bottom of the spread. She hurried toward the stairs. The old black cat was at the foot, sitting looking up the steps. Go ahead, she said, as she passed. You can go up there now.

It was Carolyn at the Free Press office. First the condolences, the murmured apology, then the point. Since the paper comes out tomorrow, today's the deadline for any notices . . . .

Yes, I'll see to it. Yes, we can have it in by four-thirty. Victor will be back from his route any time now. I'll have it ready for him to take in. Thank you. Yes, it's hard. But she's out of pain now. Yes, we appreciate it. Thank you.

* * *

COOPER

On Thursday, April 19, pioneer resident Constance Cooper of Fernie passed away peacefully at her home at the age of 79 years.

Funeral services for the late Mrs. Cooper will be held at Christ Anglican Church on Tuesday, April 24, at 2:p.m. with Rev. Brock Waye officiating.

Mrs. Cooper was predeceased by her husband Angus in 1942. She will be sadly missed by her daughter and son, Myrtle and Victor Cooper, both of Fernie.

MOON

"What's another song you'd like to hear?" He had just finished *By the Light of the Silvery Moon* and he was twisted around in the saddle looking back at her over his shoulder. She could see every detail of him and the horse. Was it true you couldn't make out colours in moonlight? Was it just that she knew his jacket was blue, his neckerchief grey? And that the horse was a buckskin? (Beanie, the buckskin. She'd never liked the name.) Maybe it was true — just the sense of light and dark, light skin, dark mane and tail. Maybe that's all you could tell by moonlight. And her horse — all dark movement under her. Hard to tell where the mane left off and the shoulder began. Queenie. That wasn't much of a name either. Of course, the two of them already had names when they got them, and the names themselves were bad enough. The fact that they rhymed made it just plain silly.

She leaned forward, resting both hands on the horn, and called to him. "There must be another one about moonlight. Look how beautiful everything is. It's so clear you can even make out the rocks up the slopes." She pressed her legs against the girth and reined the bay mare alongside. The moon had softened his face. She couldn't make out any of the lines at all. She wondered if her face could possibly look that smooth and youthful. "Do you know any more moon songs?"

"Oh, I'm sure. There should be lots about the moon." If he'd kept smiling she could have counted his teeth, it was that bright. But he closed his lips, changing his mouth into a twisted shape to help him concentrate. "There's *Blue Moon* for one."

She said, "What about *Swiss Moonlight Lullaby?* and *That Old Devil Moon?*"

"That's right. And there's always," (he started singing) "'When the m-m-moon shines, o'er the c-c-cow shed . . .' Well, that's a lot already. Can you think of any more? Let's try for a whole list. Then you can tell me which one you want to hear. That is, if I happen to remember the words."

"Isn't there a *Buttermilk Moon*?"

"No, that's *Buttermilk Sky*. Hogey Carmichael. But I have one. *Moon over Miami*. And isn't there a *Carolina Moon*?" He crooned the first line in a Sinatra like way. "Carolina moon keep shining . . ."

"And *Moonlight on the River Colorado*." She lifted the reins slightly to move Queenie forward a little. She was always slower than Beanie. "Why are all the songs about places in the States? Imagine something like," and she looked around for inspiration. "Well, *Moonlight on the Elk*, or *Fernie Mountain Moon*, or something like that?"

"Why not? It's just that most of the songs are made up by Americans. Why *wouldn't* they write about their own places? And we do have *The Blue Canadian Rockies*." He leaned forward and straightened out Beanie's mane, the part that had flipped over to the wrong side with the last toss of his head.

"What about *Big Rock Candy Mountain*?"

"Well, that could be American. They've got the Rockies too. But I'll bet we could make a song out of Fernie Mountain Moon. That sounds like a good title."

They were both silent for a while. The horses' hooves clomped softly on the dirt trail. Queenie's saddle creaked as she walked; Beanie gave a full snort to clear the dust from his nose.

"Fernie Mountain Moon." He said it slowly. Then he sang it slowly, making two syllables out of moo-oon.

She thought, it's what you could call a tuneless tune. But without really concentrating, she was going through the alphabet testing for rhymes: boon, coon, dune, goon, loon, noon, soon, tune.

Of course it wouldn't *have* to rhyme with moon. If you just finished the line with something else. "Fernie Mountain Moon you light the valley." She said it out loud, realizing after that she had sung it to his no-tune.

He said, "Great," and repeated it, adding "Shining on the river and the trees."

And she, with a laugh, sang, "Shine down on us riding our way homeward."

And he added, immediately, "Beanie, Queenie, my dear love and me."

They both laughed and, giving a couple of whoops, trotted the horses side by side along the trail.

At the crest of the next hill they stopped. He swung down from the saddle and came to her. He put both hands around her boot, stirrup and all, and stood looking up. "I wasn't going to mention it, but now that we're almost home, you do know, don't you, why Terry and Pam pushed us out on this ride tonight?"

She slipped a hand around the back of his neck. "I have a pretty good idea. After all, it is the twelfth of May. But I didn't think you'd catch on. You did remember?"

"Well, you come on down here, lady." She shifted her weight to the left stirrup, swung her right leg over and leaned into Queenie's side. As she freed her left foot for the jump, he caught her and held her close. Then, keeping one arm around her, he turned her to face the brightness. "There she is — our old Fernie Mountain Moon."

"More of a Coal Creek Mountain Moon, I'd say, by the direction."

"Right. No matter. Maybe a few more minutes of her will help for what's in store. They're all going to be giving us presents, you know. All gold-coloured stuff that we don't have any use for, like trays and goblets and plates."

"Oh, well, we'll survive." She squeezed his hand. "We'd better get back, I guess. There'll be a houseful there already. Just don't forget to act surprised."

"First, my lady," he said, "I want to give *you my* present." He raised her chin to the light. "Tonight I give you the moon. That great golden orb. It now belongs to you."

"Is it really yours to give?"

"It is. I promised it to you long ago. Now it's yours."

"Thank you, that's all I've ever wanted." She stood tiptoe for a quick kiss, then poked him in the ribs and reached for the reins. When they were both mounted she said, "There's just one other thing. Now that I own the moon, I'm going to change Queenie's name. I'm going to call her Goldie. Don't you think that would be a nice commemoration?"

He walked his horse up to hers. He leaned out of the saddle and kissed her cheek. "Some name for a bay, but, my queen, you do whatever you like." After a moment he added, "I think I'll change Beanie's too. From now on I'm going to call him Oldie."

"Good, now I can go back to calling you Old Bean."

He slapped the ends of the reins against his thigh. "Okay, and they can be Goldie Oldies like us." And they trotted off into the moonrise.

MARS

Squinty held the glass with his left hand, pressed the handle with his right, careful of the angle and the pressure. You had to have just the right amount of foam. He set the glasses one by one on the tray. How could something smell this good coming out of the spout, then become so sickening right away? Sometimes he thought he couldn't stand the smell of another beer. He raised his apron to wipe his eyes. They were always watering. His mother had told him it was because they were too close together. And she said that was what made his hair so springy and unmanageable too. His slight body moved around the counter. He picked up the tray. Six beers for Blackie's table. Blackie was sitting with a bunch of the other guys from the mill — Cal and Joe, Ben and Pete and Lee Choy. They'd been there since quitting time. Funny, Blackie hardly ever stayed so long in any one bar. As Squinty approached his table, Blackie yelled good-naturedly, "It's about time Squinty, goddam you. Us boys are all dry here."

He set the glasses down one by one. As he gathered up the empties, Cal put a five-dollar bill on the tray. "Oh no you don't." Blackie grabbed the bill and shoved it back at Cal. "When I'm the one that orders, I'm the one that pays." And he slapped his own bill in its place. "And Squinty, you get yourself a beer out of that. Don't you go taking some other fucker's money when I'm the one that ordered."

As Squinty made change, he caught a movement two tables away. It was Ellie signalling to him by pointing at her empty glass. She had on her denim shirt with the embroidered roses, the one he'd given her last Valentine's. Andy Taylor and his wife Daryl were with her, and also her best friend Rita. Rita was wearing a short-sleeved sweater, in an olive green colour, and her heart-shaped locket on a silver chain. Long silver earrings dangled out of the wispy hair at her shoulders. And there was another woman, someone he didn't know, who had just joined them. She had on a red blouse, the kind of material you could see right through. The straps of her slip and brassiere showed underneath. It was all kind of bulging white lace through the red nylon.

Ellie looked up with a weak, rather slanted smile. "Couldn't you see we all need refills here?" Her eyes were bleary, sort of red around the edges. She put her hand on his arm. "This is my boyfriend, Squinty, I was telling you about," she said, looking toward the newcomer, and then, to Squinty, "This is Andy's sister, Gloria."

"She's from Creston." It was Rita's voice. "She just came in on the bus and she had a hard time finding what bar Andy and Daryl were in. So she's desperate for a beer."

"Like the rest of us," Ellie said. They all laughed. "And we're all desperate for your company."

Squinty reached across the table to shake Gloria's offered hand. She looked up at him, smiling. Her fingers fluttered as she released the pressure on his palm. "Five beers coming up," he said.

"I'm gonna take a break," he said to Hoojoo at the bar. "Can you handle it for a bit?"

"Sure thing." Hoojoo gave a knowing look in the direction of Ellie and Rita. With a jerk of his head toward the back, he added, "Her old man's in here, you know."

"Yeah, I know."

As Squinty passed the near table, he lifted one of the six glasses from the tray in a mock toast to Blackie. Blackie saluted him elaborately in return. His eyes weren't quite in focus.

Rita and Ellie had pushed their chairs close together and dragged in one from the next table so Squinty could sit between Ellie and Andy. He set out the glasses, leaned the empty tray against the table leg, pulled up his chair and raised his beer. "To all concerned," he said. He was looking directly across at Gloria who was between her sister-in-law and Rita.

He knew he was the envy of most of the guys in town, at least the ones who spent time in the bar, but sometimes he wished his life was a little more simple. It was nice having Ellie for a girlfriend. He could go pick her up anytime he wanted, right at the house even. Her husband never said a word about it. Of course, everybody knew Jake Cameron just wasn't able to do what Ellie needed any more, not the last couple of years. He was still getting DVA cheques for what happened to him in the war. Ellie said they never even talked about her and Squinty and, anyway, he'd know better than to make any kind of trouble because she'd just walk out, let him have custody of the kids and everything. Squinty had thought it over many times. That part of his life was simple enough. He could take Ellie anywhere he wanted — out the Cokato Road, up the trail by the Pest House, down by the river, over to the coke ovens; and if the weather wasn't good, well, he could always throw the canopy on the back of the pickup and put in a mattress and some pillows.

No, Ellie wasn't the problem. It was Rita. In the beginning he had tried to discourage her, because of her and Ellie being best friends and everything. But Rita kept insisting it was okay, she'd never ever tell her. After all, she didn't want to hurt her either, her best friend. But she couldn't help herself. She just wanted Squinty. And when he found her leaning out over the tailgate one night when he'd closed up at the Castle, he knew there was no use resisting any longer. The Cameron kids had chicken pox at the time, so he hadn't been with Ellie for over a week. And Rita was so warm and misty and clinging from quite a bit to drink and from having to wait so long for him in the truck, that there wasn't much else he could do.

That's when his life became complicated. Not that Rita had ever betrayed any signs of their relationship. She always made sure Ellie sat in the middle when they were driving with him and she never expected him to spend time with her if there was a chance for him to be with Ellie. Even once when Jake had to go to the coast, for some DVA checkup at Shaughnessy Hospital, Rita stayed with the kids any time Ellie and Squinty wanted to be together. He was sure a lot of people knew about him and Rita. So, even if it wasn't Rita who told her, Ellie was bound to find out one way or another, any time now.

"Well, Squinty's the one who can tell you all about it." It wasn't until he heard Ellie's shrill voice, using his name, that he was aware he hadn't been listening to the conversation.

"Tell who all about what?" He sipped beer through the foam.

It was Rita who answered. "Gloria wants to know the story about the hotel. We've told her that it's named after Castle Mountain, but isn't there more to it than that?"

"No, that's about it. Old Abe Britney built the place in 1905, right after the fire. There was a big fire in '04 that wiped out the whole business section. It was all made of wood. After that, everyone had to use cement, or stone, or . . ."

"I don't mean that kind of thing." Gloria was leaning toward him. The way the red stuff of her blouse hung down, one side looked dangerously close to poking into the top of her beer glass. "I mean what's with the Castle idea? You got that tower and fancy trim outside, even those fake steps going up, and narrow windows at the top, so you expect something special like knights and ladies at least, or a prince and princess. Then you get in here and it's just like any other dark stuffy old bar."

Squinty had his handkerchief out. He dabbed at his eyes and took a gulp of beer. "You're absolutely right, and that's just what I've been trying to tell Hoojoo, ever since I been working here. At least put in some long wooden tables, I say, so it looks like the Middle Ages. And it wouldn't hurt to throw some bearskins around," (he moved his handkerchief in a circle) "or cougar, and have some old barrels in the corners...."

Gloria slid her glass to one side so she could lean even further forward. The two rounds of her lacy slip were pressed against the table. "And you could put in those old-fashioned lamps. You know, like they used to have on the carriages."

"Yeah, or even just lanterns...."

"And you should have some long spears, or what about armour?" She turned toward the wall to her right. "What you need is a big fireplace right here," (she shaped it with her hands) "all full of crackling logs, and then suits of armour on each side, and maybe...."

Andy had turned sideways with one arm flung over the back of his chair. His wife was searching through her purse for more cigarettes. Ellie and Rita sat very straight, side by side.

Squinty was leaning forward now too. "Atmosphere, that's what we need. I even told Hoojoo it would be a good idea to get in some mead and serve it in those big metal cup things. Aren't they made of pewter?"

Gloria put up a hand to stop him. "Did you say Hoojoo? What kind of name is that for someone who owns a Castle? That's something else that needs changing."

He laughed. "Yeah. Right again. You see, that's the biggest problem. He was always stingy as hell. All the rest of us used to tell him he was a Jew, even when he was a little kid. And every time anybody'd say 'Jew' he'd say, 'Who Jew?' So the name just stuck. His real name is Bruce. But he's still stingy as hell."

Ellie and Rita drained their glasses in unison and set them down hard side by side on the table.

Gloria held her glass in her hand now. It was still half full. She kept looking steadily at Squinty. "Have you ever thought of buying him out? Or at least going partners? With all your good ideas you'd be sure to improve the joint."

Squinty tapped the top of his glass with his fingernail and just as he looked up, ready to answer, Ellie cut in. "Hey you two. Do you think the rest of us want to sit here listening to this kind of crap?"

And Rita said, "Yeah, can't you see all this flighty talk is bloody boring?" She put her elbows on the table and rested her chin on her thumbs.

"Oh my," Gloria said with a throaty laugh, still looking directly at Squinty. "I guess, brave knight, that you are not paying enough attention to these damsels in distress."

"Right." Squinty jumped up. "I'll get you all some more beer. My break's over anyway, and Hoojoo's getting pretty busy."

Andy turned back, emptied his glass. Daryl took a cigarette out of Gloria's pack but her hands were unsteady and she was having a difficult time lighting it. Gloria watched Squinty as he walked to the bar. Ellie and Rita looked at each other. No one said anything.

Then Squinty was back. "Here you go Daryl. And one for you Andy. No, no. Put your money away. This round's on me. And two for the damsels." He was staring at Gloria's lacy bosom as he placed the glasses in front of Ellie and Rita. He set Gloria's glass down with a flourish, took a step back and bowed over the empty tray, saying, "And one for the lovely princess."

Gloria bobbed her head and smiled. "Thank you, Sweet Prince."

Squinty excused himself and, once he'd slipped the empty glasses into the soapy sink, headed for the long hallway that led back to the washrooms.

No one could say afterwards how or why it happened, not even Ellie or Rita. Talking about it later, they knew it started with the talk about the Castle. After that, it was partly because of the way Squinty looked at Gloria, partly the way she looked at him, and maybe because he had called her "lovely princess," and certainly because she had called them "damsels in distress" and him "brave knight." But mostly it was because of that dammed red see-through blouse and the lace. The hussy. Coming over here from Creston in a thing like that. Her "Thank you, Sweet Prince" when he was making his stupid bow was definitely the last straw.

As with a school of fish who react simultaneously as though from a hidden signal, the two leapt up and dived at Gloria. As they sent her sprawling, Gloria clawed desperately at the air and seized the one thing that was seizable, Rita's necklace. The silver chain broke and the locket slithered off across the wooden floor.

The next thing to go was the red blouse. Rita and Ellie must have grabbed the collar, one from each side, at the same instant. How else could it have ripped straight down the middle? Hoojoo picked it up later and noted that, although the sleeves were ripped too, the buttons at the back hadn't even come undone. They were both sitting astride Gloria, Ellie pounding on her head and Rita gripping her ankles in an attempt to pry off her black suede platform shoes, before Andy realized anything was happening, even though Daryl had been screaming, "Andy, Andy, do something" for several minutes, and other drinkers had scraped back their chairs and someone had made an attempt to grab at the flailing limbs of the two women.

It was the mill crew who finally broke it up. Cal and Joe grabbed Rita and set her back on her chair. Ben and Pete succeeded in pulling Ellie off Gloria but they had to get Lee Choy's help. He crouched down and, squeezing her hands as hard as he could, he finally broke her grip on Gloria's hair. Blackie managed to stand, both hands on the table to steady himself. When Andy and Lee Choy raised Gloria to her feet, and Daryl got her shoe back on her and smoothed her hair, Blackie raised his arms shakily from the table and managed to free one, then the other from the sleeves of his jacket. As he took a step toward Gloria, Cal steadied him by one elbow. "Here Honey," Blackie said. "You take my goddam coat and you put it on." Once his hands were empty, he positioned them energetically so he could strum an imaginary guitar, and he smiled broadly as he sang, "The gold rush is over and the bum's rush is on."

When Squinty came back along the hallway from the can he still had that warm feeling that Gloria had stirred. All those exciting ideas about fixing up the Castle. Maybe he'd stand them all another round. As he swung open the door, he saw at once that Ellie and Rita were alone at the table. They sat side by side staring straight ahead, not even talking.

He grabbed two beers off Hoojoo's tray at the bar. As he made his way over, he ignored the raised fingers and calls for service on each side. He set the glasses down in front of the two women. "What happened to your company?"

The question acted like a button pressed, a switch turned on, a lever shifted. They both unlocked their stares, looked at him, then at each other. "Oh they had to leave." He saw that Ellie's hand was clenched into a tight fist on the table.

"Flew the coop," said Rita, her fingers drumming up and down the side of her glass.

"Went to see a man about a dog." Ellie nodded and looked down at her beer. "Made bail."

"Okay, okay," Squinty said. "You don't have to tell me. I've got to go anyway. Looks like everybody's dry in this bloody miserable beer parlour." As he turned away he yelled, "Okay Blackie, keep your shirt on. You're next."

Ellie and Rita moved their chairs a little apart, just so they could look at each other more comfortably. In unison they relaxed their mouths into knowing smiles, raised their glasses in a clinking toast and took several gulps. Ellie moved her hand a bit to the right, opened it, and said, "You'd better have this back." She set the silver locket on the table in front of them. It was open. Out of the heart shaped frame, a colour image of Squinty smiled up at them.

"Oh, Ellie. Now you know."

"Oh, come on. I've known all along, even before he gave you this."

"And it didn't make you mad?"

"No, why should it? You're my best friend, aren't you?"

"You are a wonder. Why didn't you let on?"

"Oh, I guess I didn't mind seeing the two of you feel guilty. I think I was even enjoying it."

Rita picked up the locket, snapped it shut. "I just hope I can find the chain. Maybe Squinty . . ."

"No, listen." Ellie laid one finger on the locket in Rita's hand. "Let's look for it ourselves. Squinty doesn't have to know. Okay?"

Rita's eyes widened, then her face relaxed into a knowing smile. And they clinked their glasses again. Together they said, "To our sweet prince."

DIANA

James Morgan stopped the axe in mid swing. Was that a car in the driveway? Shoot! Somebody dropping by and him wanting to get the wood split. He really didn't like having visitors when his wife wasn't home. He gave a quick stroke, embedding the blade in the chopping block and, straightening his collar and smoothing the hair over his bald spot, walked across the yard to the side of the house. It was the pickup. "Hey Honey, it's you! What are you doing back already?"

But she didn't hear him. At least, she didn't answer. She was still in the cab, turned away from him, working at the gun mount on the back window. She slid out with the rifle in one hand, a lunch bucket in the other, her plaid jacket over one arm. "Hey Hon," he said again. By now he was at the front of the truck. "You must have had some luck if you're back this soon. What'd you get?"

"Nothing," she said. "Nothing at all." She slammed the truck door with one elbow. "And I'm just fed up with hunting. I'm never going again." She started for the side door.

"Here," he said. "Let me give you a hand." He reached for the gun but she swung it out of his reach, so he hurried to get a few steps ahead to open the door for her. "What do you mean? Did something get away? Or didn't you see anything at all?"

She went through as he held the door open, saying nothing. She dropped the lunch box on the counter and threw the jacket at the nearest chair. It hit the side of the seat, then fell to the floor. He stooped to pick it up.

"It wasn't that anything got away. Let's just say I missed."

"But you never miss. You're one of the best shots in the whole dammed Elk Valley."

"Okay. I didn't miss. Whatever you say. If you must know, I didn't even fire." She stared down at the rifle in her hands. "I didn't fire a single shot."

"You couldn't have been far . . . I didn't expect you back so soon . . ."

"I wasn't far. Just out by Morrissey." She moved toward the hall. "Let's leave it at that, eh? I just don't want to talk about it. Not ever again. Out by Morrissey, you got that?"

He heard the boots clumping along the hall. She went into the little room at the back, the one she wouldn't let him call her "trophy room." A snowy mountain goat hide on the floor, heads mounted on the walls: moose, elk, two deer — one a mule deer, one a white tail — a bighorn sheep; various hides on chairs, the pelt of a black bear over the small couch.

"I'll put on some coffee," he called. He could see into the room from where he stood at the sink. He could see her sitting on the couch, her legs out straight, the rifle upright between her knees. Why would she be so busy cleaning the thing if she never fired a shot? He held the kettle under the tap. Oh well, sure. She's probably afraid she's got some dirt in the barrel. She's always been real fussy about her rifles. He could see her pulling the cleaning rod through the barrel, over and over, as though she'd need some powerful signal to make her stop.

Strange she'd driven all the way out to Morrissey. Usually, on the first day of hunting she just went down to the salt lick for a fast kill. And that was in the opposite direction, north of town.

Oh well. He moved toward the stove. Maybe the coffee will help.

END

Blaze and Babe

CHAPTER ONE

DOORS

I notice when someone is writing a story that there is a certain kind of movement (it wasn't anything I ever thought about before doing all that reading), a movement from telling things in a general way to telling them in a specific way. The reason, I figure, is that an author cannot tell everything in detail; some things just need to be there in the background to give a feeling of what it is like for the most part. Then there are certain incidents, or people, or places, that call for a lot of attention. And in those cases, the writer must be very precise, giving as accurate a rendering as possible. The trick is to go back and forth between these two methods.

If I were to give YOU all the details about what was going on in the house in that first year in Fernie, YOU would probably get bored. That would be one thing. But if I were just to tell you generally what I thought was the state of our relationships, well, what reason would you have to believe my version of things? I have to ask that question because I know that even those of us right there — Blaze, Bertie and me — did not agree on much about what happened. Each of us interpreted things in a different way. And I am certain that Syd, Randy and Jackie had their own private versions too.

Dad was not talking to us, as I said, for some time before Christmas. That part continued. Bertie seemed exasperated with him, at least she complained openly about how he was acting and especially about how he was getting worse with the older children. At the same time Blaze and I had the feeling that she was in both camps. For we would hear her and him talking for hours in the night; and Blaze was increasingly suspicious that Bertie was reading her diary.

Now that I have told you these things in a very general way, I can give YOU some close looks that will let YOU gauge the situation better.

In Fernie there are very few people who lock their doors. Oh, if they were to go away, right out of town I mean, they might lock up, or at least get a neighbour to go in once in a while, but more to feed a cat or dog, or water plants, than to guard against burglars or vandals. There is the story about Peg Robertson who came back after a few days in Lethbridge. She had taken her dog over on the bus to get his rabies shots. She came home at midday. Even before she opened the door of the front porch she could tell someone had been in. There were spots of blood on the steps, blood on the door handle, blood across the porch floor and on the knob of the main door. The floor inside was covered with blood and a red trail continued along the hall.

As she told people afterwards, not once did she think of any sort of violent act, partly because she was busy keeping Cody — that was her German shepherd — from licking at the blood, but mostly because it never occurred to her that anything outrageous could happen. She admitted she was curious because, as she said, it isn't every day you come onto such a bloody scene in your own home. When she saw that the phone, on the little table at the end of the hall, was covered with blood too, it was clear what had happened. Someone had got hurt and needed to call for help. It was that simple. She put Cody in the basement, filled a basin with cold water, tore up a couple of old towels, and got on with the clean-up.

And she was right. As it turned out, Moke had come by in his old Ford to drop off a hind quarter of mule deer. He'd been lucky the day before, and had skinned out the animal that morning. Somehow, as he was getting the chunk of meat out of the back, the trunk door had slammed shut on his hand. He didn't make afternoon shift that day. After the phone call he went straight to the hospital. He lost the tips of two fingers on his left hand.

So, ever since we arrived, our door was never locked. All Dad did was tell everyone to close it real hard, even lean against it until you heard it click, so it wouldn't blow open if a wind came up. I am saying *the door*, in the singular, because as I've explained the front door was never used. I couldn't tell you if it was locked or not, or if it even had a lock. We were used to coming home, even late at night, opening the door without ever giving it a thought. Can YOU imagine, then, how it felt to turn the doorknob and have it refuse to open? And that first time, it had to be me.

I was on shift at the Diamond Grill until ten o'clock that week. Usually I was home by ten past. But that night, Gordie and a couple of the guys from typing class were in having sweet-and-sour pork and fried rice and we were kidding around a lot because there weren't any other customers. And they said why don't we go for a little ride when you get off because it's full moon and everything's so bright. The next day was Saturday and I didn't have to be up early so I said okay. All we did was drive up to Fairy Creek and look at the falls coming out of the reservoir in the moonlight. It wasn't even a quarter to eleven when I put my hand on the knob and it wouldn't turn.

I tried the window to our bedroom — it faced onto the back porch — but he had locked it too. I tapped on the glass but Blaze must have been sound asleep. Anything rather than get him up. But there was no other way. He didn't turn on the light but I could see him in the moonlight that was coming in the kitchen window. His long underwear moved like a white shadow across to the door. He unlocked it, swung it open, stood aside. Neither of us spoke. I went immediately into the bedroom. He closed the door firmly. And the key turned again in the lock.

That was when we had to come up with our rope plan. At bedtime, whichever one of us was at home would dangle one end of the rope over the sill and close the window on it, then go to bed with the other end of the rope tied around one wrist. The one who was out could simply raise the window a little and give a tug on the rope. And, because the opening of the window was rather noisy, as was the unlocking of the door, a necessary part of the plan was that it be completed during the rattling by of the freight train.

He must have wondered, but no one ever said a word. And neither he nor Bertie ever discovered the rope. We kept it hidden in a Kotex box.

CHAPTER TWO

BOYFRIENDS

Another generalized run-down I can give YOU is about Blaze's boyfriends. And I'll remember to give specific instances, too.

I've mentioned Herbie Weiss — he was the first one — but she went out with him only a few times. Once was to the dance at Roosville; and they spent one day hunting in the South Country. The best thing about that day, she said, was that she got to see the Kootenay River. She even wrote a long poem about it but the only part I can remember is: "Across the mighty Kootenay/I gazed with unbelieving eyes." The main point of the poem I think was that she preferred live animals to killed ones. Also, Herbie bragged to everybody about how she could walk and climb for all those hours without getting tired. He said he could hardly keep up to her. I know she liked that part too.

The other time with Herbie was when they went up the trail to the Saddle on Coal Creek Mountain after grouse. It was the first time Blaze ever used a shotgun. They came back to the house with half a dozen dead birds. Herbie plunked them down on the kitchen table and then launched into a long description to Bertie and me of how Blaze had shot them all, picked them right off where they sat still on branches. Bertie said, "Oh, you mean they're just fool hens," and the two of them laughed.

For some reason Blaze pretended she didn't know a thing about what to do with fowl. She shot a warning glance at me and said, "Shouldn't you be getting some homework done?" So I knew better than to say anything about how we'd had to stand by while our uncle approached the hen, hanging upside down by its feet, its wings locked into each other behind its back. He used a special knife. He forced open the beak with fingers and thumb. The thin sharp curve of the blade entered the mouth, moved back to the throat, slit the jugular. We always turned away. Sometimes the wings came unlocked. Then we had to grab them and hold them until they quieted; quieted and stopped. At the instant of death we were to start the plucking.

    Herbie was happy enough to stay, and I could see at least three reasons for that: he liked to be around Blaze as much as possible, he felt important showing her how to prepare the birds, and Bertie said he could eat with us. He had difficulty getting all the feathers off. Of course. They had been dead too long. Jackie stood by with a gunny sack, making sure that not one little piece of curled fluff got away. He wanted to make a pillow for himself. Then Herbie and Bertie cut the birds open and cleaned them, making a game of counting up the pellets as they extricated them from the flesh.

    Blaze had excused herself saying that since Syd wasn't home yet she'd better do his chores. She brought in an armful of kindling, then two buckets of coal. Then she took a long time in the bedroom changing from jeans and boots into a cotton skirt and slippers. After that, even though it was too early, she filled the boiler for her bath, this time carrying the water, dipperful by dipperful from the sink to the stove.

    It was the first time I'd ever eaten wild fowl. However Bertie had cooked it, it was real tasty. But I noticed that Blaze didn't eat anything but the potatoes and carrots.

    After Herbie it was almost as though she had decided to try out the whole racial spread of the town. The shy one who had so wanted to meet her when she first started working in the grocery department of Trites Woods turned out to be Polish. That made sense because Reginald in Menswear was Polish. He motioned to Blaze one day just as she was on her way upstairs.

There was a lunchroom up there, next to the ladies' washroom, and she was heading for a coffee and a smoke. So she went back to Menswear with him and he introduced them. His name was Bogdan Chernowski but, of course, he went by Dan. He was tall, thin, pale, and freckled. As she told me, he had a nice smile that showed some edging of gold along his upper left incisor and first bicuspid. She said it was the nice bridgework that decided her to go out with him. He worked in his father's insurance office and had the use of the family car. Often on Wednesday afternoons (all the businesses in Fernie closed Wednesday afternoons), he would drive her out the highway — either west as far as Cranbrook, or north to Sparwood. Sparwood was the new residential area for the mineworkers down the Pass. The Coal Company wanted, eventually, to move all the workers and their families out of Michel and Natal, the two old mining towns that Blaze said were actually much more interesting. Dan took her to local dances — at the I.O.O.F. Hall and the Legion — but mostly they just went to the Vogue (there were three shows every week). They always came into the Diamond Grill after and stayed as long as they could, working on vocabulary. If she hadn't had to get home (on nights that I worked late) before Dad locked the door, she could have learned a lot of Polish.

    The next one was Italian. He was a nephew of Mr. Martinelli although he didn't have the same name. Maybe his mother was Mr. Martinelli's sister, or maybe he was on Mrs. Martinelli's side. I knew at the time because he used to work at the store some Sundays (it wasn't officially open but you could always ring the bell and someone from the family would come out from the living quarters at the back). His real job was looking after the lockers at Fernie Frozen Foods. Anyway, he was Tony. He was dark, thin, brown-eyed, and he couldn't look at anyone without flashing a smile. His teeth were very white and even. Blaze said he had a couple of cavities along the lower gum line, but then she didn't go with him long enough to feel the need to suggest dental work. The highlight of their time together, as I remember, was a horseback ride in from Hosmer one night. She told me how romantic it was when they leaned out of their saddles to kiss, and how handsome he looked in the moonlight. On horseback he'd seemed taller. She learned quite a bit of Italian in those few weeks — common words and phrases. And when they stopped going out, Tony said she could keep the little grammar book (It was one his mother had used in school in Italy), and he gave her a picture of himself. He was on a tall sorrel and he looked quite a bit younger. On the back it said, "To Blaze" and was signed "from the Italian Stallion."

I should mention that she went out with Blackie too, early on — a week or so after Syd brought his message home to Blaze. She had noticed in the *Free Press* that there was some musical concert on at the hall in Michel on the Tuesday. So when Blackie said he wanted to take her to Michel Tuesday evening and was mysterious about what for, she assumed he had tickets for the concert. When it turned out that his idea of a surprise date was an evening in the beer parlour of the Michel Hotel, she changed her impression about the exciting experience of going out with a native Indian, or at least one who was mostly Indian.

There were two others — Terry Dvorak who was Czech, and Mitch Shaw who was Slavic on his mother's side. Actually, the two were good friends or, as they termed it, "partners." They both worked at Fernie Brewery. Together they would plan places to take Blaze, mostly on Sundays. And most of the places they went were parts of the Elk River: the deep part down by the cribbing, or the spot where Lizard Creek flowed in, or the big bend where you get the first view of the Three Sisters on the way up from Elko. Blaze really learned how to fish from those two. All they ever seemed to catch was grayling. I had never heard of that kind before so I looked it up in an old dictionary Dad had.

All it said was "a silver grey fresh-water fish." They weren't very big but they certainly were silvery.

It was cold weather by the time Blaze started going fishing with Terry and Mitch. The river wasn't frozen yet but there was snow on the ground. They showed her how to find something they called scratchers that were good for bait. They lived under rocks at the edge of the water. As near as I could tell they were some kind of small crayfish. The only problem with scratchers was that as soon as you took them out of the water, they froze; and since grayling were interested in live bait only . . . well, they showed Blaze how to hold the scratchers in her mouth, between teeth and cheek, to keep them warm and, therefore, alive. I went along with the three of them a few times, but certainly didn't have Blaze's determination for jumping into every new experience that came along. But, as I said, I didn't have her obsession about becoming a writer either.

They had a smokehouse too or, at least, that's what they called it. Actually, it was an old beat-up refrigerator in a shed back of Terry's house. They had rigged it up so they could make a fire in the bottom, with different kinds of wood chips, and then lay the fish on the racks up above. They did make money out of the set-up. They had a dozen or so steady customers — mostly heavy drinkers, who would stock up on payday. Later in the week, when their money ran out, they could use the smoked fish for collateral in the bars. Blaze and Terry and Mitch would all go to the smokehouse and sit around on blocks of wood and exchange fishing stories and discuss at great length the different smells of wood smoke. As I remember, Blaze's favourite was alder.

Another person I should mention, although Blaze didn't really go out with him, was one of the new Mounties. The RCMP detachment was very small — a corporal and two, sometimes three, constables. The corporal was fairly permanent, but the constables tended to come and go. I think it was a policy of the force to have fairly frequent change-overs so no officer would have time to get too pally with the locals. Some months after we arrived in Fernie a new man joined the group. We first saw him in the Diamond Grill. Blaze and I were in the very back booth. It was an evening when I wasn't on shift. She had got a nickel stuck in the coin slot of the selection box and was leaning across the table banging on the metal sides, trying to jar it loose.

I saw him come in. He was with Sandy Gordon. They were both in uniform. In Ontario we were familiar with the scarlet uniform only; that was because we saw the RCMP only at official functions. They weren't the regular police for a town the way they are here. We had the Provincial force for that. So Sandy and this new guy were in their khaki uniforms. The only thing the same as the ceremonial dress was the yellow stripe down the outside of each pantleg.

They came right to the back, but Blaze didn't see them. She was kneeling on the seat, one elbow on the table, banging at the box and flipping the coin return. Sandy smiled at me as he slid into the booth behind her. Raising his chin toward Blaze he said, "What's with her?" The new guy was still standing but I could see on his face that Blaze had turned around, for I had observed that look many times before on faces seeing Blaze for the first time. And that night she looked particularly good with the green of her print shirt bringing out her eyes, and she had just used that new White Rain shampoo that made her hair extra glossy and, even though it was turned under in a long pageboy, any slight movement swung it silkily from side to side.

Blaze and Sandy said something to each other. I don't remember what because I was watching the reaction: the sweep of the eyes, the intake of breath, the drop of the lower lip, but all giving the sense of complete control. He put his hand on Sandy's shoulder. "Who's your friend?" he said.

Sandy made introductions. "The Cassidy Sisters," he said. "Blaze and what's her name." He had teased me like that before, those times when I was on shift and he'd come in at least twice for coffee.

The new officer was Constable Southby. Robert Southby. "But you can call me Rob." He leaned forward to extend his right hand across the distance between him and Blaze. She shook it briefly and he slowly took it back across the space. I guess he thought I was too young for hand-shaking or any other kind of acknowledgment. He simply sat down beside me, never taking his eyes from Blaze. "Can we help you with that thing?" He slowly unbuttoned his jacket, careful to pull it open enough to expose the strap of his holster.

"No, I don't think it's any use. All of them stick once in a while."

He stood up. "Well, okay, just tell me what piece you wanted and I'll play it for you on this one here." He moved to the next booth and started flipping the lever that moved the little selection arms inside.

Blaze shot an exasperated look at me but said, "Well, thank you. It was *Don't Fence Me In*, number eight." I don't know why she made the change. What she'd been so desperate to hear before was *Blue Moon*.

After he had arched up to get some coins out of his pocket, he took his revolver out of the holster and stepped back to lay it on our table, first making a point of checking the safety. With a glance at Blaze he dropped one of the coins in and punched the number, just as Carmen came by with two coffees. "You'd better move that thing out of the way," she said.

"Oh sure." He pushed the gun aside with one thumb to make room for the cup and saucer. Then he sat down again.

As soon as *Don't Fence Me In* finished, Blaze got out past Sandy and reached for her jacket. Rob was on his feet immediately, helping her into it. I just twisted mine over my arm and held it there. She thanked him and added, "And thanks for playing our song." We all laughed a bit. Blaze hurried me away.

After paying Buck at the counter, she grabbed two or three toothpicks out of the holder and stuck them all in her mouth at once, chewing down hard on the ends. "What a jerk," she said.

"I thought he was kind of nice." I waved to Buck and Carmen as we went out the door. "He sure gave you a good looking over though, didn't he?"

She didn't seem to hear me. "I bet that'd be one boring man, if you could ever bring yourself to get to know him. Even with the uniform — nothing but one big walking cliché."

That wasn't the end of Rob by any means, and it seemed that subsequent encounters with him just reinforced her first impression. For instance, there was the night of the pictures. It was in the Grill again. Since Blaze refused his persistent invitations to go out with him, that was the only place they ever met, except for the night she let him drive her home in the police cruiser. He had pulled up beside her in front of Cash Grocery. If it hadn't been a wet miserable night, and getting close to Dad's lock-out time, she said she would have refused. And sure enough, when he stopped outside the house he grabbed her and tried to kiss her. She pulled away and said, "I don't know what pleasure a guy can get out of kissing someone who really doesn't want him to." She got out and he drove away without saying a word.

But back to the pictures. I was on shift and the place was pretty busy, right after *Love is a Many Splendoured Thing* let out at the Vogue, so I wasn't in on it. Blaze said he told her about a teen-aged girl who'd been axed to death in Kimberly; no one knew about the murder yet; it wasn't in the papers or on the radio or anything. For some reason he had been called over. He actually had pictures of the dead girl. He spread them out on the table of the booth for her to see. They were big, five-by-sevens, glossy black-and-whites. They'd been taken from different angles, all showing the girl lying in blood in the cellar of her home. It looked like a dirt floor. In one of them you could see the bottom of a stairway. Blaze had tears in her eyes when she told me about it. "It was just like that first time when he put his revolver on the table, such a clichéd, crass thing to do — but this time it was something too real. Right away I grabbed them up and put them back in the folder. I felt so mad. What right did he have to be putting her on display like that? All just to make a big impression?" I don't think she ever forgave him, not even later when he was such a help getting me out of town.

I've left Nick to the last. Well, that's natural because he was the last one before Blackie became permanent. As I mentioned earlier, he was the owner of the Olympos. Blaze thought he was too short, and too old (he was in his late twenties at least, maybe thirty already), and he spoke broken English, and his teeth had cavities, dark grey patches clearly visible right between the centrals and the laterals, both upper and lower. YOU will remember that teeth were important to her; she never got over that dental-nurse training she had in Toronto.

I have to admit, Nick was my favourite of all the ones she'd gone out with. But he was interested in her only. He talked about taking her to Crete (that's where he was from), about showing her the ancient Minoan site at Knossos, about taking her down some huge gorge at the west end of the island, and he never let up about wanting to see her swim in the azure blue waters of the Mediterranean Sea. He punctuated every sentence with a word that sounded like oh'-ray'-uh. He said it was Greek for beautiful. "Your sister," he would say to me . . . and he would take on a dreamy faraway look that made me feel that I was entering the blue sea of his eyes and swimming there with the sunshine on the waves around me and the mellow sounds of some Greek seabird in my ears . . . "She must come to my home. Oh-ray-uh. Your wonderful sister. Oh-ray-uh."

I asked him once about his eyes. To me they were his most striking feature. "Isn't it unusual for a Greek to have blue eyes? especially as blue as yours?"

"Not usual? May-*bee*. But people from my village, we are all not usual. Maybe because we live right by the sea in a place that is, how you say? most south? Kriti is the most south of all my country. And my village is most south of all Kriti. Many people, from all the world, they come visit to my village. Maybe that is why my eyes are blue." He smiled so wide even I could see the cavities.

Blaze spent a lot of time with him at the Olympos in the evenings. She helped out in the kitchen, mostly making salads with tomatoes, cucumber and onion all together, with some shredded white cheese and black olives on top, and an olive oil and vinegar dressing. She got some recipes from him too, for Greek dishes, and she tried a couple out at home. But she didn't keep it up. For one thing, they didn't turn out like the ones Nick served at the Olympos; for another, Dad refused even to try them.

She did keep after Nick to teach her Greek. He said that first she would have to learn the alphabet. He wrote it out for her. I couldn't believe how all the letters were so different and there weren't even the full twenty-six. She worked at it a lot. Even at home she kept practising and memorizing, and she did learn a few words. The only one I remember is oh-ray-uh because for a while she and I used it at the end of just about any sentence that had anything at all positive in it.

But then she switched all her attention to Blackie and that was the end of Nick. Well, not only Nick. It was the end of that part of her life that had been so open to all experience, languages, culture. She settled for much less: rather mindless activity, the English language only (ungrammatical at that), and a lack of culture of any kind.

CHAPTER THREE

HOSPITAL EXPERIENCE

It wasn't until it was over between Blaze and Nick that I realized how much I had come to like him. He still let me help out in the kitchen because I'd got in the habit of going with Blaze and he'd still come by once in a while to drive me home after a late shift. But it just wasn't the same. I know I kept bugging her about why she didn't want to keep going with him.

I was at it again on the Sunday morning when we'd tramped through the snow down to the cribbing. At first she gave me the list of reasons that I'd already heard: he was too old for her, too short, had bad teeth, spoke poor English. I made her admit she'd had fun with him and hit her with my list: that she liked being with him, that he made her feel good, that he was very handsome, and I even reminded her how she always sang out "Hey, good lookin', whatcha got cookin'?" every time she went into his kitchen. At last, probably to stop my badgering, she said, "He won't leave me alone." It wasn't that she looked embarrassed or that she seemed uncertain, it was the fact that she was so clear about what was okay and wasn't okay that gave me some hint of something unnatural in her, the fact that she just assumed I thought the same, that everyone was in agreement.

There were deer tracks along the trail. We followed them to the river's edge. She leaned against the trunk of a cottonwood and looked out across the narrow strip of open water that swirled around the weathered grey posts. They had been part of the cribbing when the bend of the river was in a different place. "I don't want any man touching me," she said. She crossed her arms over her breasts. "And there's no way I'm going to ruin everything by letting some guy get me pregnant, especially when I don't want to marry him."

"Don't you want to marry Nick? I think that'd be perfect." I whirled a chunk of ice at the water. It glanced off one of the posts and shattered into a shower of whiteness. "He'd take you to Greece and everything. You could both save up . . ."

"No, I don't want to marry him. He's too . . ." She stopped. I wanted to think it was because she didn't have a real reason, but she gave me such a desperate look that I finished the sentence just to help her out.

"Yeah, I know what you mean. He's too short."

"Oh come on, Babe. I don't want you to think I'm a snob, that I think I'm better or anything. It's just that I always had this idea about my husband . . . that we'd lie in bed at night and we'd read Shakespeare to each other, or Balzac, or Dostoevsky." I turned away from the river and she followed me back over our own tracks through the snow. There was no point talking about it, something she didn't even realize about herself. She was fine at handling young guys: being buddies with them, learning from them, even getting into romantic moments. But she was no good at handling Nick. His big failing was that he was a man.

But breaking off with him was some kind of turning point for her, some kind of victory. I had to work that night after it happened, but she went skiing, by herself, up toward the Saddle under Coal Creek Mountain. She told me after how free she had felt coming down the trail, slope after slope, in the moonlight. It was a frosty night in late March but she was warm and tingling. By the time she stopped, on the level part by the Pest House, she was feeling so elated that she slipped her boots out of the harness and lay flat on her back, for a very long time, staring up at the moon and the stars and that whole expanse of sparkling sky. She remembered how warm she felt, and how fresh and crisp the air was, and she didn't really notice how the cold seeped through

160

her jacket and pants. During the next few days, the only memory she had of that night was the feeling of freedom, of something going out from her body into the hugeness of the sky above her and the snow slopes around her. And later as she lay in bed (on the day she had been unable to get up to go to work) that memory danced in her head from one beribboned stage to another, as the players and streaks of colour swirled in a fever of celebration. The delirium was with her off and on, as she could say later, but at the time no one knew about it.

Shorty and Arnold were the ones who came to get her. They were the drivers of the Trites delivery truck, but they also drove the ambulance — as volunteers. It wasn't a regular ambulance, but an old black panel truck that had been fitted out to accommodate a stretcher. Bertie had sent Syd with the message the minute he got home from school. She had just got Blaze back to bed after her fainting spell in the kitchen. It had been only for a moment; Blaze swore she came to the second she hit the floor. As Bertie said, she probably would have been okay if she hadn't got up to brush her teeth.

That day I had stayed after school to do practice typing. As I neared the house along Baker Avenue, Jackie ran out to meet me. "Guess what, Babe? They took Blaze to the hospital. They put her on a stretcher and they took her away in a bread wagon."

She referred to it later as her *hospital experience*. For the first few days there was a NO VISITORS sign on the door. Dad was allowed in to see her during that period but she didn't ever realize he was there. Every time, he brought her one of those big tins of fruit juice, the twenty-four-ounce size — mostly grapefruit and orange. The nurse put them in her cupboard for her. She was the one who told her afterward where they'd come from.

To begin with she was so out of it that she didn't even register when her dinner tray had been left for her. Two of the other patients in the ward got up out of bed to help her; one held her head while the other kept the straw in her mouth — so she could at least get some liquid, they said. The nurse explained to them that in such severe cases of pleurisy and pneumonia the patient wouldn't be able to eat, or do anything much, for several days.

    I won't regale YOU with all the details of her stay in hospital. She was there for six weeks in all — too long a time to talk about if I expect to keep YOUR interest. There are a few things, however, that bear on the story; some simply because they add to the characterization of the town, some because they relate to what was happening between her and Dad, and one because, as it turned out, it changed the course of her life.

    Personally, I think Blaze enjoyed that hospital experience to the utmost. For one thing, her surroundings were suddenly improved. She was away from the smoke and grime of the coal stove, the dirt between the boards of the wooden floors, the smell of soiled clothing, towels, and diapers, and from the discomfort and uncertainty over Dad. And that constant filling and heating of the copper boiler. Instead, she was in the proverbial "clean, well-lighted place." Squinty's ex-wife, Flora, came in to wash and wax the floor of the ward every morning before the doctors' rounds. The linoleum shone in the sunlight streaming in through the wide windows. The nurses brought in with them the smells of other rooms: ether, rubbing alcohol, wintergreen, as well as the crisp bleached aroma of their starched uniforms, accented subtly by a beginning-of-shift dab of perfume. And the sheets too — smelling of bleach, changed every second day as she sat in a chair by the window, the whiteness floating toward the ceiling, settling crisp and straight, the ironed-in fold lines paralleling the sides of the bed. At first the nurses bathed her in bed, one part at a time with a soapy cloth, but once she was able to get up by herself, they let her go along the hall to the room with the tub. She would let the hot water run a long time, just to feel the warmth and see the steam fill the air.

She had no worries at all. It was like some sort of reprieve. At first she was very seriously ill, then she was just not well, then she was convalescing. Apart from writing a few letters, and typing out some of her poems, she was completely off the hook. It was a time of suspension.

There was a huge card that came from everyone on staff at Trites Woods. It was a big sheet, folded in eight. On the front it said: "the BUNCH is waiting for you to get well." The picture was of a bunch of grapes, all with smiling faces, colourfully-clothed bodies, and little round black feet. And there were pictures of these little grape people doing all the various things that the card suggested as it kept unfolding:

> Wish we could tell you just relax
> And lay back at your ease
> While someone plumped your pillows up
> And mixed your drinks to please
> And some could be the kitchen staff
> And cook up rare delights
> And you'd have lots of magazines
> And music and soft lights . . .
> We'd like to do all this and more
> But the best your gang can do
> Is wish the biggest, darndest, swellest
> QUICK RECOVERY TO YOU

The very inside — the back of the whole sheet when it was opened up — had "Best Wishes from the Bunch" across the top. Underneath were all the names — thirty-three signatures. I can give YOU this much detail because I have the card in front of me. It must have meant a lot to Blaze. She's kept it all this time.

The management let her know they would hold a job for her; it probably wouldn't be in the grocery department for they'd had to hire Rhoda back on. She was the one who used to be cashier. She had quit to have her baby. That was how Blaze got the job in the first place. Blaze wasn't getting any salary while she was off, but, as she said, it was lucky she'd waited until she got to B.C. If she were still in Ontario, she couldn't afford to be sick, never mind be in hospital. Here, her medical coverage paid the doctor's fees and the hospital costs, except for one dollar per day. Not that it would have happened in Ontario. After all, it was because she came to Fernie that she met Nick. And it was her feeling so free after breaking off with him that caused her to heat herself up skiing and then lie flat in the snow long enough for the cold to move in and do the damage. I don't think she ever told the doctor, or anyone at the hospital, that that's how it happened.

Maybe it's like that with other things. Once the damage is done, repair is difficult. When the cold sets in, the thaw is slow to come.

But, after the first while, once she was past being really sick, it was just fun. Many people came to see her, not just the ones from work. I remember one day, in particular; it was a Sunday. Visiting hours started at two. I was a bit late because I had taken longer than I thought to get the things together she'd asked for: some make-up items, her shampoo and curlers, more writing paper and stamps, and some little rock that was somewhere in our room. It was looking for the rock that held me up. I found it finally in the pocket of one of her jeans. It was a smooth black stone that she needed to hold in her hand when she felt a poem coming on. She called it her *writing stone*.

It was a fairly long walk to the hospital — from the North End to down near the highway. It was a bright sunny day in early May. There was still a lot of snow but a bit of a melt over the last week had bared the ground in a few places. On the hospital lawn, several crows stood together in one muddy patch, their eyes glinting as they looked sideways at my approach.

As I walked along the hall, even before I got to her door, I could hear the noise coming from her room. There was a ring of people around the bed. Terry and Mitch were showing Blaze something in a magazine. Dan and Tony sat at the foot, one on either side. Dan had an open box of chocolates in his hand. They were both chewing vigorously. The two young boys from Trites — Eddy and Johnny — were arranging some vases of flowers on the tray that was swung off to the side. Blackie was leaning back against the windowsill, his legs out straight in front. He had an unlit cigarette in his mouth and was just in the act of extending his pack to Rob who was standing at attention in front of him. Above the general noise I heard Blackie's laugh as he said, "Do you have to wear that monkey suit all the time, or just when you're on duty?" Rob said something but I couldn't hear it because he had lowered his head to the match Blackie had just struck into flame with his thumbnail.

I suppose the actual scene doesn't really matter, but I was aware of a couple of visitors at each of the other beds, and I remember that just as I was making room in the cabinet drawer for the things I'd brought, Blackie turned toward the window and sprang to his feet. "Well, here's the cowboy comin' a callin'." He slid the window up and yelled out, "Hey there, Lone Ranger, why don't you bring your spotted friend up here? There's lots of room." And he laughed real loud.

Blaze sat bolt upright and the others moved out of her way so she could see. Herbie was spinning his Appaloosa around in circles through the snow and muddy patches. He was waving his hat up at the window. I noticed that the crows were no longer around. Along with the others, Rob looked out smiling, then said, "Well I gotta go. Not everybody gets Sunday off to play around." He rested his hand for a moment on the bed covers as he went by, but Blaze didn't notice. She was leaning off to the side and laughing at Herbie's antics. "See you tomorrow," he said. I remember feeling a little sad for him, watching him leave like that.

They must have passed in the hallway because it was just a moment after Rob went out that Dad was there, filling up the doorway. Since everyone else's attention was on Herbie and his horse, I was the only one who saw him. He looked in. That's all you could say – he looked in. His eyes took in the whole scene. His face was still, sad, and quiet. I noticed that because it was in such contrast to all the other lively, laughing, and noisy faces in the room. Before I could reach over to nudge Blaze, he had set down the paper bag he was carrying and, in one movement, straightened up, raised his black hat to his head, and turned. The doorway was empty again.

When Blaze was discharged (after her six-week stay) it was Blackie who drove her home. He had borrowed a car from his friend, Al. His new green Chevy.

CHAPTER FOUR

DEPARTURE

I don't know if YOU have noticed or not but I've tried to vary the length of the sections. Many times when I was reading all those books, I found myself flipping ahead to check on the chapter length. Especially if it were late at night, I'd be hoping for a short piece, something I could finish off before I got too sleepy. But even at other times, I'd want to know before starting that I wouldn't have to put the book down in mid-chapter.

And now I have the feeling that it is time for a rather short one. All I want to do in this section is bring the plot to one of its natural resting places, to show YOU what changes occurred.

Blaze didn't stay long at the house after she came home from the hospital. Maybe it was the contrast between the two environments that made her realize she could not go back to living under the heaviness of Dad's avoidance and seeming disapproval. She worried about leaving me — we knew that since I was under age he would never agree to letting me go with her — but I assured her that I could manage for the little while that was left, for I had decided to go back to Ontario. I had already written home and our aunt and uncle had offered to help me with the train fare. But they were definite, saying I should keep my job in Fernie for the rest of the summer, then plan on getting into business school in the fall. Another reason was they wouldn't be able to send money until the end of August.

Blaze worried too that she (or we) had upset things for Bertie. But she did talk to Bertie about it and Bertie said no, we hadn't made it worse; he was always moody like that, had swings from being real friendly to being what he was now. She said she had learned to accept it, but she did worry about the kids.

So Blaze got a room at Mrs. Arbuckle's place and the next weekend she and Blackie came over with Al's Chev. Bertie had told Dad, but he didn't come out of the bedroom. Blaze had all her things packed and ready so they just put them in the trunk, and she was gone. Randy and Jackie stood at the window and watched them drive away. They were both crying. Syd was not home at the time. Bertie and I sat at the kitchen table. She had Tex in her lap. She reached for her pack of Exports. She shook one out for herself, then one for me. When she lit the match I could see she had tears too. They were just standing in there, behind the reddish lashes, filling up her eyes. All I could say was, "*He* doesn't know I smoke, does he?"

Dad never did acknowledge my presence after that. The one thing I made sure of was getting in every night before lock-up. I could never have brought myself to knock on the door and have him let me in.

I didn't tell Bertie about my plans to go back, so there's no way he could have known. Maybe he thought I would try to run away, once Blaze was gone, or that I'd go live with her. Anyway, it was only a few days later that I came home from school to find my suitcase on the floor in my room. A chain was looped through its handle; the other end was padlocked to the bed frame. I had to live around it for the next couple of months. When the time came for me to go, I simply packed it full, locked it and left it there. I put everything I needed for the trip in an old canvas bag I got from Blaze.

It was Constable Rob Southby who helped me. Normally, there wouldn't have been any trouble getting away; the train for the East came through once a day. All I would have had to do was get on it during the week Dad was on day shift. But about the middle of August, the mine workers voted to go out on strike.

That meant he didn't go to work at all. He took to being at the station every day about noon when the Eastbound came through. Sometimes we saw him ourselves; sometimes we just heard about it. The money had come and I had bought my ticket, but when the strike still hadn't been settled, Blaze and I decided we'd better get help.

    Blaze was waiting for me to get off shift. She had come in with Blackie for coffee after the show. It was *Shane.* He ordered a Western sandwich. Every time I looked their way, she was lighting up another cigarette. They were talking quite a bit but I was busy with customers at the counter, too far away to hear any of it. Even before he finished his sandwich he got up from the booth and went along the length of the counter toward the washrooms at the back. "How you doin' there, kid?" he said as he went by. He had a rolling kind of walk, one you couldn't mistake for anyone else's in town. When I first knew him I thought maybe he'd been in the Navy or something. "You tell that sister of yours I got some important business to attend to." And he flashed that big wide smile of his and closed one eye in a slow, elaborate wink.

    "Why don't you try telling her yourself?" I said. But he kept on walking and I heard the door bang as he went out into the back alley. That's what he did a lot. He'd just get up as though he were going for cigarettes, or to have a look out the window, and he wouldn't come back. It embarrassed the heck out of Blaze and made her feel real hurt. Sometimes he even left her sitting in the show. He'd say he was going for popcorn, or to the washroom, and not come back. She knew what it was: he had to go to the bar, he had to get a drink. But she was sure she understood the problem. He was an orphan — like her. His mother had died when he was two. And, like us, he'd been raised by an aunt and uncle, in with a family of cousins. She was certain that once they had a home of their own, the problem would be solved. He wouldn't need to drink any more. But still, she always felt ashamed, having to come out of the show, like that, by herself.

I didn't mean to digress into all that but I guess it's part of bringing the plot up to that point. It will let YOU know something about how things were when I finally left Fernie. Anyway, not long after Blackie went out, Rob came in. When he saw Blaze alone in the booth he sat down with her. That's when she told him about how I wanted to go back to Ontario and how Dad had my suitcase chained to the bed and how he watched at the train station every day. She even came over to the counter to get the letter so she could show him I had a place to go.

So it was *his* plan. I was to get on the early morning bus and go to Calgary. *There* I would wait for the train — the very one Dad would be checking on going out to the east.

It was the last week of August, on the Sunday. Blaze waited with me that morning at the Annex Café, the one that doubles as the bus station. There was nothing left to say. We had already said everything, several times. Just as the bus was pulling in, she went to the cashier's desk and came back with a package of Du Mauriers for me. We kissed each other and hugged. We didn't cry.

I was the only person getting on, so the stop wasn't long. The driver swung down off the bus and hurried into the washroom. Next, he was taking my ticket and closing the door. I found a seat just in time to give Blaze a quick wave. Drinnan Street, that runs perpendicular to the river, was behind her. She was silhouetted against it and Trinity Mountain. Her arms were tight against her, a hand on each upper arm — as though she were hugging herself.

As the bus lurched forward, the man in the seat in front of me roused himself. He had been asleep with his head against the shoulder of the woman next to him. He sat up straight and looked out the window, saying drowsily, "What Christly town is this?"

A GODDESS OF THE NORTH

King Wû, a wise and beloved ruler, fell ill and seemed about to die.... the Duke of Chow took definite steps to prevent the king's death. He...prayed to his ancestors to spare the king's life. "If he must die," he prayed, "let me die in his place.... It may be that I shall serve in heaven better than your great descendant, and it may be that he will serve better on earth."

When he had finished, the duke opened a metal-bound chest and found that the response to his entreaty was favourable — the king would recover and he, the duke, need not die. He then placed the tablet on which his prayer had been recorded in the chest and closed it.

Lee Choy closed the book carefully. The yellow pages were thin, their edges frayed. It strained his eyes to concentrate on the faded characters. He placed it on the narrow shelf below the picture on his west wall. The sun wasn't up yet but the early morning light filtered through the small window and lit up the face of the goddess. She was seated on a lotus throne. Her three eyes looked out at him, each with a different expression. The right one emanated kindness; it was a benign look, the eye of blessing. The left one sparked with anger; it was a malevolent look, the eye of demand. The middle eye — the third eye — was uninterpretable. It stared straight, yet its gaze covered the whole room, the whole of the cabin. It took in his total being. It penetrated the walls, travelled past the trees, the river, the mountains. He knew the old beliefs. It was the eye of universal cosmic energy.

This was the goddess that was called by some Tou Mu; by others, Kuan Yin. To him, she was simply the Goddess of the North. He could never look at her without counting to make sure all the arms were there. Two were extended with fingers outstretched; two were bent at the elbow, the fingers curved toward the body; two grasped the petalled sides of the lotus throne. The others were in various oppositions, each hand in a shape appropriate to the object it held: a bow, a sword, a spear, a flag, the head of a dragon, the disc of the sun, the disc of the moon, and each of five chariots. Eighteen arms in all.

This day her gaze was particularly powerful. Lee Choy sat at the side of the small table, facing her. Pushing aside the bundles of yarrow sticks, he placed his elbows on the wooden surface, his thumbs under his chin. After a long look into her face he closed his eyes.

Automatically his attention focussed. His being concentrated itself into a long thin force which pushed out through a small opening between his eyebrows. All was black. He could stop the progress of the force; stop it and focus it. At first it rested at a point about nine inches from his forehead. Then he let it out some more; stopped it. As he continued letting it go, arresting it, the hole the force was pushing out through grew increasingly larger. And as it grew it gained more light until, finally, it formed the familiar window.

Before he could see the scene clearly, he felt a pull from one side. He was facing west; the pull was coming from the right, from the north. Without opening his eyes he shifted his chair around the corner until he was sitting at the end of the table, facing due north.

Slowly the scene brightened and cleared. In the immediate foreground, in front of the tall cottonwoods, were the two shiny tracks of the railroad. Lying across the ties, covered with a grey blanket, was a body. The head rested on the nearer rail. The pull of the force now shifted to the left; a warning, he knew, of the eastbound freight. "If he must die," he prayed, "let me die in his place." As he rose, he turned toward the picture and, with eyes still shut, murmured. "It may be that I shall serve in heaven better than this person now lying on the tracks, and it may be that he will serve better on earth."

Then Lee Choy opened his eyes. He took off his slippers, put on his work boots, and went outside. The first edge of the sun was emerging from behind the right shoulder of Hosmer Mountain. Shadows still lay over the quiet of the mill yard. It was still two hours to go before any of the crew would arrive for work. The only sounds — the scolding of jays — came from the cottonwoods the other side of the tracks.

As he crossed the field he checked his watch: about ten minutes before the freight was due in town, and it never stopped there long; maybe five minutes to unload boxes at the freight sheds and it would pull out again.

The covered body was in exactly the place he had seen it, with the head resting on the near track; the blanket, grey, as he knew it would be. Something different was a piece of bright material under the head. Material with pink and orange flowers. The head was resting on a thick, puffed-up print pillow. Across the pillow was a spread of long greyish-blonde hair. It was a woman.

Lee Choy slid his hands under the armpits and pulled. With the slight lifting of the head, the pillow rolled off the rail onto the oily ties. The blanket moved along with the body, but slipped down enough to reveal the face. Even upside down, there was no doubt. It was Freida Patterson, wife of one of the town councillors.

Once he had her free of the tracks he eased her back to the ground alongside. Her breathing was deep and even but she did not open her eyes. He picked up the small amber-coloured container that had rolled out from the blanket when he moved her. Empty. No label. Lid screwed on loosely. He put it in his pocket, picked up the pillow and tossed it down the slope of the track bed — a sudden blooming in that patch of dry weed stalks.

It wasn't an easy trip back across the uneven ground to the cabin. He had managed to keep the blanket around her when he picked her up, but it was lop-sided. One corner dragged in front of his right boot. But it tripped him only once. By then he was entering his yard and he steadied himself by leaning hard against the gate post. As he lay her on his bed, there was a sudden deafening noise all around him. The eastbound freight.

Before its rattling had died away up the valley, he was back with the pillow. He eased her head up and stuffed the pillow under it. He straightened the blanket and tucked it in at the sides and around her feet. Only then did he glance toward the Goddess of the North. Her middle eye stared straight at him — not through and beyond as usual, but right into his eyes. He heard her voice, a husky feminine voice. "The lady of the tracks will recover and you need not die." He sank slowly onto one of the chairs, the one facing the bed. Now was the time for vigilance.

* * *

It was Blackie who brought the news. He had arrived at the mill a bit early so he could reposition a couple of piles, over by Lee Choy's fence, to make room for the new lumber coming off the planer. A piece of paper was taped to the seat of the forklift.

He roared up by the lunch shack where the men were standing around waiting for the big hand of the clock to creep up to twelve. He shut off the motor and leaned down to hand the note to the foreman. "Here you go Joseph. A love letter from the Chinaman." He smiled wide and laughed. "No workee today."

Joe took the note, and read it aloud. "Feel sick. No work. Please no disturbing."

"Okay you guys," he yelled. "Remember that. Don't be going over there at noon — or after work — for a nip or two like you usually do."

And Blackie cut in. "He's got his curtains shut. A sure sign he's got a woman in there." He laughed again and reached for the key in the ignition. "And if anyone's got a right to it, it's Lee Choy. His wife keeps on having babies back in China but he hasn't been there for over fifteen years. So remember you guys. No disturbing!" He fired up the forklift and wheeled it around. After that there was no point in anybody saying anything else. It was all noise.

CHAPTER FIVE

ABANDONMENT

There is nothing more disconsolate than an abandoned setting. Here we are, all the various aspects of setting, prepared to act as backdrop to the story Babe is writing about Blaze. We've been happy to lend our features, our significance, our complexities to the enrichment and furthering of the plot when, suddenly, what happens? The narrator leaves.

We know that, in actuality, Babe didn't start writing this story until after she came back to Fernie and, even then, not until after Blaze left. But time, in a work of fiction, is not actual time. It's all a fabrication. It shifts around so that what came first often comes last, or what was in the middle comes first, or what was last fits in better somewhere else. For us it is *now* — the present time of the piece — that our narrator has left us, and we are suffering these intense feelings of abandonment. Remembering that Babe let the town take over from time to time and tell various stories about the characters, and that she even let that secondary press have the spotlight, we have decided to get together and, in a cooperative way, keep the story going. We may have to fill in some information about ourselves as we go along to make our own roles relevant and to add interest, but our prime objective is to further the story Babe has been telling. That means that for now — because obviously this is what she meant to come next — we must each relate whatever we know about the main characters, Blaze and Blackie, and what we think of their being together.

That is what we have agreed on.

YOU might think that the matter of order would present a problem. All we need say about that is: where setting is concerned, all is spatial; time is not our issue. Here we can give an anecdote that may help illuminate this point. Once we heard a woman who was travelling through us (this part of the country) refer to her new daughter-in-law back in Germany as "a girl from the landscape." That is what she said. "Our son married a girl from the landscape." She meant, of course, as YOU would say in English, "from the countryside." But that distinction, the one referring to the surrounding area as if it were a painting, is what captures the timelessness of setting. So, although there seems to be some order, in that one piece is set in a sequence before another, that is simply an illusion. We are all speaking at once, giving what firsthand information we have about Blaze and Blackie. The ideas are simply drifting about through the landscape, passing each other, overlaying each other, intertwining, intermingling. We have said that the sense of order is illusion; it is YOU who creates that illusion.

ELK VALLEY SPEAKS:

How long have I lain here, the river coursing through my centre, the mountains rising at my sides? How long have I lain here watching the coming of the first peoples, the ones who came into me gently over the mountain ranges to the east, watching the others who came later, pushing them out? And did I ever interfere? I saw them building the town, the railroad, the highway and bridges — always pushing aside the first peoples, the ones who honoured me and the river and the mountains. I remained silent. I remained passive, for there was no one person who stirred me to sound or to movement, until . . .

Until the boy, the one with the darkness of the first people, the light eyedness of the later people. Once I felt his oneness with my soil, my stories, my greenery and my wild ones, then I stirred and roused myself. I noted the death of his mother, the dark one from the South. I noted the habits of his father, the lost one in the town. I felt the boy's growing feet on my trails, heard his bubbling laughter in the air, spoke his name, touched his very self — and then I cared. And once I cared, he became my focus, my passion. I watched him always. I breathed easy when he was easy, laboured when he was not, and strained myself to bend in him a force to battle the foul lightness that denied the spark of darkness. The father in him, the mother in him.

Until the train.... As soon as it came along the track by the river I knew she, who was on it, had entered my being at that turn. I felt her and rejoiced. I held her, I cradled her, I hummed the magic tune to make her stop, to make her stay. For she was the one *I* chose.

They met on my ground, they breathed my air together, they fished in my river; he took her along my trails. I chose her, and kept her, for him.

ELK RIVER SPEAKS:

I have lived so long with riversong; I am never done with riverrun. And now the glory of riverstory. I am honoured. Of course I have the time. That is the trouble. Too many confuse water and river. Water is in a hurry. Water does not have time to stop, sit down and talk. It speaks running. It takes cunning to be water, on the move in the same old groove.

But for river. River is not just water. It is water in the groove and in my case it is not the same old groove. Every year I try to change my course. My banks are here this year, but then they swerve into next year's curve. The valley is wide; first I am on one side, and then the other.

But river is not just water and banks. It is gravel, it is rocks; it is sparkle and vox (that is, sight and sound), also taste and smell and feel. Just ask the deer who come to drink it, the fish who live in and breathe it, the people brave enough to . . . I can't say "swim" because they are never in long enough for that. All I ever hear, even in mid July, is their song that goes: "ooh, it's icy cold; ooh, it's freezing my bones." So let us say that some people are brave enough to jump in even though they rush right out again. Then they sit in the sun for a long time and the rest of the song goes: "Ooh, ooh, that's so tingly" or something about glaciers (that is almost as jingly).

So it takes all of these things to describe what river is; and even so, that is just a cross-section of river; say, one slice of me, here in the valley near Fernie. As well, there is my longitudinal aspect to consider. I start — why not take part, and guess where I start? Not known to YOU? Well, here's a clue. If it hadn't been that people first discovered me at my bigger end, I might have been called Kananaski, or Rocky Mountain River, or River of the Great Divide, or Mount Joffre River — although I am not sure they had even found that mountain, never mind named it, at the time I became *The Elk*.

My infancy: I start (for I am forever starting) as snow melt, glacial melt, spring, fount; then move as rill, rivulet, streamlet, brooklet, brook, creek, stream, river — the compulsion is always to move south. Yes, I am a north-to-south river. I begin high in the Rockies, at Mt. Joffre; I empty into the Kootenay River, down below Elko. I know that my waters move onward with the Kootenay, then with the Columbia, and continuously flow until they empty into the Pacific Ocean. But all of that is not my immediate experience: my true sense of myself ends at the Kootenay, below Elko as I've said, near Dorr.

Enough of me, however. I am here to speak of Blackie and Blaze. Still waters, turbulent waters, slow waters, fast waters. And there is deep, and there is shallow. Do not think I am talking of myself again. I saw in both of them the joy and the pain. Still waters run deep. Running waters make you weep. And she was a winter person. I gave up my grayling to her on icy banks. He fished in summer, water to his waist, and his casting laughter charmed my trout out of the flow . . . What else do I know? Only that she was one of the few who swam — swam into my bosom in her rainbow-coloured suit, and I nudged her, then pulled her, and would have kept her, safe forever in one of my deepest parts. But he came splashing after and hooked onto her as though she were a thrashing trout, and reeled her back into the gasping air.

The loss was mine. But not all of her got away. I carry her along as part of my song. She lends a glory to my riverstory. And that is all I have to say.

THE MOUNTAINS SPEAK:
1) Trinity Mountain
The others have agreed that we should be the ones to speak for all the mountains — we, meaning, in the plural sense, The Three Sisters or, in the singular sense, Trinity Mountain. We feel abandoned particularly because we know that we were to have a definite purpose in the story. We are the element in the setting that was supposed to parallel the Cassidy girls. Our narrator did introduce that notion, but before she could get back to it and explore it properly, she left. So we are now prepared to explore the possibilities from the other direction. We wonder what those three sisters have in common with us.

US. We will have to explain some things about US. Babe described our configuration, situation, relation to the town, and so on, but she didn't have any sense of our personalities. YOU must keep in mind that even though we speak here as one, we have, like any other trinity, three distinct and separate selves. Of course, she did not know our names, for no one knows the innate names of any of the mountains, only the man-given ones.

We don't mind being called Trinity, or The Three Sisters, because those names have meaning for the people and, of course, there is a certain amount of truth to them for us too. We are sisters, and we are three. But our real names are, from west to north, Yufi, Thal, and Ag. Yufi is the oldest. She is tall and thin, even pointy, and she has a daughter. The daughter is the angled peak tucked in under at her right side. She is not so noticeable because she is smaller, but the resemblance is striking. Her name is Rosyn.

Thal is in the middle. She is the one who makes herself noticeable, pushes herself up and spreads out. Self-important you might say. The snow always lies on her most dramatically; the sun strikes her surfaces in the most flattering way; shadows enhance her crevices and promontories most subtly and appealingly. Because she is in the middle she thinks she holds the whole configuration together, that she is the important one. And maybe she is.

Ag, the youngest, has a beauty of her own. She is more symmetrical than Yufi or Thal; she is less ostentatious; she has a personality endowed with humility. If we were to put it in human terms, we might say she is the one with *mind*. Some kind of inner brilliance shines out from her that the other two don't have.

We don't really know the Cassidy Family. Oh, we look in on them, the same as we do with all the families in town. But they are newcomers. Blaze is the only one of the sisters who has been near us. She came partway up, just under the peak of Rosyn, with her father Tare, one day last autumn. And she has come up as far as Fairy Creek Falls several times — with Blackie.

Now Blackie is someone we do know. His ancestors on his mother's side were the first people to come across the mountains into the valley. They have lived here for centuries. We remember the day he was born; we have watched him every day of his life for he has never been far out of Fernie. Even as a little child he always looked to us, and we could feel the pull; we knew that as soon as he was able, he would come . . . . It was always with him, that urge to climb up here. And he tried many times. He'd climb to the falls; he'd make it partway up to Rosyn, once even to Yufi's base. It wasn't until he was in his teen years that he came all the way. Another youth came with him, a few years older. A cousin. Tom was his name.

Together they found the secret passage — the chimney in behind Yufi's straighter side. That took them to the foot of Thal's broad slope. It was springtime but there was still a lot of snow and the going was hard. They brought mirrors. Every little while they would stop, point them to the sun, and flash reflections back to town, to the house of their family. We three could see the uncle and aunt, the other cousins, in the back yard. We could tell it was an exciting time for everyone.

They went right to Thal's top. That is what any climber of Trinity Mountain would do, of course, because it is the highest point. Not that there have been many who have made it. Of the few who have, once there on top of Thal they would turn back and go down the way they had come. And that is what Tom insisted on.

But he did not persuade Blackie. He wanted to go down Thal's northern side; that is, he wanted to keep going. It was a steep way but it would take him to the ridge that swept across to Ag. That was where Blackie wanted to be. He and Tom parted. He went on alone. In all our centuries of memory, Blackie is the only person whose feet have traversed all three parts of Trinity Mountain.

What is there to say of him and Blaze? We do not know her well. We grant that. What we say is simple: there is no one yet, maybe there will be no one ever, worthy of Blackie.

2) Coal Creek Mountain

While the Sisters have been speaking, I have recorded some of my thoughts about Blackie and Blaze.

When first he knew her, Blackie brought Blaze up along my saddle to Swinging Valley. He sat with her beside snow patches on a dry grassy knoll. He picked a handful of my glacier lilies and gave them to her.

And later, they came for blueberries. And once they came with a rifle and binoculars. They watched a grizzly tearing a stump apart. It was far down the slope on a ridge below the saddle. They did not shoot.

There is a hollow spot, in his back, just at the belt line, that she calls Swinging Valley. The glacier lily is her favourite flower.

FAIRY CREEK SPEAKS:

I had to plead with the others to let me speak. I had to convince them that I have something important to add. I promised to keep it brief.

About myself. Fairy is my man-given name; it was after the daughter of Sandy McDougall, a well known lumberman. He was the first person to hold rights to my waters. My original name was Coral Secret, because I have coral fossils imbedded in my rock.

Century after century I have splashed down the slopes, all the way from the feet of Yufi, Thal, and Ag, right to the Elk River. Splashed and bubbled, free and joyous, until . . . People came to the valley, built a dam. Then my waters backed into stillness. A quiet meeting place. In 1912 Fernie Council voted money to build a high board fence to keep the mountain goats from swimming in the reservoir. Now the goats stay high on the mountains. The fence is gone.

Blackie brought Blaze to see me. Every time they came he told her about the goats. But he did not tell her the legend: "If any unmarried couple strays in the spray of Fairy Creek Falls, they will be married within the year."

And she always said to him, "Why do you make me go so close? I always get soaking wet."

All he ever said was, "I wish we could have seen the wild goats swimming in this pool."

PRESS

CONVERGENCE

When E.J. Pratt wrote his poem, *The Titanic*, he went to a lot of trouble to fill in the background of both the iceberg and the ship. He starts right back at the moment the iceberg was born and at the moment the construction of the ship began: "The glacier calved . . .," and he describes the iceberg's journey out to sea; "The ship was launched . . .," and he describes the ship's course across the ocean. What he wanted to do was show that the two were fated to come together, at that particular point in the Atlantic, in that particular disastrous way.

Well, we had something similar in Fernie: two people who were on just such a pre-destined collision course. It was Mac who told everybody the story once the disaster occurred and, of course, it had an immediate impact on his listeners. But, just as with the iceberg and the Titanic, for those who don't know all the facts that contributed to that inevitability, the story needs some filling in.

Shortly after Harriet Shaw and Jamie MacDonald were married in Falkirk, Scotland, in 1908, they set sail for Canada. Jamie had the promise of a job as an apprentice carpenter in Estevan, Saskatchewan. The couple settled into prairie ways and soon became proud to call themselves Canadians, although they never did try to lose their Scottish way of speaking. Since Jamie was a steady worker and a lad known not to drink too much, he was soon noticed by the town undertaker who took him on as his assistant and taught him the trade. The biggest part of his job was building coffins on the premises; they were cheaper than the bought ones. After two years in Canada, Harriet gave birth to a baby boy. They gave him the first name of Sean; the second was Shaw, after his mother. The couple felt fortunate indeed because their livelihood was secure, they were pleased with their position in the community, and they foresaw no problems in the future for themselves or their son.

Helmut Weiss was a young man in Germany in 1920. It was a grim time for the country, and his town of Mittenwald, near the Austrian border, had nothing to offer him. Although the war had been over for two years, there was little employment, especially for young, inexperienced people like himself. He had gone to nearby Garmisch Partenkirchen to look for work but had no luck. He had just decided to go to Munich when he happened to see a small poster in the window of a bank. It was an offer of a job that the poster promised would be lucrative, exciting, as well as rewarding in every way. It was a mining job ... in Canada, passage paid. The promise of that poster was what drew Helmut to Fernie where he was immediately taken on by the Crows Nest Pass Coal Company. Feeling was still high among Canadians about people "we fought against in the war," but there was one German family in Fernie and, luckily, they took to Helmut and encouraged him in his courtship of their daughter. So Helmut married Gisela Goetzsky, and they lived with her family until their third child, Rudolph, was born.

Little Sean MacDonald was a delight to his parents. He seemed such a healthy and sunny child, but he was afflicted with a condition for which there was no medical help. He had a cleft palate. His condition affected them in several ways: their love and concern for him increased, they determined they would put everything they could into educating him for some profession that would allow him to be self-sufficient despite his handicap, and they vowed not to have any more children. When he was ready, they sent him to the university in Toronto. He went into dentistry. After getting his DDS, he spent the summer with his parents in Estevan, waiting for replies to various applications.

The letter that showed the most promise was an offer for him to take over a practice in a little B.C. town he had never heard of. Its name was Fernie.

    Rudy Weiss did not think of himself as German at all, growing up in Fernie; not even when the children at school called him Kraut. And he didn't mind the way they rhymed his name with mice or lice. And he didn't care if they pronounced the W like a W and not like a V as in Vancouver the way his dad said it was supposed to be in German — as long as they didn't mess up his hair or get his clothes dirty or put coal dust on his shoes. All he knew about his future was that he wished never to be a miner like his dad. So, when he quit school to get married to a girl from Natal and had to go to work, he realized that wish. The Company took him on at Coal Creek but not as a miner. They put him in the boiler plant. Maybe because he had two older sisters, or maybe because his mother was compulsive with him, Rudy was a real stickler for cleanliness, neatness, orderliness. So this job suited him very well. Not only did he not get dirty, he got to wear white coveralls. It was well known about town that his wife, Linda, could never keep those coveralls white enough to suit him, even though he was furnished with several pair and he never wore them more than one day between washings. It was also well known that it was impossible for her to keep the house clean enough or neat enough for him. There were many people who could report they had actually seen him come in after shift and run his finger along some part of the furniture — even the top of the fridge where she couldn't reach — and then hold it up for her to see the dust on it. Millie McNay, a neighbour, vows that he once yelled at Linda because two of her shoes, of a pair, were facing opposite ways in the closet. All the women in town, and some of the men too, were constantly telling Linda about new, improved washing products (soaps, bleaches, cleansers) they'd had success with, or some new squeegee mop or long-handled duster. And no matter how much other wives complained about their husbands, they would invariably end their commiserating conversations with: "Well, at least he isn't fussy, like Rudy Weiss."

Now the iceberg has moved very far southward and the Titanic is well on its way across the Atlantic. The moment of impact is not far ahead: Rudy has a Saturday morning dental date and Doctor MacDonald is taking all his appointments despite a very severe head cold.

Mac wasn't able to tell the story until Monday morning although he'd heard about it not long after noon on Saturday. He was the first person Blaze saw when she came out of the office, and she just had to tell someone. She worked for Dr. MacDonald on Saturdays. She'd been a dental nurse before, back East somewhere but, of course, Peggy Neidig was his permanent assistant, so he hired Blaze just for Peggy's day off.

So, Monday morning found Mac at the post office door, cap in hand. "I guess you didn't get a chance over the weekend to hear about Rudy's appointment with Doc MacDonald?"

"No. What happened? Did he make Blaze scrub up the cuspidor so it was clean enough for him to spit in?"

Or, "No. What happened? Did he get a spot of blood on those precious white coveralls?"

Mac twisted his cap a bit, looked into the listener's eyes and said, "No, it was this way. Doc had a bad cold and you know how he is . . . he doesn't have any feeling anywhere around his face?" He moved one hand over his upper lip. "Well, there's Rudy, his head way back and his mouth wide open and Doc bending over working away with the drill, and his nose, unknown to him, starting to run down . . ."

And the listeners. "No. Don't tell me he got him."

"Yep. Blaze said she was just hurrying a kleenex to him but it was too late. It got him. Plop! Right in!"

No one needed any more information. The scene was complete enough, and they were off to tell someone else about it.

So that's maybe further than the parallel should have gone. It's not sad or tragic like the iceberg hitting the Titanic, but it just goes to show how inevitable Fate can be, even in a small town like Fernie.

CHAPTER SIX

INTERVIEWS

CPR TRACKS

- I have absolutely nothing to say. I think it's unfair of you even to ask. Do you know how much country I transverse? Just all of it, that's all. From sea to sea. I'm here for the trains, nothing else. And you expect me to tell you about some couple who happen to live in *this* town? Do you know how many towns I service across Canada? If I had to pay attention to the people in them, I'd hardly be able to do my job, would I?

- I don't care if I am part of the setting too. That doesn't concern me. You've already condescended enough by pointing out that I am in the sub-category of "man-made setting."

- Of course I know about the sun and the moon and all the planets. I see them up there in the sky. I lie here looking up all the time, don't I? But a Lotus Flower Game? It's not my fault if you got left in the lurch by some girl narrator. A game? No, don't take up my time with such irrelevancies. I've got to get ready for the next train.

- Well okay. Yes. I do remember this Blackie guy. He's walked my ties all his life. And yes, I remember Blaze.

- Sure I know he proposed to her. It was right here between my rails, just before they turned off to go up McNab Draw. They had rifles.

- All right. I do remember a bit more. She said yes but she wouldn't let him give her the ring. Just refused to take it.

- Why? Yes, I know why. Because of the location she said.

- Sure, I admit it hurt my feelings, her thinking the railroad track wasn't a romantic enough place to get engaged. The last I heard was her telling him to keep the diamond until the weekend. They'd climb up somewhere more appropriate and he could give it to her — maybe on the top of Fernie Mountain, or some place like that. Why a mountain top is any more suitable than a good solid railroad track is beyond me. You probably don't agree.

- No, don't ask me anything else. That's the last thing I'm answering.... Except that some time later she crawled up into one of my boxcars, hauling herself up, out of the darkness of the outside into the darkness of the inside. It was car Number 62W. He said she just stayed there nearly all night. The car was on a siding at the time, right by the Queens Apartments, just a block or two away from the station. He figured she was someone who wanted to get away from the town but somehow wasn't clear about the schedule for moving out. He wasn't to get hooked up for a trip until the next evening. He said she just sat in there and cried. About 4 a.m. she climbed down and left.

Well, that's enough. I can feel the afternoon freight coming. I've got to get to work. There's no more time....

CROWSNEST HIGHWAY

- Sure I'm happy to contribute. After all there are lots of roads in literature already. Think of the *Road Books* themselves, and there's *The Road to Ruin*, and some titles such as *The Road Not Taken, On the Road,* and the song, *On the Road to Mandalay*. So why not me? One thing though, I don't like so much being called by a number. Number Three! I much prefer Crowsnest Highway. So could you put that in? It's more memorable, don't you think? I always thought that's what should be on my road signs. Maybe even with a picture of a crow on its nest. So is this a road novel you're talking about?

- Oh, the town is the star. And is that the title?

- Well, do you think there's any chance they'll make it into a movie? Remember all those Bob Hope-Bing Crosby movies with Dorothy Lamour: *The Road to Rio*, *The Road to Bali*, *The Road to Utopia*? This could be called *The Road to Big Rock Candy Town*. And that would work coming in from either east or west. You know, don't you, that I run all the way from Hope to Medicine Hat? Through some of the greatest scenery in the country. But I guess you'll agree with me on that. Nothing better than what's right here around Fernie.

- Blackie and Blaze. Yes, I knew them. The worst possible combination.

- Well, I'll tell you. I'd be a lot happier highway if people like them would just stay home, or walk to wherever they're going. I swear that this stretch from Fernie to Elko is about the worst part of me, for my whole length. It's the combination of the drinking town — imagine eight hotels in a place this size — and the terrain I run through. In so many places I have to cling to the mountainside myself, and then there are all those rock cuts the other side of the tunnel. And, of course, it's straight down to the river. It takes a sober driver to take those curves, even going slow. And it seems the more a guy has to drink the faster he wants to go. All the accidents on that stretch. It doesn't look good on my record.

- No, it's not just Blackie's drinking, although that's bad enough. It's her too. When he's drunk she insists on driving. You'd think that would be safer. But no. He makes her drive fast, and then faster. It's not as if they have any place to go. They're just driving out here for something to do after the bars close.

- No, she doesn't drink. At least she doesn't get drunk. But she's just as dangerous. And what's that bull shit about him *making* her drive faster and faster? Hell, I've felt them taking some of my turns at over eighty. It's her with that stupid notion in her head that she has to do what he tells her. You'd think she wasn't a goddam person herself. She goes in the car with him because he'd go without her and probably end up in a wreck. But don't tell me she can't go slow. What's he going to do? How can he *make* her drive fast?

- Bull shit! That's what it is. I'm sorry about my language. I never talk like this over in Alberta, or around Cranbrook, or on the Hope-Princeton. It's just this part of me. They make me so mad.

- I guess you're right. That's about all you need to hear. I don't want to talk about Blaze and Blackie any more anyway. Bullshit drivers!

THE UNITED CHURCH

The day of the wedding was the only time either one of them came through my doors. I hadn't seen them before. No, I'm wrong; they did come in for the obligatory talk with the minister, but that I've tried to forget because it ended up in an untruth. Blaze had always thought she and Blackie were born in the same year, that his birthday was three months before hers. But when Reverend Carter asked for their birth dates and Blackie gave his as September, 1933, she was so incensed to think he was nine months younger — and to think he had led her to think otherwise — that she gave her date as 1933 too. December, 1933. And that lie went right down in my records. It's still there.

You should know that as long as people are within my walls, I have the power to see into them — into their souls, you might say. That means that I know everything about them: their thoughts, their experiences, their memories, their aspirations — everything. And I can tell you Blaze and Blackie's wedding itself wasn't really truthful or right. For one thing, the father wasn't there to give away the bride. That job was done — and this is highly incorrect — by the groom's uncle. How can it possibly be acceptable to have a member of the *groom*'s family give the bride away *to* the groom? It's not even logical.

Blaze was unhappy about having her older sister as matron of honour. She hadn't asked her. The sister — Pearl Anne her name was — had elected herself for the role, had told Blaze what kind of dress to buy for her, and had come all the way down from Edmonton for the occasion. And it was because she came that the father refused to attend. They had had a serious falling out and were not on speaking terms.

On top of all that, both the best man and the bridesmaid were Roman Catholics. Italians!

But maybe worst of all was the dishonesty between the bride and the groom themselves. He was a drinker. He had promised to stop drinking once they were married. He had promised not to drink before the wedding. She had never had any experience with alcoholism so she believed that she (or their life together) would be his cure. The bride, in her white lace wedding gown, came up the aisle on the arm of the uncle, stepping in time to the Wedding March, stepping closer to the groom who, in his grey gabardine suit and blue tie, waited at the altar, his Catholic Italian best man at his side. Blackie turned around to look at her and he cracked a wide smile and — can you imagine this behaviour in church? — he winked!

She could tell he was drunk. He had broken his promise. I could feel her impulse to stop right there, say NO, I will not marry you, NO the wedding is off. But she did not have that kind of bravery. People had already given them presents. People had come out to see the wedding. There was a lot of food prepared back at Mrs. Arbuckle's, including a wedding cake topped with a little ornament of a bride and groom in a bower. She kept moving along. The minister began the ceremony. When he came to the part "Who gives this woman . . . ?" the uncle stepped forward, cupped his hand to his ear, and said, "Eh?"

What else? They were married. Everybody followed them down the aisle and outside. My doors closed. That's all I know. I have never seen them since.

THE GRAVEYARD

I don't pay much attention to the live people who come through my gates. They are not a happy lot. Mourners mostly.

Blackie brought Blaze here. Showed her my acquisitions from the wars. She took a picture of my cenotaph, tribute to the dead of WWI, moving around to get it lined up with Trinity Mountain. She walked through the white-crossed section of the WWI victims. Even stepped on some of the plots.

He pointed out most of the miners' graves, especially the ones in my new part. I am more fortunate than most cemeteries because I have this extra, fairly steady supplier.

He showed her the family plot but, apart from his older brother who died in the Fernie Hospital from pneumonia at the age of fourteen, he didn't have any person in my ground that he really remembered.

They had come past the Pest House, on their way up to mountain. They were just passing through.

B

FERNIE BAKERY

Howland Avenue was bumpier than usual. Lois had to pedal hard to keep the bicycle from stopping in the loose gravel that had washed over the pavement in last night's rain. And there were potholes to avoid. Even so, she was able to study her hands. The way they gripped the handlebars pulled the skin tight and showed up the brown liver spots more than usual. And the position of her arms made the skin hang down. A definite flabbiness between elbow and wrist. When had she lost enough flesh to cause that? *Où sont les neiges d'antan?* She had indeed become one of Villon's women: *Des Dames du Temps Jadis*.

Her name wasn't really Lois. That was the Fernie version of the romantic name her mother had given her – Héloïs. Héloïs, after one of the women in the ballad, the one who was in love with her tutor, Pierre Abelard. *Des Dames du Temps Jadis*: women in days of old.

Every once in a while as she pedalled, Lois slipped her left hand off the handlebar to pull her skirt down over her knees. Women in Fernie, at least the older ones, did not ride bikes, so she had to be careful. And she had never got used to wearing slacks. She was thankful she'd been able to bring her own bicycle with her – the model without a crossbar and, of course, it had a guard to keep her dress from getting caught in the chain or the spokes.

Where she grew up in northeastern France, everyone rode bicycles. For the children, learning to ride was as natural as learning to walk; for the old people, the bike was simply an extension of their own limbs; as long as they were able to walk, they were able to ride. And they bicycled everywhere — in the cities, in the towns, in the countryside. But here! The people of Fernie had the attitude that the bike was a vehicle for the youth — a plaything, a sport thing. Or, beyond that, they were the vehicles of the poor, the ones who could not afford a car. *Air prétentieux!* Just as in her village on the Nied, some of the older men took their bikes along the river trails to fish, children rode their bikes to school, young people had biking excursions. But when it came to older women it was different. To bike uptown in Fernie to do her shopping? *Mon Dieu*! Maybe it was because of their penchant for dressing up. Comfortable, serviceable clothing did not belong in uptown Fernie.

As if to coincide with her thoughts and provide a ready example, a figure in the distance caught her eye. Lois recognized it as that of Ebba Kasmir. Both of them happened to be crossing Pellatt Avenue at the same time, but Ebba was five or six blocks over. In that last block, Lois had to raise off the seat to get enough momentum for the incline up to Main Street. The heels of her brown oxfords locked securely against the pedals as she pumped.

Although she hadn't been close enough to make out what Ebba was wearing, it was easy to see her exactly in her mind's eye. The image of Ebba floated in front of her, somewhere just beyond the handlebars. Ebba in her mid-forties. Ebba in her navy blue suit. A saucy red hat perched jauntily on her greying head. The red veil swept down across her forehead at eyebrow level. A red scarf tied in a bow at her throat, red gloves clutching a shiny red purse; and red shoes, their high heels spiking into the gravel to bring her out of the West Fernie street, along the highway's edge to the bridge, across the bridge click clicking, into the ruts and mounds of Wood Street, up the hill past the courthouse and, finally, to the sidewalks of uptown Victoria Street. And not even for shopping, but, as everyone knew, for a round of the bars. Lois could imagine the red gloves and purse shoved to the dark edge of a round table to make room for foul-smelling glasses of beer and butt-filled ashtrays.

Any woman who would go into a bar! But then, any woman who would drink beer, even at home. With wine so much more sophisticated. Not the Dago Red stuff of this town, but *real* wine, good French wine: Burgundy, Moselle, Bordeaux, Chardonnay. Oh the light, zesty, fragrant wines of France. Pleasant to the eye, to the nose, to the tongue. She was the only one who bought them at the liquor store. Special order. Not even the other two French families in town — the Poiriers, the Armands — well, they were from St. Boniface, Manitoba, and Maillardville, B.C., not from France.

But something else assailed her nose at that moment. She looked at her watch. Eight twenty-nine. Right on time for the bakery to open. Her two great loves: aged wine and freshly baked bread. Héloïs turned toward the curb, braked, and dropped her feet to the ground. She lifted the bike up onto the sidewalk, wheeled it over to the store front. Baked goods — tarts, pies, cookies — sat in rows inside the window. Okay for now but not later when the sun shone in. Not good for food. Surely he knew that. Especially the things with cream in them. But all she wanted was bread anyway.

She leaned the bike handle against the glass, at the spot where there used to be the sign that said "Helmut's Konditorei." She could still see the outline left by the glue. Too many customers kept asking him what it meant. Too many said, why not have it in English? Now there was only the bold printing across the window: FERNIE BAKERY. She took her shopping bag out of the carrying basket and moved to open the door.

But the door didn't open. It was stuck. She could see through the slit that there was no one at the counter. She knocked and called out. "Hello. I can't get the door open." She could hear voices coming from the back, but a second and even a third knocking produced no results. She pushed gently. The door gave a bit at the top, but seemed anchored at the bottom. Crouching down, she slid her hand through the narrow opening and felt along the floor inside. Sure enough, something was stuck there. After a few unsuccessful tugs and some jiggling of the door, she managed to free it. It was a short length of metal, a plate with a screw hole at each end. The one screw still holding was what had jammed under the door. And there was a strange little lever protruding. Of course, part of the signal system. It was set up to buzz when a customer came in. As she closed the door behind her, she looked up. There was the buzzer attached to the top of the frame. And right below it, on the door itself, a small rectangle of unpainted wood with two splintered-out screw holes.

As she turned to the counter, Héloïs was aware of voices again. Funny, she hadn't noticed before that they were speaking German. Now that there was nothing else to pay attention to, she heard them clearly. A woman saying something about needing money, and the man, yes it was definitely Helmut's voice, replying something about giving her enough — enough if she didn't go spending it in the bars all the time. The words weren't easy to make out, maybe because she was trying not to listen. And it was a Northern Deutsche, not the soft Southern Deutsche that she was used to hearing near Metz.

She was trying to decide whether to call out, or maybe ring the service bell on the counter, when she heard words there was no mistaking. The woman was shrill: "I'm the one who has all the work and all the shame." Then his voice, in a shout: "How much can it take to keep a retarded kid, anyway? When he can't even go to school!" and hers, answering in a shriek: "Well, he has to eat, doesn't he? and wear clothes? He's your kid too, don't forget!"

Without realizing it, Héloïs had moved toward the door. Now she opened it quickly and slipped out. Then, remembering, she stooped and set the buzzer part on the floor, aside just enough so that the door cleared it when it closed. She threw her shopping bag back into the carrier and was about to wheel the bike off the sidewalk when the door opened wide beside her, hitting against the back wheel.

There was the blur of navy and red of someone rushing out. It was Ebba. When she saw what had happened she stopped, grabbed the door, and slammed it shut, saying, "I'm so sorry. I didn't know anyone was here. Oh, it's you Lois. I'm so sorry. Did I hurt you?" Her fingers were clenched tight around the shiny red purse. The edges of her eyes were moist. "I shouldn't be in such a hurry. I just came for a little help in German — before he opens up. You know, I used to speak it when I was a girl? Before my mother died. Helmut tutors me a bit when he has time." She was breathing hard. "Are you sure you're okay? Did the door hit you?"

Héloïs smiled as broadly as she could. "Oh, no," she said. "It barely touched the bike. No, really, I'm fine." She leaned the handlebar back against the glass. "Helmut's open now, is he?" She reached for the shopping bag. "I was just coming for some of his good fresh bread."

CHAPTER SEVEN

BY MAIL

I wrote Blaze a postcard from the station in Calgary to tell her I was getting on the train okay, and sent a letter when I arrived home to tell her I got there and to fill her in on my plans for starting business school. Aunt Dora and Uncle Stu were so mad at Dad that they said they'd never ask him for another penny for my keep. They said they'd cover my fees themselves and I could pay them back later when I got a good job. And Aunt Dora wrote a real severe letter demanding that Dad send my things at once.

I was desperate to hear from Blaze to find out how Dad reacted to my getting away so slick. Blaze's letter wasn't long coming. It was dated September 5:

Dear Babe,

Just feel like writing in pencil — glad to see your pen is still full of green ink. I got both your card and your letter & sure was relieved & glad to hear everything is going O.K. But I must get on with all the details. I saw Rob Sun. noon just before I went to the Grill and he asked if you had got away OK & said that they had heard nothing (Dad's a lot dumber than we gave him credit for). I ate with Carmen and when we came out, Rob and Sandy pulled up. They had a picture of you, the one with Rover (did he have to go into your suitcase for that?), your age, etc., & Gordie's name. Rob says "You don't know her, *do* you?" I said, "Well, she used to work at the Grill." "Yes, we heard that — we'll check there." We came down home here — they passed us again. Rob said "We're still looking. Think we'll throw out a dragnet" (laughing like everything). They even asked Mrs. Arbuckle if you had spent Sat. night with me. She said "Well, I don't know. I don't see much of them." Anyway, around 4 p.m. (still Sunday) they cruised up again very officially and Rob said "We can't find any trace of her around town. Do you think you could give us any information?" I told him he might as well tell Dad that you had taken the bus to Calgary. Yesterday morning (Tues.) I saw Dad & Bertie coming out of the Welfare Office. I went up on my noon hour because I wanted to be sure Mr. Rutherford heard both sides. They were there then, so I left. Dad & Bertie came into the Grill just as I was finishing lunch (I saw that old black sombrero bobbing over the partition). He really looked mad & Bertie was right at his heels. He said, "Listen. I'm giving you *one* warning. Keep your nose out of our business," and then of course he lumbered off again. I just had time to say "I *am* keeping it out. I'm just looking after my sister. She's *my* business," but of course, since then I have thought of thousands of things that would have been better. I phoned over and Inez (girl in Welfare office) said Mr. Rutherford wanted to see me anyway. After we talked he said, "You did the right thing — the only thing." He said that he felt Dad wasn't genuinely interested in your well-being or he could have asked me re your whereabouts. He thought his biggest worry was that he figured Uncle Stu and Aunt Dora were going to demand financial aid for you. I explained that they had looked after you *well* most of your life with very little help from him. Also, Dad told him he didn't know whether you were going home to Orillia or not so I assured him I had got the ticket myself — Calgary to Orillia (Well, I had to explain how we'd got the ticket to Orillia from *here* but then had to change plans and you took the bus to Calgary). Dad told him he was worried that you ran around too much and once again I assured him that you were very sensible — popular & had a good time, but in no way wild, and added too that he never allowed friends to the house & got mad when you met them anyway. He told Dad that all he (Mr. R.) could do was to write U.S. & A.D. and make sure you arrived, but after he asked if I could vouch for them and I said I certainly could since they'd brought me up too, and also since I convinced him you were really going there, he said he wouldn't even bother to do that. So — that's that and Dad can't do a thing. He's pretty mad at me — good, but he (Mr. R.) says that's just because we pulled a fast one on him.

He went over to Smiths' Sat. night. Gordie wasn't home & apparently he talked to his dad telling him that Gordie was to leave you alone & let you concentrate on school or something to that effect. Imagine how foolish he'll feel when he learns you aren't even in town. Just think! He didn't even suspect what we were doing. I guess he thought he'd just show *you* on Sunday for not coming home Sat. night, and have the cops pick you up. Imagine how furious he'd be if he knew the cops were in on it all along and thought it was a good joke. Oh, boy — we really enjoyed it. Blackie says if he'd been there when he came into the Grill he'd have fixed him. Yeah, for sure. Remember how he always talks about giving someone "three in the eye."

Well I'm going to leave you for a while. I just washed my hair (Wed. p.m.) and am now going over to see Scotty. Blackie says he'll be out of hospital by the weekend. Too much drinking. Like son, like father, no? Bye for now.

Back again — feel like using ink now. I see you didn't use up all the green bottle after all.

Everyone inquires about you. Gordie's mom was in to see me yesterday. Telephone Mike said you told him you were going to send him a postcard, so don't disappoint him. I hope you know his last name. If not, send it in care of me and I'll give it to him.

I see Randy rushes up to the mail at 8:29 every morning. I guess they're afraid you might get a letter. The P.O. girls are keeping any of your mail for me anyway. *Haw!* including Bessie.

Clancy came in yesterday to ask me to sign some things at the station re your cancellation and refund. I guess they have to have a pretty good reason. I sure laughed when I went over there. He had it all filled in — the ticket was cancelled due to illness and the passenger went by car to Calgary, etc. I asked him how long it took him to think *that* one up.

Actually we didn't do a heck of a lot over the weekend. Blackie was to meet me in the Grill before 10 to see the parade. He didn't arrive. I watched with Dan a while, then with Al and Reno. Then lo and behold, there was Mr. Blackie — marching with the Fernie Band — packing Tony D'Amico's bass horn. What jokes were made of that all day!

The Labour Day parade was really good. One float was a boat with Old Tommy Thatcher as captain at the wheel. They had flattened one front tire of the truck underneath, and the opposite back one so it rocked like it was on a stormy sea. I'm sure they were all sea-sick when they came ashore. The geologists had a big truck with a sign — "Be safe while you work." They had a bunch of equipment up on top and they all sat around with guns and bows and arrows etc. A pot hung over a fire (really burning) at the back door (closed-in truck). A roll of toilet paper on a nail at the back, x's and o's all over the doors, and one of the guys was tied by a rope to the truck and was struggling along on foot with beer cases piled I don't know how high on his back on a packboard, sporting the sign, "I'm just an Engineer." The whole thing was quite good.

Well I really should quit although I could talk on and on forever. I guess I just miss having you here. Blackie gets paid today and wants me to meet him at the Olympos so you know what that'll mean. Not really orayuh.

Mrs. Arbuckle gave me another dresser so Blackie and I spent last night moving the new one in and the old one out and Blackie put new handles on all the drawers (of the dresser).

Have you heard from Gordie? He says he just wishes he had the money, he'd get the train to the East and just forget about school for a year.

Give all my love to everyone and write and tell me *all the details* of your arrival.

Love
Blaze

P.S. I'll try to get your shoes away tomorrow. Be sure to ask for your suitcase (or get A.D. to do it) because I know darn well he won't send it unless he "knows where you are."

B.

PRESS

KISSIN' COUSINS

It was written up in the *Fernie Free Press* the following Thursday under the heading: "Two Fernie Men Not Kissin' Cousins." That term, said the article, would have to be changed to "Shootin' Cousins" since the accident on the weekend when Alfredo D'Amico Jr. managed to shoot his first cousin, Reno D'Amico, in the left forearm. The two were after gophers up by Fairy Creek, and, according to the RCMP, who were notified when the injured man was admitted to Fernie Memorial Hospital, the first Mr. D'Amico inadvertently stepped into the line of fire just as the second Mr. D'Amico pulled the trigger after having lined up a gopher at the entrance to its burrow on the hillside. The weapon in question was a Cooey twenty-two. The two had been accompanied on their Sunday afternoon excursion by Al D'Amico's fiancée, whose name was not given. The item ended with the assurance that Mr. Reno D'Amico had not sustained serious injury to the limb, and that he would likely be released by Thursday evening.

Of course we had all heard a different version — the correct one — three days before. Monday morning, Mac, with no cap either on his head or in his hands, stood humbly at the post office doors, beginning this time with "Lily" (that was his niece who was a nurse) "was on duty yesterday when they brought Reno in with his arm shot up."

"Which Reno?" some asked.

Mac didn't bother to acknowledge a question that insignificant; he just went on with the story. "Al brought him in. And that Jenny girl of his off the reserve." The listeners could figure out for themselves who he was talking about. "His arm was shot up bad. And Al was telling Sandy and Rob how *the gun had accidentally gone off* when he was shootin' at a gopher on that bench up by the reservoir."

Everybody knows Mac pretty well. We can always detect, in that slowing down of speech and that deliberate emphasis on several words in a row, his own special brand of irony, or just plain scepticism. So that particular sentence brought responses such as: "What really happened then?" or "Give us the real scoop, Mac," or "Yeah, there'd be no accident like that with Al."

Mac continued. "Well, they might have expected the cops to swallow their cooked-up story. But all the family was there. All the D'Amicos, and the Bulfones too — both sides — with the mother and grandmothers crying over Reno (you know those Italian women) and the father and uncles threatening Al, even though they are all more related than most. (Al's and Reno's mothers are sisters and their dads are brothers.) Al couldn't take all that, especially from the grandmothers. And even before Reno was out of the operating room, he admitted he hadn't done it. He'd just said he did because he was trying to protect his girlfriend. Seems Jenny was the one who shot Reno — just fooling around and acting smart. She thought the safety was on when it wasn't. Lucky thing it was just a twenty-two, and lucky thing it was just shorts, and lucky it was just in the arm. Even a short could do a lot of damage — say in the heart, or in the head."

Mac was a bit more long-winded that day than usual, explaining how Blackie and Blaze — even though they were just back from their honeymoon at the lake — drove the girl home so Al could stay at the hospital. Mac seemed quite caught up in the story. And if he saw anyone getting impatient — jingling a post office key or starting to edge away — he actually stayed him with a hand on the arm. "Don't go off now without hearing the best part. Lily said that when Al finally came clean about who shot Reno, his old man, Alfredo, said, 'I'ma warna you about takin' up with a Indian squaw. You see what's justa happen to Reno all becausa her? Are you gonna marry with that kinda trouble? You be more like Blackie and getta yourself a reala nice Canadian girl.'"

CHAPTER EIGHT

WEDDING PLANS

It was strange being so totally away from Blaze. Sometimes I wondered if we'd ever see each other again. I tried to work hard and do well at business school, even though I wasn't very interested in the courses, because that seemed the only hope of getting a job that paid more than waitressing, and then, who knew? maybe I could save enough, in the first year or two after paying back Uncle Stu, for train fare to Fernié again. Maybe I could even get a job there — in the Coal Company office, or with one of the lawyers or something.

And Blaze wasn't any better off. She still worked for Trites Woods, in the Ladieswear now, but her salary was about the same as when she was in Groceries. We wrote back and forth all the time, so I kept up on the Fernie news. I kept waiting for her to say she and Nick were getting together again but no, her letters were all Blackie, Blackie, Blackie. He'd left the mill to go into the mine, something he'd vowed he'd never do. But, as she said, he was bettering himself — getting bigger pay so they could get married. He was doing it for her. So I guess my dream of having Nick for a brother-in-law was never going to come true. I heard regularly from him too. He hardly ever mentioned Blaze.

I don't like to be narrating events in this long distance way. It would be better writing if I could give YOU more immediacy. But what can I do? I wasn't there. I was 3,000 miles away. And letters were my only source of information. I can give you the first-hand accounts (I've kept all the letters) but for all I don't believe in being critical, I must say Blaze set down everything in a pretty matter-of-fact way. I would have thought that, with her having that image of herself as writer, she would have tried to express herself more vividly. For example, here's what she wrote about their engagement:

"It wasn't any surprise when Blackie took the ring out of his pocket because he had told me he was going to Healeys to get it. And even though I'd said definitely I didn't want a diamond (I mean, that's what everybody has for an engagement ring isn't it?) he went and got one anyway. It's nice enough — the stone is set up high with a kind of lacy bridgework under it. Gold, of course. (I didn't want gold either, remember?) He just pulled it out Wednesday in the middle of supper at the Grill. We'd ordered hamburgers and chips. So I made him put it away again. I told him I didn't want it to happen like that, to make it more romantic. Then the next time he tried, we were on the tracks with our twenty-two's — on our way to shoot gophers down past Lee Choy's. Honestly. I said maybe we could wait and go up Fernie Mountain and that would be a good place. But it was still too cold by the weekend so on Sunday we went over to that lot that we both like, you know the one up the riverbank above where the old skating rink used to be? You can see right over the river and West Fernie toward the Lizards. It'd be a nice place to build but it belongs to the Coal Company and they won't sell it for a house because it's on such a slope. I know because I went in and asked Mr. Powell about it. Anyway, that's where Blackie gave it to me. I wear it all the time. Nobody was very surprised, but they all think it's a beautiful ring."

In a letter soon after that one, she wrote to say that she had run into Dad. She was on her way to the North End to meet Blackie at the soccer game when she saw him coming toward her along Victoria Avenue. This is what she said:

"He had his head down and I'm sure he was going to pretend not to see me. I felt scared but I said hello to him anyway and I showed him my ring. All he said was 'Blackie, eh?' I told him we'd set the date for June 17th. I don't know what got into me but I asked him if he and Bertie would come and if he'd give me away. It seemed like the right thing to do. A person should be able to have her father give her away, don't you think? He looked uncomfortable, but he said, 'Yeah, I guess so.'"

She kept sending me updates on her wedding plans. She hadn't wanted to have a white dress (she couldn't afford it anyway) and she hadn't wanted to get married in a church. But Blackie insisted on both counts saying it would be nicer to remember it that way — her in a long white wedding dress and everyone there at the church to see her. So, she was going to do it for him. Neither one of them ever went to services but, since the United Church was the one his aunt and uncle belonged to, that would be the one. They went to see the minister and got it all arranged.

She picked out a dress from the bride catalogue one of the salesmen brought and he ordered it for her. With her twenty-per cent discount, the price wasn't too bad. Blackie had a suit made to order in the Menswear but he couldn't put it on her account because they weren't married yet. So he had to pay the full price.

Every week there was another letter with additional problems. First it was who to have for best man and bridesmaid. Blackie wanted his best friend Al D'Amico, of course, and since Blaze didn't have any special woman friend in Fernie, it was natural to decide on Al's girlfriend Jenny. The blow came when they both refused. Al's family was devout Catholic. They could not condone his taking part in a Protestant ceremony. And they were convinced Father Morley wouldn't approve anyway. Jenny was Catholic too. Her family didn't live in Fernie. She and her sister had come by themselves from a reserve somewhere in the West Kootenays, and got waitressing jobs at the Diamond Grill. That was after I left so I didn't know them. She could have been bridesmaid all right, but she didn't want to go without Al.

Al's cousin Reno was also a good friend of Blackie's. And he was Carmen's brother. Carmen, the one I worked with at the

Grill. He said it wouldn't bother him to be best man in a Protestant church and he even suggested that Carmen be bridesmaid. She was more my age. I had always admired her. Curly black hair, dark brown eyes, slim straight nose. What you think of as a classic Italian beauty. Blaze didn't know her very well but I was sure, since they were a lot alike, there couldn't be any problem. They were both the type everyone tended to like, the type who got along with anybody. Part of the reason, I guess, was their looks. Even a dress for Carmen wasn't too difficult. There were some fluffy formals left over from last year's grad selection that were marked down to half price. Blaze got Carmen to come in and look at them. The one that fit was mauve, in organdie and lace.

With Mrs. Arbuckle making the cake and putting on the reception in the dining room of her rooming house — all as her wedding gift — and with Rudy and Linda Weiss offering their cabin at Rosen Lake for the honeymoon, the whole thing was beginning to look manageable.

But then the other glass slipper dropped.

Blaze wrote immediately: "Like I said in my last letter everything was coming together nicely with all the arrangements for the church and the reception, even the cabin at the lake. But can you imagine what awful thing has happened? And only a month away? PEARL ANNE! Of course I wrote her about the wedding — the date, the plans, and everything. But I didn't really invite her because I know she can't afford to come down here; just like I didn't actually invite you — even though that would be my dearest wish, to have you here to stand up with us. And as you know, it isn't my dearest wish to have her! So what happens? She says she's coming! And not only is she coming, but she's going to be matron of honour! I never once mentioned that. I don't even want a matron of honour, not when I've got Carmen for a perfectly good bridesmaid. I don't even know if you're supposed to have both. And that means I'm going to have to buy her a dress too. And on top of that, she's bringing Shelley to be my flower girl. I have to admit that will be kind of nice, to have a pretty little four-year-old flower girl. And she does have a dress for her to wear — something she's making over.

"But it's just awful. I don't even know where they can stay. Can you imagine the three of us in this one little room of mine? Blackie says it'll be nice for me to have my sister here. But he doesn't know her like we do. I just told him it's the wrong sister, that's all. How I wish it was you coming instead."

And that wasn't the end of her problems. She had to see Dad to fill him in on final arrangements. So she went to meet the train from Coal Creek. It was a Wednesday, her afternoon off; she knew he'd be on dayshift that week. She said she had that awful feeling of embarrassment, the same as she'd had when she was in high school, when she saw his black cowboy hat. He was in behind some of the other miners coming off the train. He didn't look surprised when he saw her. Just nodded. She walked beside him across the tracks. There are quite a few sets of them there — for both the CPR and the M.F.& M. She didn't give me their conversation but the gist of it was that once he heard about Pearl Anne, he said he wouldn't be going to the wedding. When she asked if he meant he wouldn't be giving her away, he said, "Not if she's going to be there." He just kept on walking. When they got across the tracks he turned onto Baker Avenue and started right for the North End without even saying goodbye.

"Blackie says not to worry. His uncle will give me away. I'm not sure if that is proper, though. Anyway, the point is — a person should be able to have her own father. I wonder what it's all about. We knew they'd had some kind of trouble up in Mountain Park, remember? years back? and they haven't been in touch since. But I never thought it was so bad he'd stay away from my wedding because of it. I guess I just have to accept that whatever feud they've got going is more important to him than giving me away."

And there was a P.S. "Sometimes I think I should have taken your advice about Nick. He used to say we could just get married at the Court House and then go straight to Greece for our honeymoon. That would have been so much simpler."

My heart jumped a bit at that. But I knew it was too late.

CHAPTER NINE

APOLOGY

"There she is. She's all ready to go." Blackie laid the rifle across his knees and looked over at Blaze where she sat picking dead leaves off the geranium plant on the windowsill. "You want to have a look?"

She turned to him, wadding the dead leaves into a ball and flipping it into the waste basket. "You know I told you I wasn't fussy about having my name on any gun."

"Yeah, I know, but after last night I just wanted to show you how much you mean." He ducked his head down slightly. "You aren't still mad about last night are you?" He picked up the few metal tips from the chesterfield beside him and placed them, one by one, in the grooves in the wooden box on the coffee table.

"Mad isn't the word. I'm just so disappointed. What about your promise that you wouldn't drink any more once we got married?"

"Well, I still promise that. You know I've never had a home of my own before. But I couldn't help it. It just happened last night because I had to go to the bar to pay some debts. You wouldn't want your husband to forget about his debts, would you?"

"You said once we had a place of our own...." She looked around the apartment. "Well, this is it. A place of our own."

"Once I get all my debts paid up, I won't have to go there any more." He stood up and held the gun out to her. "Come on, Blaze. Have a look at it."

She took it in both hands. The letters of her name burned into the wood of the stock. On the left side. Was that because he was left-handed, she wondered. "Well, that is nice. You got them all so straight and even."

"Yeah, and deep too. It's burned right in. No one will ever be able to sand it off, or scrape it, or get rid of it in any way."

"What if you want to sell it?"

"I'll never sell it! Never! There's nothing like a two-seventy, you know that. Your old man's got one for Christ's sake. And now with your name on it. Actually, that makes it your rifle. So how could I ever sell it? Come on, give us a hug." He took the rifle and stood it against the wall, holding out one arm to her.

She moved in against him and leaned her cheek against his. "It is nice to have a place of our own, isn't it?"

"Yeah, and you know what I like best? From this high up you can see all along the tracks and down past the mill." Suddenly he stepped back, gripping the sides of her arms. "Hey, let's go down there. Come on. We can do some target practice."

Blaze looked at him steadily. "I don't know. I thought we'd do some more painting when you finished with that. We could get a start on the bedroom ceiling. I've got the star pattern cut out."

"Aw, come on. That can wait. We can do it later." He leaned over and picked up the rifle. "I want to try out this baby now that she's got your name on her."

"Well, okay. I'll grab my jacket."

As they closed the door behind them he said, "It'll help us forget about last night. You know I'm really sorry."

She put her arm through his and they started down the stairs.

It was into early summer but everything still had the fresh green look of spring. And spring in her step. Blaze liked to think of how one word could trigger more than one meaning and open up a whole new line of thought. They were on their way back to town. She was stepping along the left-side track, real fast, keeping her balance by resting her hand on Blackie's shoulder. He carried the rifle over his other shoulder and he held two pieces of cardboard out in front. "Actually, now that I look closer, you did better than me. Look, here's your target. You know when you thought you missed altogether? Well, look at this. There's two shots in exactly the same place. You can see the hole's just slightly bigger and kind of overlapped. I mean, it's more than if it was just one hit. So you got one right on centre, one at the outer lower edge, and the rest of them in a good cluster and only a little bit high."

"Well, what do you expect? It's my rifle, isn't it?" Just as she jumped down to walk beside him, something caught her eye far off to the right through the trees. It was a shiny surface with a strange ripple on it. "Hey, is that some kind of pond in there? See, over past the trees? I've never noticed it before. And it looks like something moving."

"Oh yeah, I see where you mean. It's a bit of a backwash from the river. Al and I used to try fishing in there for rainbow."

"What is it then? See that kind of V-shape, like something swimming?"

"Yeah, it's a muskrat, I think." He handed her the targets, raised the rifle. "Here, let me get a bead on him."

"Don't you dare! Don't you dare shoot!"

But the report drowned out the last words and he was saying, "Don't worry. No way could I hit it. That's two, maybe *three* hundred yards away."

Even before he finished speaking, she saw the hit on the water. A white spray, a slow settling, and then a reddened surface spreading out evenly from where the point of the V had been.

"Oh, Blackie. How could you?" She grabbed the barrel with both hands. Her eyes filled with tears. "You've killed him. Oh God, look at the blood everywhere, and bits of pieces. And all he was doing was just swimming along."

He twisted the rifle away from her. "I didn't mean to do it for God's sake. I was just sighting him in. There was no way I could hit right on at that distance." She stepped away. "Honest to God. I'm sorry. I couldn't help it Blaze."

He turned to follow her. But she was already far ahead of him, striding between the shining rails, taking two ties at a time.

CHAPTER TEN

ORILLIA

Time and distance are strange things. My year in Fernie seemed very far away, in both senses, from my current life. Not that so much had happened since then. I was still in school (but it was business school now), I still had a part-time job waitressing, and I was still a teenager. The actual distance was the same, of course – about three thousand miles – but it seemed much more. Both the time and the place had become more remote with each passing month.

And then it all collapsed around me. (That seems like an inappropriate metaphor, I know; maybe the time *collapsed*, and the distance *contracted*?) Anyway, Fernie and my time there were both suddenly brought very close. All because Dad showed up in Orillia.

It shouldn't have been a surprise. It was early October, our grandfather had just died, and various members of the family were gathering for the funeral. I had gone over to the funeral parlour for the second evening's viewing of the body. Several of my aunts and uncles and a few cousins were there. The room was heavy with the smell of flowers – the sweet, stale, overriding odour of roses. The coffin was oak, dark and shiny. I leaned down to kiss him, his cheek icy cold and hard as granite.

As I raised my head, my whole being jerked to sudden attention. Coming in the door was the black hat.

It hit me at once how Blaze had felt when she had to walk with him on Main Street when she was in highschool. I felt the same kind of embarrassment or shame and here I was in the midst of family. But added to that was a jolt of fear. I was right back in

Fernie, under his roof, dreading all over again that silent and threatening presence.

His first look was toward the coffin. He saw me just as he was removing the hat. With it in one hand, down at his side, he came toward me. "How are you, Girl?" he said. Neither one of us made the slightest move to touch. "Is everything going okay for you now?"

"Yes," I said, "fine. How are you doing?"

He looked toward the coffin again. "Hard to see the old man laid out like this, even though he did make it to ninety-two." And he moved on past me.

At the funeral, he sat in the front row, the one for chief mourners. He was with Aunt Addie and Uncle Ed. They were the ones who had taken Blaze in at first. She had been very fond of them, especially Uncle Ed. She said she had often told him that she thought of him as her real dad, and he always said, "Well, we spent some important years together." I was never sure why but, after having her with them for quite a long time, they passed her along to Uncle Stu and Aunt Dora, the ones I lived with. I think it was because he didn't send anything toward her keep, and they just couldn't afford to look after her any longer. Uncle Stu and Aunt Dora had taken me right at the time of our mother's death. I was fourteen months old. They couldn't really afford it either but, somehow, they managed to look after me, and then, later, Blaze. It was well-known throughout the family that Dad never sent any money, other than maybe a few dollars at Christmas for us to buy presents with. I think now that he might have meant presents for ourselves; at the time, we thought he meant presents for other people.

All I could see was the back of his head, but somehow I couldn't look anywhere else. Without his hat, he seemed smaller, greyer, older. I wondered what his life was like now. I knew through Blaze that Bertie had left him. She had gone to Vancouver

Island where her ex-husband worked in the coal mine at Cumberland. She wasn't with him or anything, but he had agreed to take Syd and Randy. She had Jackie and Tex with her. She worked as a cook at the air force base in Comox. I had visions of her serving up Steve's cabbage rolls and Mrs. Megale's spaghetti, and all her other great dishes, to hungry servicemen.

The back of his head. Thin short hair. I don't think I heard anything of the service. I hated the new feeling that was growing in me. It was pity.

That feeling, though, was short-lived. I didn't see him again after the funeral. He was staying with Aunt Addie and Uncle Ed. Their farm was on the far side of Orillia. He wasn't there long, and he didn't try to get in touch with me. The next news of him was from Blaze, who was livid. Apparently he had convinced Aunt Addie and Uncle Ed that he had sent money for her keep all the time she was with them. He had post office money orders to prove a great number of payments. Since there would be no indication as to sender or recipient, Blaze figured that he had just kept all his stubs from anything and everything he purchased by mail (and that would be most things when he lived in Mountain Park, it was such a remote town) and then produced them as evidence. He said the only possible explanation was that Blaze had intercepted the money orders, cashed them, and spent the money, all without the knowledge of our aunt and uncle. (One thing that was never clear to me was in whose name did he claim they were made out? She certainly could not have cashed them had they been in their name. And how could he admit he had been so foolish as to send those amounts to a child?) She was angry with him for pulling something so shoddy; she was even angrier with them for believing him.

I hope all this isn't too circuitous for YOU to follow. I realize that I am suddenly introducing new characters from our Ontario life, but it's necessary to the story because it's important for YOU to see the connections between our lives in the two places, to see how Dad could cause such trouble for us in both provinces. Both Dad and I were born and brought up in Ontario. Blaze was born in B. C., brought up in Ontario. All of us ended up in Fernie together. Later, once I have gone back to Fernie, it will be simpler again. But there is more about this business.

Blaze first heard about it through letters from Aunt Addie and Uncle Ed. She sent me copies that she wrote out by hand. Aunt Addie started off with one date, as though she was writing the letter before Dad talked to them. Blaze said she probably did that because there were some things she needed to deal with first, such as thanking her for the birthday present she'd sent, and mentioning Grandad's death and funeral. That part was dated October nineteenth. Then, on page two, under October twenty-ninth, the bombshell. Blaze said she was sitting on Blackie's knee, reading the letter to him, and it was like a steam roller going over her, over both of them.

This is the part she sent me:
October 29
For some reason I never got this letter finished. I guess it was just fate that held me back at first, but for the past week I have just been wondering how I could ever finish it.

Up until then I steadfastly refused to believe that the years you lived here with us, that you were not sincere & decent, but now that we have the definite proof, there are so many "pieces" that fit into place that at the time I wondered about, but still went on believing in you. More fool I.

How a child could go along so gaily, accepting all the things and chances that Ed and I sacrificed to give you. Even to postponing a family of our own, so that we could give you a chance.

Well the whole thing is completely beyond me.

Well I guess there's not much point in continuing, but for once I can truly understand why your Mother was spared from knowing how you turned out.

For myself I feel more or less sympathy for you. You have hurt yourself more than anyone else in the long run, and I guess I still can't help feeling a little more for you than my other nieces.
As ever -
Addie

Then Uncle Ed's letter. More direct, more condemning:

Orillia, May 29th

Blaze,

Your guilt has just come to our attention. Why did you steal the money your father forwarded to you to assist us in your upbringing? Then recently as a climax to all your despicable behaviour comes your announcement of your betrothal to a really wonderful guy. The fact is, you have betrayed us again by marrying a drunken bastard, and an Indian at that.

It always seemed like an awful tragedy that your poor mother was snatched away so suddenly. In the light of your behaviour it now appears to have been a great mercy. Her poor heart would have been broken. Next, you have wronged your father shamefully. We could not help but lose our respect for him when he apparently was not showing any direct interest in his daughter's welfare. Did you not realize or care that he risked his life every time he went into the mine to earn a living and an education for you? There is no reward in this world or the next for such behaviour. Sin pays no dividends. Addie and I gave to you freely in your need, our compassion for you was true and we hold no bitterness. You have wronged yourself a thousand times more than anyone else.
Yours etc,
Edward

Space and time, as I've said, are strange things. Blaze and I were so far apart. Dad had presented great untruths, ones that overthrew old trusts. He had come all that way to bury his father and, in so doing, had heaped trouble on his favourite daughter. I had watched him at the funeral and felt pity. The damage he caused was irreparable. He had rearranged the past.

Blaze wrote back to them, indignant that they could believe such charges. Resorted to logic. How could she cash money orders, have money to spend, without their knowledge? What could she have bought with the thousands he claimed to have sent without their seeing any evidence of her spending? Reminding them that it would have been the spending of a child.

In the end, nobody knew what to believe. When Blaze saw Dad again in Fernie, and tried to straighten things out, he said, "Listen, Girl, you'd better come clean." Her protests were useless. And then he paid her back the hundred dollars he had borrowed to help him with the trip to the funeral.

CHAPTER ELEVEN

UNWRITTEN LETTER

Blaze threw the pen down, crumpled the page, and stretched back in the chair. How boring it would be for Babe to hear about the apartment again. An update on the progress of their decorating. The beginning so long ago. What had seemed daring and exciting was now just absurd. A yellow and brown bathroom. A mauve kitchen. She had always hated mauve. And then the crazy idea Blackie had of dividing the livingroom wall diagonally with burgundy on the bottom and dove grey on the top. Putting stars on the bedroom ceiling had been her idea. Grey stars, only three, on a midnight-blue background. Even to tell that to Babe would be just too embarrassing. More than embarrassing at this moment, with him passed out in there, snoring and filling up the whole room with the stink of the bar. Maybe try thinking of a letter with all the things in it that she would never tell her. How would that go?

Dear Babe. The first thing I want to tell you is that I was stupid to get married. I was stupid to think he would stop drinking once we had our own place and he had someone to care about. I knew better even as I walked up the aisle with him waiting at the altar. He winked at me and swayed — already drunk. Stupid, stupid, but then we never knew anything about alcohol and the problems it can cause, not the way we were brought up in Ontario, did we? It seemed wild if someone had a drink of sherry or port at Christmas. And he drinks all the time. Beer mostly — he's always in the bar — but hard stuff too, anything he can get his hands on. They do say Indians have low tolerance. Even though he's only part Indian, his tolerance is extra, extra low. He's dead drunk right now, in under our starry sky, after a whole evening in the bar. He stayed drinking until closing time. Pay-day today . That means he went straight to the Roma from work. Every week he runs out of money and so he borrows from the rest of the guys. Then the biggest concern is getting them paid back immediately, so his credit is good when he runs out again. It's hard to keep the bills paid. I have taken an extra job on Saturdays, at the dental office. My meter-reading for the city wouldn't be enough by itself.

And here's another thing I'll never tell you. We got back together with Dad again. He stopped coming around after his trip east and all that trouble last year. I was glad to leave it at that but then Uncle Ted and Aunt Florrie came west with the two kids, you'll remember. Well, they were asking around town trying to find Dad. Nobody seemed to know where he was. I guess it was because he had just moved from the North End to one of the coal company houses in the Annex now that he's on his own again. Anyway, somebody told them where they could find me, and I couldn't very well let on that we weren't speaking, so I took them down there. They stayed only the one day but I felt I had to invite them here for a meal, and I couldn't very well not invite him too. That was the start. Now he comes by all the time and I swear he's doing it on purpose. He keeps talking Blackie into drinking, even on nights when he hasn't figured on going out. Not that it takes much persuading. And he's back to glomming all over me the way he did when we first came to Fernie. You'd think we might pretend we're not home, but he just slides his jack-knife in the side of the door and releases the lock. These damned old apartment buildings.

So those are the men in my life. I remember reading a thing in *Reader's Digest* by a woman who was praising men, saying you just couldn't have too many around. I can't remember all the adjectives she used to describe her list but it was something like a *doting* father, a *thoughtful, loving* husband, an *applauding* brother, a *supportive* friend, an *entertaining son*, etc., etc. Well, I have the father and the husband, although I wouldn't choose any of those words to describe them. My brother is a half brother who's three years old and far away, male friends can't stick around a married woman in a town like this, and there is no son.

That's another thing I will never tell you. We tried for a while right after we were married, but nothing happened. Blackie even came home with a good old Chinese remedy. You remember Lee Choy? He told him what to do. That was when Blackie was still working at the mill. And for quite a while, every time after we had sex, Blackie would hold me up by the feet and shake me like a sack. That's what Lee Choy said would help get me pregnant. It was quite a joke, but then we got tired of it. The way things were going, I was glad it didn't work and I even went to the doctor and got fitted for a diaphragm. The last time I saw Lee Choy he said, "You no baby yet?" He rounded his hands to indicate a big belly. When I said no, he said, "You no need baby. You already got one. That Blackie. He baby enough for you." Now how could I ever tell you that?

The last thing, and this is *definitely* something you'll never know, is that he gets really mean when he's drunk. He throws his hunting knife. We've got marks in the wall. He's held a loaded rifle to my head, more than once. The first time, I got out of the apartment and actually went to the police station. It was Sandy on duty. He said he was sorry but they had no jurisdiction in the case of domestic trouble. Since then....

Suddenly Blaze sat up straight. There was a shuffling noise in the hall. Oh, no. Not him. She switched off the table light and moved quietly to the door just as the buzzer sounded. She sidestepped into the bedroom and ducked into the clothes closet. Maybe he'd go away if she didn't answer. Maybe he'd think they were asleep. My God, it was after one-thirty. The closet had no door. She hunched down in the corner, covering her head and shoulders with something that was hanging down far enough. Blackie's trench coat. She heard the knife pushing through between the frame and the moulding, then the click of the lock as it opened. There was a stumbling sound and then the door banged shut. He was in the hall, he was coming into the room.

Only now was she aware of Blackie's snoring. It was loud and drawn out. Her father stopped at the foot of the bed. She moved the fabric of the coat aside. She could see him dimly in the bit of light that made its way up to the fourth floor from the street light. The curtains were still open. He seemed to fall. No, not quite. He was simply lowering himself down at the side of the bed. She could see his arm reaching out toward the snoring, toward the mound under the covers. Then his voice, hoarse and cajoling. "Come on, little honey. Where's my little girl?" Blaze wrapped the coat closer about her shoulders.

When his hand made contact with the bedspread, the mound suddenly jerked into sitting position and the arms flailed out. Blackie shouted in a very loud voice. "Fuck off! Whadda ya think you're doin'? Fuck the hell outa here.!"

Blaze breathed deep. She found the swinging belt and jammed it against her mouth to keep from laughing. She saw her father rise, rather unsteadily but fairly fast. He backed away from the bed, turned, and staggered out of the room. The door clicked open and then shut, and he was gone.

Blackie threw himself back down on the bed, made a half turn, and pulled the covers over his head. She was sure he hadn't even woke up.

Back at the table with the light on again, Blaze resumed the letter that she would never write. And, my dear Babe, that is something else you'll never know.

PRESS

THE ARENA

Last year, *The Fernie Free Press* ran a very interesting series about sports in Fernie over the years. They started with a comment someone (they didn't say who) had made about 1900: "Fernie has always shown a keen appreciation of true amateur sport and few towns can boast of so many liberally supported clubs." The article then went on to treat the various sports, saying that "although just about every sport has been staged here, hockey, soccer, baseball, curling and golf have proven to be the most enduring. More recently, skiing has captured a great deal of interest and will, with the growth of good facilities, hold permanent favour."

Our arena was recently reduced to rubble by a fire which also claimed the life of one of the juvenile players. Since the tragedy, everybody has become greatly absorbed in the history of hockey in this town. Many people have gone to the newspaper office to ask for back copies of the sports series, particularly the articles on hockey, which have become the main topic of conversation around town:

> The first arena was built on the "41 block" about 1900, and by 1903 the Crow's Nest Hockey Association was organized, with teams from Pincher Creek, Cranbrook, Moyie and Fernie doing battle for the beautiful "Liphardt Cup," which Fernie won.
>
> The first rink was destroyed by the great fire of 1908, but by 1909 a new rink was ready at the river bank site across the river from West Fernie. Here in 1911 the locals hosted

the Nelson team in an exhibition game. Playing for Nelson were hockey immortals Frank and Lester Patrick, who later achieved fame and fortune in the N.H.L.

The pinnacle of hockey success in Fernie was achieved by the ladies. In 1923 the "Swastikas" journeyed to the Banff Winter Carnival and returned home with the "World Championships" for women.

The 1924 senior men's team won the East Kootenay championship at Kimberley but lost to Rossland, the West Kootenay representatives. In 1928 The Fernie Junior Rotarians were crowned B.C. champions.

In 1952 hockey got a real shot in the arm when the new artificial ice arena was completed. The Fernie team, by now called "The Rangers," competed as intermediates with teams from Great Falls, Coleman, Michel-Natal, Cranbrook and Kimberley.

It was the 1952 arena, the pride of the town that was, as I said, "reduced to rubble." So, most people, even those who were not particularly interested in hockey before, have become authorities on the subject. Their keenness has led them to believe that the sport is what has given the town its character and reputation. Such fervour is what has contributed to the immediate decision, on the part of the town council and the citizens alike, to build a new winter sports complex.

Had there been a psychiatrist in town, he might well have noted that the avid concentration on hockey itself and on plans for immediate rebuilding of the arena, was indicative of an urge, shared by everyone, to sublimate the grief the town felt over the boy. He was Fred Yip, thirteen years old. He had been born in

Fernie. He and the family were known to the whole town; they owned the Diamond Grill. Fred was a strong player, now felt to have been a potential star, one who would have undoubtedly gone on to achieve "fame and fortune in the NHL" like his predecessors, Frank and Lester Patrick.

The practice had just ended; the team was in the dressing room. The suddenness of the outbreak, the speed and force of the blaze, the just-in-time moving back of the parked ambulance to save it from burning up too, the inability of the fire crew to get any control over the flames – afterwards everyone talked endlessly of such details. And of the players themselves: how they came rushing out the side doors into the spray from the hoses, beating at their flaming uniforms; how they plunged into snow banks, how the ambulance crew dragged them clear. They were all out; they were all safe. Then the unbearable part. One turned back. Everyone said it at one time or another afterwards: "It was Fred. He was already out, and he went back in to get his skates."

Finally, it was Mac who made it bearable. He stood, on one particular morning, at the door of the post office, his cap stuffed into his back pocket, his shoulders a little more stooped than before. But he was not greeting people with the usual verbal message. Instead, he handed them a clipboard and a pen. It was a petition stating that "the citizens of Fernie make an urgent appeal to the mayor and town council that the new sports complex, which is slated to be finished in time for the beginning of the new hockey season, be named, in memory of our esteemed and departed player, the *Fred Yip Arena*."

Every person who read the petition signed it.

Had that psychiatrist been on hand, he would have noticed a marked change in the mood of the town. Everyone smiled a little brighter, stepped a little lighter, and said to each other, "That Mac. He sure knows what to do."

CHAPTER TWELVE

UNREAD STORY

When people move from one place to another they tend to leave pieces of themselves behind. And they take pieces away with them too, of the places they left. I know that when I went back to Ontario I thought about Blaze all the time, and my friend Gordie, and Nick, too. And I missed the mountains, and the river, and the whole town. Fernie was the only place I had lived in other than where I grew up. Whatever there was before the farm I didn't remember. How different it must have been for Blaze. She had been moved about within the family constantly, ever since she was seven, when our mother died. She ended up at Aunt Dora and Uncle Stu's with me, but that was just in her late teenage years. Before that, she was with Aunt Addie and Uncle Ed, and before that with Dad's oldest sister over on Uhthoff Line, and before that... well, that's when I was still a baby. When I was home again, some time after my year in Fernie, Aunt Dora said there was a boxful of Blaze's school things that she wanted me to have a look through. Now that Blaze was getting married, maybe she'd want some of them sent out.

I took the box to my room. Mostly it was stuff from high school: her history notebook, all in neat handwriting with underlined titles and dates; geometry theorems and drawings; French and Latin and Biology notebooks and texts. At the bottom of the box was a thick folder full of essay booklets from her evening courses at U of T — assignments she'd done on various literary topics: one on *Joseph Andrews*, one on *Great Expectations*, one on the poetry of Emily Dickinson. I didn't look at them all because, under the folder, there was an intriguing slim binder with a birch bark cover. It was tied securely with thick string.

The strands crisscrossed each other from top to bottom, and from side to side, and were knotted and reknotted so many times that they were impossible to undo. I had to cut them with a knife.

Inside was a story with the title "Saturday," about eight pages long. There were no written comments on it as there were on the essays in the folder. I read it, and I wished I hadn't. It was about a young girl. No one had names, but I knew it was Blaze's story because I recognized the place, the aunt and uncle, *and* the *boy*, our cousin Lyman. They were the ones Blaze had lived with before Uncle Ed and Aunt Addie.

It was something Blaze had left behind, a part of her she hadn't wanted anyone to know, and I had read it. I couldn't unread it. I would have to find some similar string and try to duplicate the crisscrossing and the knots. She must never know.

SATURDAY

Where an apple tree had fallen and crushed the fence, a shaft of sunlight splashed across the muddy lane. The tree had died, leaves withered, trunk split, roots bared. The desire for life had been ignored, its responsibility unheeded; its death was premature, and had left half-formed apples on the dead branches. In the sunlight, a young girl sat on a rock, her arms pulling her knees tightly against her chest. Beside her, the wind wiped muddy water from the upturned faces of pebbles; behind her, a reckless robin straddled an apple and pecked the stem free from the twig to which it clung. The girl did not move. She was crying. Each sob shivered the length of her slight body, slipping through the straight dark hair of the bowed head, down tanned neck, through faded flowered dress, down bare brown legs, stopping briefly in the curl of the toes before it was flattened against the waiting rock. The robin pecked viciously at the apple. The girl raised her head and saw him. He flew away.

She looked toward the road where she had watched the car disappear and, tracing its course in reverse, came to the gate that had closed behind it; to the lane which picked its way past the fallen apple tree, then cavorted through the orchard to the clump of lilacs, to the tall spruce trees walled in front of the house. She was relieved she could not see the house. The protective slope of its low roof, the sympathetic glance of its windows, the call of the creeper-clad doorway would have tempted her to beg for refuge it could not offer. But crying was no weapon now, and she wiped her eyes with the hem of her dress. Earlier that morning it had been different. Then the crying had purpose and might have achieved for her triumph; here on the rock it was the useless, resigned, Saturday sobbing of failure.

Almost as long as she could remember, Saturday was a morning that awakened her with dread – the same dread she felt the day the boy up the road killed his cat with a hammer while she watched. Always the realization that it was Saturday again snatched away the usual morning warmth of home-made quilts over her, leaving her stripped and shivering in her brass-posted bed. Then she would get up, dress quickly, and hurry down the steps to the kitchen. This morning she had remained in bed a little longer than usual, reluctant to leave the safety of her own familiar room with its white walls and curtained window. Tracing the flowing, bumpy route of the wall-paper border, searching for evasive figures and scenes long ago discovered in the watermarks on the ceiling, she had wanted to put off forever the moment when her longest toe must touch the floor.

When she pushed open the door at the bottom of the stairway, the kitchen was empty. Alone, she ate her porridge. A mottled cat jumped into her lap, settled itself, and purred. The sun, climbing the August sky, flooded over the top of the barn and pushed its warmth to touch her hunched shoulders at the window. But it was a Saturday sun. She shrugged it off and, settling the cat on a cushioned chair, cleared the table. She was tip-toed, hanging the last of the dried cups from the top shelf of the cupboard, when the back door opened, admitting her aunt and two foam-topped pails of milk. The woman was not much taller than the girl, heavier of body, with greying hair. The brown eyes, seated in crinkles of good humour that had become hardened into wrinkles of something wiser, stared vacantly ahead in a sort of saddened surprise. She set one pail on the floor and hefted the other to the cream separator bowl, which yawned wide, swallowed the warm milk in one hungry gulp, waiting for the second helping. Without a word, the girl moved over and began to rotate the separator handle. It turned slowly at first, but warmed with the increasing speed until the whole machine was humming, then shouting, as her arm flew in faster circles to keep the handle from slipping the notch. Her aunt's voice darted through the noise, tagged her ear, then dropped out of reach. "I'll need all the butter we have to make up enough for the market. You churn that cream that's in the cellar, so we'll have some for tomorrow. You'll have to feed the hens too. I won't have time. There's that stew in the pantry for your dinner." The voice turned its back and left the room.

    That was when she had started to cry. Up to that moment there had been hope, hope that she would be allowed to go with them to town, hope that she would not be left alone with Saturday. All the waiting for this moment, when she would know for sure, crowded from her in an uncontrollable torrent of tears. Anger, hate, fear, terror, fisted their way out. The fury transmitted itself to the separator which suddenly spat milk from one spout and cream from the other. Savagely, she kept the handle turning, her mind whirling with her arm, her crying strangled by the machine's noisy digestion.

    She was aware of her uncle's presence; the sudden smell of cow manure followed by a pair of dirt-stiffened overalls carrying more milk for the gaping mouth. For a moment, watery blue eyes level with the emptying bucket peered at her from beneath winged eyebrows overlapped in flight. "What you cryin' fer girl?" The sand-coloured face was drawn, weather-beaten, and dirty. Sand hair poked greasy strands from under a sand hat. "I don't know why yer always carryin' on to get to town. Rather be home myself than standin' in that dirty market tryin' to sell eggs and butter and spuds and yer aunt's bakin' to people always wantin' everythin' cheaper. Damn 'em! Like to see *them* runnin' a farm, scrubbin' the dirt with a plough – nothin' growin' proper fer the rocks." He held the empty pail under the milk spout while he moved the full one aside with his foot. "Yer ten years old now, girl. Old enough to stay home and do a bit of work fer yer aunt. Not as if yer alone even. You don't see *him* belly-achin' to get to town." The smell didn't quite follow him out.

It was the same every Saturday, wondering whether they would take her to town or not. They did not understand; she had failed to make them understand. It was her fault. But how could she make them see that she was crying not because she wanted to go with them, but because she didn't want to be left; that her tears were not for a marketplace she could not haunt, but for the farm where she must remain? She was old enough to stay at home. She would not be alone. Alone she would have been content – to churn the butter and feed the hens, to tidy the house, or clean the calf pens at the barn; she was old enough to do the work. Alone would have been glorious, with the grey gelding waiting in the stable for his currying and brushing, the creek eager for her exploring feet, the cornfield impatient to walk her through its tall, tunnelled rows. But she would not be alone.

She had followed the car out the laneway, closed and barred the gate behind it, watched the cedars hasten its disappearance before the bend in the road. She was thankful she could not see the house. She was more than thankful she could not see the barn beyond it. The boy would be there now, finishing the chores and waiting, and smelling of cow dung like his father.

His odour was one thing about him that would not let her forget that first day, the awful ancestor, sire of a savage line of Saturdays. Even on weekdays, or Sundays, she had only to get the faintest whiff of him and it was Saturday again, that Saturday in the stable – the sudden surprise of his presence, the desperate struggling on the chaff-covered floor, her beating of fists and screaming. Pinned down, screaming, the hurt, the terror. And when it was over, the smirking face under sand-cloured hair drifting away above her, the cows moving restlessly in their stanchions, a row of cud-chewing curious faces. "Mom! Mom!" The piercing voice was a frenzied thing, dashing itself against beam, post, and manger.

"She's *my* mother," hissed the boy, "not yours. So you can't tell her." He stood over her there in the feed passageway, hoisting the straps of his overalls into place. "And yours is dead, so you can't tell *her*. And you can't tell your dad when you don't even know how to write yet." His smell was there, pungent and sickening, swinging about her like a suspended rope, circling free of the other stable smells.

Now on the rock in the lane, it was four years later, and Saturday again. There had been no way of telling his mother (her aunt) or, even when she had learned to write, her father. School had taught her no way of telling on Saturday. When she rose from her rock, the wind was busy shoulder-shaking the withered leaves, but the tree would not waken. Some of its apples, which had rolled into the lane, lay flattened and tire-marked. The robin had returned. Urgency flitted with him and he swooped about her, accompanying her along the lane toward the house. The cellar door could be locked, the churning done; when he came she would hide safe and still and never open the door. Past the lilacs, past the spruce trees, around the corner of the house, through the back door, across the empty kitchen....

    He was upon her like a ragged rock shot from a giant slingshot, ripping from the direction of the pantry, hurtling against her, knocking her to the floor. His body flattened her fear into panic. Fingers grasped her shoulders, knees pinned her legs; the smirking face, the hateful smell swinging round and round. The leering line of Saturdays joined hands and looped in a leaping circle about them, watching.

    She struggled, scratched, pounded, while a tiny fleck of her mind soared free, and hovered above and outside herself. Somehow, the fourteen years of the boy were not so overpowering to her now, not as his ten years had been to her six, or even his thirteen to her nine. The fleck sped back. Doubling her knees under him, she forced them sharply up, sending him sprawling to one side. She was on her feet. The cupboard. The drawer. He rolled over and was up too. But like a dog jerked to a stop at the end of its chain, he hung in the middle of a lunge, eyes wide, staring at the long pointed blade of the butcher knife in her hand.

    "I'll kill you!" Her voice swung on the room, the cowering Saturdays, and the panting boy who turned and ran, clumsy and yelping, out of the house and across the barnyard, with her shrieking from the back door, "I'll kill you! I'll kill you!"

    She did not see him again until suppertime. Sobbing and shaking, she had clutched the knife through the unending morning, expecting his return at every moment, at any sound. When he did not come, and it was well past noon, she remembered the hens and edged her way to the chicken house to feed them, flipping the wheat from the pan with the blade of the knife; remembered the churning and went down into the welcome coolness of the cellar, locking the door behind her, and teetered the knife on her knees as her feet treadled the barrel churn with its sloshing cream. By the time her aunt and uncle turned into the lane in the late afternoon, she was beginning to feel that it was not Saturday at all, but just any day after school, and slipped the knife back into its drawer.

He slumped at the window while she set the table. At the stove his mother was turning sausages in a pan. "Poor boy, you look tired," she said. "You shouldn't try to do so much work, when you're home by yourself."

The girl looked sideways at him then. He screwed up his face in mockery, silently mouthing, "I'll kill you, I'll kill you." Turning to the cupboard, she opened the drawer and slowly drew out the knife, and moved to the end of the table so that the shiny sharpness of the blade pointed straight at him. As she saw the leap of terror in his eyes, she reached for the loaf and, deliberately and laboriously, sliced the bread for Saturday's supper.

CHAPTER THIRTEEN

MINE TALK

After Blaze left for the coast, I found several small scribblers among the things she left with me. Some of them had poems and parts of stories; a couple had drawings of scenery, mainly mountains, and of local plants and flowers; one was a recording of bills paid and "to be paid." The one that intrigued me most was one entitled "Conversations about the Mine." She must have set things down as they were being said when people were over and got to drinking and talking about the mine.

Here are some of the conversations.

April 30. Present: Blackie, Moke, Tony

MOKE: As far as hydraulic mining goes, it's a cheap method of mining. You have no haulage. It's always... through the crusher... the coal bucket [I can't hear all the words. They're slurring already]

TONY: I'm a hundred per cent right. Convention mining, you have to leave it seventy-five per cent to sixty per cent coal right on the ground because you can't get in, can't do it. You get killed in some... and hydraulic. Oh she's seventy-five per cent this way, power this way and this way. Other mining you have to.... These timbers go rotten and break and... [His Polish accent makes it difficult to catch the words.]

MOKE: I'm not talkin' about timber going rotten and breaking in your arches, Tony. I'm talkin' about the gas and conditions that are in there. You can't go

	too far, otherwise you're going to get accumulation of gas there and somethin's goin' to happen.
TONY:	In small seams they get almost a hundred per cent. Do you remember Number Four Moke? Far back as you could see, all posts in there and all the roofs up.
MOKE:	When your roof caves in, that's took the pressure off the places when you're drivin,' y'know, as yer goin' out, and the way the mine works is on a thing like this, you drive your incline and then let her cave. Then toward the end of it that's when you get yer... and yer pressure and everything, but as far as hydraulic mining, they're not getting as much coal as what they figure they could. Mind you, they're gettin' *cheap* coal. Y'know what I mean, Blackie? First they haven't got the guys on the long haul and yer not takin' these lifts like you did with the mining machines.
BLACKIE:	When the roof comes down, you can still wash quite a bit of the coal out.
MOKE:	Oh yeah, but you get rocked out when the place caves in, and at the same time you're behind it and then after it caves an' that, you just knock out a few more parts and keep on comin' back *and then* put your monitor in again and set it up again to cut the coal and everythin'. But at the same time it's cheap coal for what they're gettin' out. Two guys can dig 2,000 ton of coal like nothin' with that monitor system but at the same time you've got yer safety regulations to go along with... Sure likely to get locked out an' everything, when them rocks fall.
BLACKIE:	But do you know the problem behind it? Say all those big rocks come down. They stay hot for a

	while. You can get an explosion in there. And not only that, you can get a flood in there. Y'know if it plugs up or somethin' the pump will stop but at the same time you've got a big block-up and when that breaks loose, you got all these guys in there.
TONY:	Never been happen yet so far.
MOKE:	No, well, they've been very lucky. It's just like an explosion. It's the same thing. *It's the same thing.*
TONY:	No, I think it's a very very good method to mining. Good for the people.
MOKE:	At the same time you've got yer Fire Boss in there. You got yer Pit Boss in there. He's regulatin' the gas and everythin'. Say a cave comes or somethin', or somethin' does happen. Sure he's got an easy job sittin' there but at the height of it you could be snuffed out like that, with an explosion.
TONY:	Look now, you been workin'...but if you need two men. Twelve ton. I mean twenty-four ton. Oh, you work man. What's now? three thousand ton, then they give you cigar?
MOKE:	Sure you can get three thousand ton from two guys there but you're only gettin' twelve ton from what's drivin' the place. And they're just sittin' there. But it's hazardous. Three thousand ton versus twelve ton.
BLACKIE:	It only takes one bloody mistake...

[I can't get any more. They're all talking at once. Some argument over couplings.]

May 5. Present: Blackie, Dad, Moke

MOKE: My grandfather used to be Fire Boss at Coal Creek. I got a picture at home I'll show you. He signed his name on the board. The picture's right there in front

	of him, and I'll tell you who else's picture's there. You remember Pete Dawson? Well his father, Douglas Dawson, was a Fire Boss at Coal Creek. And they're both standin' there signin' their names. I got that picture at home right now.
DAD:	Where's Pete Dawson now?
MOKE:	He's on the Island. He was in town at Christmas but I didn't see him. He was in about a year ago. I just went to the mail, and he jumped out of the car and said 'I gotta see you.' Pete Dawson. He's a nice fella, Pete. You remember Pete Dawson, Blackie? You too Tare? Used to be secretary of the union.
DAD:	He's the one I got a job through when I came in from Alberta.
MOKE:	I remember when you got a job in Coal Creek. You come up on the train. Now let me put it this way. [All three talking at once]. Wait a minute. Let me talk. You were standin' in front of the train with a cowboy hat on. Y'know, your same cowboy hat on and you got hired on. Am I right or am I wrong?
DAD:	Well the way it was, I was supposed to contact Dawson and I couldn't find him, so I went up and talked to the Super myself...
MOKE:	Well that's when you were...
DAD:	Then Dawson came rushin' in...
MOKE:	And I saw you comin' in. When I was comin' off work. You were there and you had a black cowboy hat on. And you got a job there. Right in front of the office at the mine.
DAD:	It was all cut and dried before I ever came down here from Alberta.

MOKE: Yeah, I know, but I saw you there the day you got hired.

BLACKIE: That's the point, Dad. Moke was right there that day and saw you.

MOKE: I was comin' off work and you were there with a black Stetson hat on, and you went in the office. Am I right or am I wrong?

BLACKIE: But *he* didn't notice *you*, Moke.

MOKE: No, it's pretty hard to.... I didn't even know him then! And I didn't know you, Blaze, either. But I sure to God know you both now. That was a long time ago. I'll tell you who was there the same time. We were diggin' coal together. Rex Flannery and I. He was ahead of you. And then you came up and you walked into the office, and I said, 'There's a fella with a cowboy hat on.' And the next thing.... Where did you go to work? In Number Three right off the bat?

DAD: Uh-huh.

MOKE: Number Three and you remember it too. Number Three, am I right or am I wrong? Remember the time we was night shift there and I was runnin' the dinky and, Jesus Christ, I piled up. Charged six hundred pounds pressure. Remember I used to run the dinky?

BLACKIE: Wasn't that when you worked in the Michel mine?

MOKE: Yeah. It was in Michel. There's always things you want to reminisce and talk about. I'm goin' on nineteen years. It'll be twenty in September, since I been in the mine. Long enough to be gettin' three weeks' holidays.

[End of mine talk. Discussed wedding, during holidays, of Eric, Moke's son]

May 12. Present: Blackie, Dad

BLACKIE: When I'm walkin' in the mine –three different shifts now - I see footprints. Just like flour in there, y'know, on the floor... It's rock dust?

DAD: That's rock dust.

BLACKIE: What's that? They're usin' it for safety?

DAD: The reason they put rock dust in there is your modules of rock dust, nine pieces of rock dust and one piece of coal dust, will stop a fire. You understand what I'm talkin' about? And that's why they have it in there. It's rock dust. Mind you, there's places where they water down and everything. Water is the same thing.

BLACKIE: The guys were sayin' they were ready to fire Mickey because he was puttin' that stuff — rock dust - in there. They say rock dust was floatin' in the air, and coal dust was floatin' in the air.

DAD: Mostly they're runnin' cheap. Any time there was dust in the air, they tried to cover it up and make it look good.

BLACKIE: Well, when Vic got killed...

DAD: Y' mean Vic Hornquist?

BLACKIE: Yeah.

DAD: If the motor'd been where it should have been, he'd have never got killed. A man coulda seen it. If they'd had the proper light in there...'Cause I ran the same motor but I was on a different shift.

BLACKIE: But about Vic that day.

DAD: Vic. Well, he went down to fix that chain up or somethin' and then he was walkin' in the mine and who comes next behind him is Pete Polanski with a dinky and pushin' these ten-ton cars, no light flashin' or nothin' and the next bloody thing, poor Vic got killed.
BLACKIE: So it was Pete's fault?
DAD: Pete was goin' in with the motor, *pushin'* the cars in. You don't go on the front end and your ... The only time you're on the front end is comin' out.
BLACKIE: You should be on the front end goin' in too.
DAD: See how he got away with it though. It wasn't right. Anyway, when you're workin' in the mine – and you don't know yet, Blackie, 'cause you're just startin' out – that's the kind of thing you gotta get used to.

    I guess this kind of recording meant something to Blaze — her old habit of being overly interested in "the experience."

CHAPTER FOURTEEN

BLACKIE SPEAKS

I'm getting sick of hearing how I'm the luckiest guy in town. I've been hearing it ever since Blaze and I started going together. And no one's let up, not even after we've been married all this time. They're always saying how come I got the most beautiful girl in Fernie, and how come she puts up with me, and how come she hasn't left me by now. Of course I know they've got reasons for coming out with that stuff. First of all, I'm an Indian guy. Only part Indian, but that doesn't make any difference. How can I be good enough for a white girl, especially if she's great looking and got an education and, on top of it, she's from out of town? And second of all, I'm a drunk. Not that anyone ever makes either of these observations to my face, of course. But that's what's behind it all. No one stops to consider that maybe Blaze interfered with my life. If she hadn't come to town I could have been quite happy just going on being an Indian and a town drunk. It was a good life. At least I was free.

I should have known right from the start that she was after me. Sure I liked her, and I asked her out — got that step-slow, step-brother of hers to start things off. On our first date I took her to the bar at the Michel Hotel. But when I could see she, herself, wasn't very interested in drinking (she had only one beer the whole time – and just let it sit there and go flat), I thought I'd better forget about her.

I didn't ask her out again but she started timing it so she'd walk with me on my way to work in the mornings. She had a job in the grocery at Trites then and it's just the next block past Cash's place. She'd come up from behind and slip her hand into mine.

There wasn't much I could do but let it stay there and keep on walking. She was a looker all right; tall and slim, long dark hair, green eyes. She said she liked it that my eyes were the same colour. It meant we had something special. Next thing I knew, we were already in the habit of meeting uptown after supper, mostly to go to the show or, on the nights we'd already seen the picture, just to sit in the Diamond Grill and drink coffee and smoke. She was sure good at both those things. Once in a while I could talk her into going to the Olympos or the Roma but she'd always get mad because she said I'd leave her sitting alone at the table. Well, how's a guy supposed to be in a bar and not drink with the guys? It wasn't my fault ladies weren't allowed in the men's bar.

And another way she changed me. I had a kind of weird tooth in front. It got broke off and sort of twisted around when I was a kid, playing lacrosse. It was really just a half tooth, but it was no problem for me. It never hurt at all and I could eat real good with it. But Blaze said I'd look better if it was whole and white and evened up with the rest. She made me Saturday morning appointments and Doc MacDonald took what she called "an impression" before he yanked it. That way he had a little plate with one tooth on it all ready to slap right in. It was bloody sore for a long time and I hated the feel of the hard stuff covering the whole roof of my mouth. But Blaze said it looked great and that I'd get used to it. What she didn't know was that when she wasn't with me, especially when I was drinking after coming off shift, I took the damned thing out and kept it in my pocket.

There's no doubt about it, she was a gutsy girl. One Saturday night, way before we were married, I asked her if she wanted to go hunting with me next morning. I was going up Coal Creek Mountain to look for deer with my partner, my best friend Al. She said "Sure!" right away, even though I'd told her we'd have to get an early start, about five a.m. Well, I'd had a few drinks and when morning came and I was more sober, I just thought, I can't be bothered. Who wants a female along on a trip like that, and probably she wouldn't be up anyway, and I sure didn't want to wake up her old man on a Sunday morning. He was okay, I guess. Blaze kept saying we'd probably get along fine, mainly because we're both left-handed. She thought that was special somehow. But he was a lot bigger than me and I'd heard he could be real miserable, even when he was sober. Blaze insisted he didn't have a drinking problem. Said she'd never seen him drunk. Well, after all my experience around bars, believe me I can spot them – the ones that never look drunk. For sure, they're the worst kind. Anyway, we went without her. And do you know? When we didn't show up at five o'clock, she took off by herself. Walked down the tracks to McNab Draw and went right up Coal Creek Mountain, sticking to the creek bed. Right to the top. Now it's not as high as The Sisters, or Mount Hosmer, but it's got to be over seven thousand feet. Fernie's at thirty-three-o-five, so that means she climbed damn near four thousand. Some of the girls in town go up the slopes for blueberries in the fall but none of them would ever even think of actually climbing a mountain. I heard about it that night from Al's cousin, Reno. He was up there with his old man. He said they couldn't believe their eyes when she came walking up to them. The first thing she said was, "I thought Blackie and Al would be here. Are you with them?" They gave her a couple of their sandwiches. All she'd brought with her was a pepperoni sausage. She had the last bit of it in her hip pocket. Said she'd had a few drinks out of the creek on the way up. I told her after that I was sorry, that I thought she'd figure we weren't real serious about expecting her to come. But she didn't seem to mind, said she'd enjoyed the climb. She came down by herself too, but by way of the Saddle. An easier route. At least there was a trail.

Things weren't too bad while we were going together. Maybe because she didn't come to the bars with me. I mean, she wasn't around much when I got drunk. Oh, she'd get mad any time I'd leave her and go to the bar. But what else could I do? I'd get feeling desperate for a drink in the middle of a show (I'd tell her I was just going out for a smoke), or when we were in The Grill (I'd say I had to go to the john and then I'd slip out the back door to the alley). It ended up that she'd just go home. She said it made her real embarrassed, especially to be coming out of the show by herself. The next time I saw her she'd be mad for a while but it never lasted.

It was after we were married that she started making up stories about how bad it was. That was because then, no matter how drunk I got, I had to go home to her. Even when I was real quiet coming into the apartment, she always woke up. Or maybe she'd never even gone to sleep. Every morning after I'd been drinking she'd have something new. She started telling me about my foul language. She said I cursed her something awful, and she even repeated some of it just to show me. There's no way I believed it because that kind of language I might use, but only around guys. I sure didn't like to hear those words coming out of her mouth. And she said I accused her of shacking up with someone else, usually some *Wop* was what she said. Now that may be, because I thought the way she liked sex so much, maybe she'd had other guys. But *Wop*. That was one word I knew I'd never used. Anyway, if I'd said any of that stuff I would have remembered. I've always had a first-rate memory.

One of her stories was that I passed out on the floor. She said she tried to put a pillow under my head and a blanket over me but that I got so violent and loud she just had to leave me there, cold all night. But I don't believe that because when I woke up in the morning I was in bed the same as usual, all covered and warm.

Another story was that once when I came home I went right into the bathroom and ran the tub full. Next thing she heard me letting out a bunch of screams. She said I had the water boiling hot and then fell in. She might have been a bit right that time because I sure did have some bloody sore scald marks for the next few days. That was when we had the substitute caretaker, Roy Hicks, and he'd left the tanks in the basement turned up away too high. The way she told it though made it sound like I did it on purpose. And there was another burn story. It was about how I went to sleep on the bed with the sun lamp on me and didn't wake up. Well, that was probably partly true too because for a week or two afterwards you could see the outline of my hand across my stomach. It was burned red all around it. That was sore for a long time too.

But my shit on the kitchen chair? She didn't have to blame me for that. When she showed it to me in the morning I was so disgusted I took it right down the hallway and chucked it out on the fire escape balcony. Even that didn't make her happy. She said everyone would know whose it was because we were the only ones in the whole of the Queens Apartments who had that kind of chrome chair, the one with the tulip design on the plastic of the seat. I said how come there wasn't any crap on my clothes if it was me, and she said because I had all my clothes off. Then I said how come there wasn't any mess anywhere else in the apartment, and she said because she'd cleaned it up. Did I think she'd leave something like that in the kitchen? And I said then how come she left it on the chair? And she said so I'd know she wasn't making it up.

As I said, no one knows how much she has interfered with the way I was used to conducting my life. Lots of times there were fights in the bar and, I don't know, it seems to me you do what you can to help out the guy that's been hurt. But Blaze never saw it that way. The night I came home without my shirt on she wouldn't even believe that I'd ripped it in strips to put a tourniquet on Davey Albo's arm and bandage up his hand after Corky went for him with a knife. All she could think of was how she'd washed it and bleached it and ironed it so I'd have something nice to wear. Why did I need a white shirt to go to the bar anyway? She never once asked how Davey was doing or made any remark about how it was the decent thing to do.

All she talked about was why did I drink all the time. And she kept reminding me how I'd promised that once we were married and I had a home of my own I wouldn't need to any more. Well, that was a surprise to me too. I told her I was being honest when I made that promise, but that I just couldn't help it, any more than a dog can help rolling in something rotten, or a mama bear can keep from attacking anything that's threatening her young.

Of course, she didn't know about Al's old man and his wine. His cellar was a dug-out space under the kitchen. He had to raise a trap door and go down a short, straight ladder to bring up a bottle. He always said, "Here we go boys. The last of the wine." He said he needed Al and me to test it. Probably from the time we were seven or eight years old. I remember I was never sure if he was saying "test" or "taste," he had such a heavy Italian accent. Sometimes he didn't even use the right words. He would say he was going to "*rape* the side of the house" when he meant "rake," or "have a little *snake* in the afternoon" when he meant "snack." Anyway, I always went home with Al after school and we tested and tasted an awful lot of his old man's what they call *Dago Red*. It was real powerful. Every bottle he brought up was "the last of the wine." By the time we got to Al's mom's big platter of spaghetti, we were pretty tipsy.

And then there was *my* old man. "Drunk from the two wars," he always said. He got himself into the army, and overseas, in 1914. He was several years under age. In the Second War he stayed in Canada and was at a camp on the Prairies in charge of

German prisoners. Somewhere in between, he married my mother. She had two children before me and died when I was two, of alcohol poisoning, they said. Our grandmother wanted to raise us on the reserve but that stubborn old Scot wouldn't have it, brought us to town to his sister and her husband. Buddy died in the hospital of pneumonia when he was fourteen. Marie got away as soon as she could. Went down to the coast and became a prostitute. My old man has a room at the Proctor Hotel and is drunk pretty well every day.

So there we have it. I am the son of drinkers, one Indian, one Scotch. I think the world of Blaze, and I'm glad we're married, but how can she imagine, no matter how much I promised, that it's possible to give up the booze for her? Actually, she is interfering with more than just *my life*. She's meddling in a long-set-up pattern. It's like my grandmother used to say: when the recipe is in the pan and already in the oven, you can't take it out and unmix the ingredients and start over. That would take more power than Blaze has, or *we* have, even the two of us together.

It's probably just as well we don't have any kids. I remember not long after we were married and I was down visiting folks on the reserve. One of the old guys, the one they call Barney Google, said, "Well, Blackie, I hear you tied the knot." And when I said that was true, he nodded all smiles and went on, "And you got six kids already." Blaze laughed so hard about it when I told her. Right that day she started giving names to all the six, and calling me "Daddy." So then I memorized their names and began calling her "Mumma." It's kind of nice. Maybe we don't need kids.

C

TO THE BALL PARK

Ollie Daniels closed the door to his room and shuffled down the hall toward the stairs. Maybe the felt slippers weren't a good idea for such a long walk, but he couldn't stand the pressure of hard shoes around his toes any more. Yolanda greeted him as he reached the lobby. She liked to sit just outside the main door. If she kept moving her chair she could stay in the shade of the overhead sign all morning. It read: *1908 Roma Hotel Prop. C. Ciriani.* "Isn't it too soon to be off to the ball game already, Ollie?"

He stood for a moment with his hand on the back of her chair. "I like to be able to take my time gittin' there. Y'know how it is. Not so young as I used to be. Goin' on seventy now, both of us, isn't that right?"

"Yes, that's right. Me in August and you in October. Even so, like as not some of the team'll want to talk things over with you before the game."

"Oh, I'm not so sure about that." He turned and began moving along the sidewalk. "They got a real good coach now, Sam Eckersley. Some of them, the younger players, they don't even know me."

His direction along Victoria Avenue (Main Street) was to the northeast. He raised one hand to shield his eyes from the sun. He passed the Vogue Theatre. *Duel In The Sun* was playing. Jennifer Jones and Gregory Peck. He'd like to see that. Jennifer Jones was beautiful, and she could really act. He remembered *Song of Bernadette*. Anyone who could play a nun like that. Ralph Blakely appeared at the open door with a broom. "Early for the ball game isn't it, Ollie?" he said.

Ollie smiled and tipped his cap. "I like to take my time gittin' there."

He crossed Hemmil Street and stopped at the empty lot on the other side to look at the bulletin board. The important news items of the town usually made their first appearance there. Dance at the I.O.O.F Hall Saturday. Miners' Picnic a week from Sunday at the North End Grounds. Old Cyrus Brinks dead. Finally. His ninety-seventh year. He looked ready to go when I first came to town, Ollie thought. Almost thirty years ago.

As he moved toward the Imperial Bank, something ragged caught his eye. He stepped into the empty lot for a better look. It was a bramble-like plant straggling out of the rocks piled along the brick wall of the bank. The leaves were puny things, not even a good green, and there were flattened, hooked prickles along the stem, and some little fruit things, like berries. Some were a dark reddish brown, a dozen or so were black. He picked the black ones, put them in his mouth. Well, I'll be darned. They're blackcaps! Haven't seen any of those since Saltspring Island. As he walked past the bowling alley, he moved his tongue around the familiar taste. Imagine them growing here. Well, I'll be darned.

Along the front of the Trites Wood Company he noted the five separate departments: Drygoods, then Men's Wear. The grocery in the middle. Beyond that, the hardware, with the Ladies' Wear next to the West Kootenay Power office on the corner. As he crossed Wood street and stepped onto the curb at the Bank of Commerce, a voice called to him from across Main. "Hey, Ollie." It was Jack Cleary, out on the sidewalk with a bucket and rag, washing the front window of the Meat Market. "A little early for the game, isn't it?"

Ollie yelled back. "I like to take my time gittin' there." He was still tasting the blackcaps. Along that whole block – past the Diamond Grill, The Trinity Hotel, Geo. Rahal's Ready-to-Wear, and Cash Grocery – and even across Cox Street and into the next block – the Shell Service Station, the Fernie Bakery, and on to

Wilson's Transfer – he was working out the puzzle of the blackcap bush. It was an unlikely place for it to grow, but there it was, struggling but alive, even with berries on it. There was a word he wanted, something to describe its being there. Niche. That was it. The plant had found its own, proper niche.

He shuffled a little faster now. He was beyond the business blocks, passing houses that were along that end of Main. Thinking: I'm like that bush. The family out of Missouri; underground railroad to Canada; farming and living free on Saltspring Island. That was their niche.

I came here in twenty-two, the year the Crow's Nest Pass Coal Company took over the sponsorship of the Fernie team. I was near forty then. Baseball was my niche. All those years playing with the Negro League in the U.S. and then coaching in this town. A real rocky place. But by 1925 the Fernie Falcons were one of the finest teams in the west. We even defeated Edmonton for the Alberta championship. We had an awful struggle, got defeated by that powerful aggregation at New Westminster. A major setback. We didn't get the western title but we kept trying. Like growing out of rock. And then the war. No baseball during the war. In forty-seven the Fernie Baseball Association was formed, but by then I was too old to start coaching again. Now the Falcons are in the reorganized Crow's Nest Pass League – a five-team city league: Pincher Creek, Hillcrest, Blairmore, Coleman, Michel/Natal. All from Alberta except the Michel/Natal team. No wonder Fernie wanted to secede from B. C. and join Alberta. Now the team's into all that, and here I'm seeing myself as a blackcap bush. Well, at least I never had to settle for Red Cap. As he laughed inwardly at his own little joke, a voice startled him out of his reverie. "Hey there, Ollie!" It was old man Martinelli, sitting on a stool just inside the entrance to his store. He had a fly swatter in his hand. "Aren't you a bit early for the game?" He looked at his watch. "Like, say, about two and a half hours?"

"Yeah, I guess. I like to take my time gittin' there, but I must be just about to the North End, if I'm at your place already."

"Well, you got some time to kill. Come on in and have a pop. And you can tell me what you think the Falcons are going to do to those guys from Pincher Creek."

When Ollie pried the cap off his Pepsi, he still had the taste of blackcaps on his tongue. His thoughts went back to the bush growing out of the rocks. Martinelli said, "The way you're smiling, I guess you're predicting a good win. Right?"

"Yeah, I sure am. What's more, I predict they won't get a single hit off our new pitcher." He put the bottle to his mouth, saying to himself, I sure can't tell him what I'm really smiling about: talk about being a big black frog in a little pond. Yeah, I got my niche all right.

CHAPTER FIFTEEN

BLAZE SPEAKS

No WAS WHAT I SAID TO BLACKIE AT FIRST OVER SEVEN YEARS AGO but then I changed my mind and said Yes or maybe I said I guess so and here it is a nice sunny Sunday in May but theres no chance of going anywhere or doing anything interesting with Blackie still in bed sleeping off last nights stupidity why cant I get him to stop drinking? there must be something wrong with me Al has stopped already for Jenny and theyre just going together not even engaged just talking about it is there some secret that I don't know about? maybe something to do with sex? I've heard some wives or girlfriends keep saying no until they get their way whatever it is they want I could never do that its not that I am overly crazy about sex or anything but to use it that way would be pretty low or unnatural at least unnatural thats the way I have always thought about flirting too I would rather be direct with a person well I mean a guy not resort to some behaviour that was calculating well growing up with aunts and uncles the way I did I never got anything very clear about how boys feel about things even girls or about how to act with a boy Blackie was my first and it was easy with him because he made it seem very nice he said it was perfectly okay because we loved each other he even set up a little hose that he fitted to the bathroom tap in the place where I stayed so I could rinse out afterwards and that way he said there was no fear that he would be knocking me up before we were married that's a laugh now married six years and no baby except for him thats what Lee Choy told me I don't need any baby because I have got Blackie and maybe I do withhold sex sometimes thats what they call it withholding sex but its only because he smells so bad with stink coming from every orifice I swear even the pores of his skin thank goodness he is never interested in having sex when he is actually drunk the drinking is probably enough of a satisfaction for him so here I sit on a May morning with nothing to do but put these few last rolls of pictures in the album I am glad I took this one of him and my rapist hobo the news on the CBC that morning was all about the escaped rapist and all they knew was that he had turned up in Creston and raped a young woman and then left they warned people to be on the lookout for a short burly man in a plaid shirt and there was me looking out the window with that clear view of the tracks from the fourth floor and didnt I see someone terribly suspicious coming out of one of the boxcars that were standing on the siding just down from our apartment building I could see he had on a green plaid shirt and dark pants and then when I got the binoculars out I could see that he looked really seedy burly too and he was going back and forth into the boxcar just as though he lived there and one time he came out with a shiny tin can and went over to a puddle by the other set of tracks and filled up the can and took it back next he gathered up some twigs and dry leaves and got a little fire going he held the tin can over the weak movement of flames for about five minutes then he set it on the ground and rummaged in his pack beside the boxcar and next thing I knew he was shaving he was doing it with one hand because he held up a tiny mirror in the other I watched for a long time and when two little boys went walking down the main tracks not far from him I thought maybe I should alert someone especially when he beckoned to them and they went over to him but he put something in the hand of one of them and they left right away and I watched long enough to see them come back they brought him a bagful of something I think maybe it was chips or Cheesies and maybe chocolate bars well I became increasingly concerned and I called to Blackie that I was going down there to see who he was and I told him I thought he was the escaped rapist Blackie was battling a hangover that morning too just like today but he got up and said he couldnt let me go down there alone and that he would come with me he downed a raw egg first to make himself feel better when we approached the boxcar there was no sign of any life but I knew he was in there because of looking with the glasses the last minute before we left Blackie made me stay back a bit while he went to the opening then he yelled well for fuck's sake if it isn't old Dumdum I havent seen you for a coon's age what are you up to man? and he hauled himself up into the boxcar and told me to come on it was just Dumdum one of the Christafio brothers and he hauled me up too the man looked pretty scruffy even though he was clean-shaven but Blackie knew him so I thought it must be okay and he explained that he had been riding the rails for quite a while he was just passing through Fernie and he would appreciate it if we didnt let on to the family because he was kind of on the outs with them and he didnt want any handouts nothing would do but Blackie had to insist that he come up to the apartment at suppertime and fill up on my spaghetti he said youve never tasted anything like it she uses Mrs Megales recipe well maybe you have because your mother but he didn't finish that sentence he turned to me you wont mind making up a big platterful will you Mumma? I don't mind that he calls me Mumma but I would rather he didnt in front of anyone else its more of a private thing so Dumdum hung around for a few days and Blackie made sure he came for supper every night until I guess he figured it was time to leave and he hopped another freight I felt good that Blackie was so generous and hospitable he even helped with the cooking and washing up here is the picture of the two of them I took at the boxcar when we went back down to visit him for the longest time after that Blackie kept singing "On a sunny day/in the month of May/ a burly bum came hikin'" he knew I liked that Big Rock Candy song Babe and I used to sing it a lot together he changed the next lines to tease me about my first impression of Dumdum "rape on his mind/ he couldn't find / nobody to his likin'" Blackie is funny he can be real miserable but he can be real generous too here is a picture of him a flash that I took when he came home from the bar late one night with no shirt on he had torn it up for bandages when Davey Albo got hurt in a fight with Corky it didnt matter to him that it was his best white shirt although why he has to wear a white shirt to the bar I don't know they take so much bleaching and ironing to make them look good I wish he would save them for something special now heres a picture of him with the two little Pierson girls I took it at Edwards Lake that Sunday two weeks ago when he was feeling good enough to go somewhere it's a nice close-up of them all I wish it was in colour so his green eyes would show up he sure is nice looking being so dark with green eyes its too bad we don't have kids he is so good with them except it wouldn't do with his drinking but I remember the time just before Christmas when he told these two Evelyn and Susan that he had seen Santa out in the South Country in his sleigh and that Santa had told him to tell them he was coming with something special for the Pierson sisters they were absolutely wide-eyed and they hung onto his neck the both of them and asked him all sorts of questions about Santa and especially about his reindeer theres a song that always sticks in my mind it could have been written about him

>
> Everywhere you go
> Sunshine follows you
> Everywhere you go
> Skies are always blue
> Children love you
> They seem to know
> You bring roses
> Out of the snow
> The whole world says 'hello'
> Everywhere you go

thats him all right he livens things up wherever he goes the way they say 'lights up a room' is right for him I have seen it so many times when people are sitting around not knowing what else to say to each other and in he comes and right away everyones talking and laughing Im probably remembering the early stage of his drinking hes like that to start with and then he gets a bit meaner a bit more aggressive until hes picked a fight with someone or is at least cursing and swearing I wonder what the difference is between those two words why we always use them together it's a shame that he spoils everything by drinking its as though hes two different people when he is sober he cant believe all the things I tell him hes said and done he doesnt even believe that he uses foul language to me when he sobers up hes so sorry for it all and really means it when he says he wont drink any more its got such a hold on him his Aunt Flossie told me it was Mr D'Amico that got him started he was giving wine to him and Al when they were just kids I try to make him agree to get help but he says he doesnt need help he can do it himself once he put himself on the 'Indian list' (ha for that expression) and it just ended up with him getting friends fined for buying booze for him and once I appealed to Dr East that was when he was seeing him anyway about bad pains in his stomach Dr East agreed to talk to him and as it turned out he put a real scare into him by telling him that because of the condition of his stomach he wouldnt have long to live if he kept up drinking well that worked for a little under two weeks when he decided if he was going to die anyway he might as well drink up to the end after a few months he thought it was quite funny that he wasn't dead yet I can see the good in him and I can see the bad in him I love the one side of him and am disgusted with the other Im afraid as hell when he gets violent especially with a knife or a gun and something that really bothers me is that I can see him bringing out the bad in me heres an example right in this picture I bought him a record player for his last birthday and a whole album of

Jolson records because thats who he enjoys most hes always singing his songs doing take-offs on his style he is pretty good too especially with 'Sonny Boy' and "Mammy' he makes his voice tremble and warble just like Jolsons he loved the present of course and he made me take a few pictures of it with him holding up the album so the printing would show he played the records over and over which was okay except that one night he came in drunk and brought Al with him so he could play them for him I was desperate to get some sleep because it was a Friday night and I always work at the dental office Saturday mornings I asked him several times to shut it off or turn it down at least and each time I went out of the bedroom I could see that both he and Al were getting drunker and drunker I went out again in the middle of 'Goodbye Tootsie Goodbye' Al was passed out lolled back on the chesterfield and Blackie was at the fridge pouring two more drinks I grabbed up the arm that holds the needle and I twisted and twisted it I was surprised it took so long to break I thought he would go for the rifle or at least grab me but he just laughed real loud and said thats the way to do it Mumma shut down that Tootsie for good he raised his glass to me gulped down the drink and started singing 'Id walk a million miles for one of your smiles my Maaaaaaaaammeeeeee' back in bed I was shaking with anger but maybe with another feeling too it was kind of exciting just to wreck something but it was mixed up with being sorry because it was my present to him and he liked it so much but was that really me? I had never before destroyed anything intentionally in my entire life how can I stay on in this kind of situation? how can I possibly get out of it? maybe it has been my fault all along I shouldnt have eased myself into his life the way I did he would have been content alone he would have kept drinking the rest of his life but hes doing that with me in it anyway I should have known when I saw he was left-handed like my dad even in the church I could have said no you promised not to drink before the wedding and there you are winking at me coming down the aisle already well on your way why couldn't I have had the guts to do that? I was too worried about everybody else is it too late to worry about myself? no one ever let on I might deserve any better than this no one told me anything about making bad choices no one told me anything about alcohol and what it can do I want to be more in this world than the wife of a town drunk I cant end up saying yes to this kind of life no I say no I won't stay NO.

CHAPTER SIXTEEN

WINTER NIGHT

SCENE ONE: Blaze and Blackie's apartment

We have a livingroom which opens, upstage right, into a kitchen area. A low counter running out from the right wall is even with the chesterfield which is against the back wall. Between the couch and the counter is access space to a kitchenette. Along the right wall there is a draped window with a long radiator under it. That's about all we need to know. YOU can put in a couple of armchairs, a coffee table, a few lamps, some bright cushions, two large pictures. To the left, a door to a hall where hanging coats are visible. Another door on left wall leads to the bedroom.

    Blackie comes in from the hall dressed for cold weather: heavy car coat, heavy boots, wool work pants, wool cap with ear lugs down. He has been drinking enough to affect his speech and his movements. Actually, we hear him calling *before* he enters. "Mumma. Come on Mumma. I need your help." Then he enters. "Hey, Mumma. You in bed already? Come on, get up. I need you." He crosses to the kitchen and begins taking bottles of beer out of the fridge, putting them one by one into his coat pockets, talking all the while. "Come on. Get up for old Daddy. We gotta go out."

    We hear Blaze's sleepy voice off right. "What on earth for? What time is it anyway?"

    "I don't know. Come on, come on." He tries to put another bottle in his pocket but there isn't room. He puts it back into fridge and slams the door. "We gotta go help your old man."

    "What?"

"We gotta go help your old man I said. He's broke down and he's got Frenchie Brisson with him and he promised he'd drive him home after the bars closed."

As he walks to the bedroom door, Blaze appears tying her dressing gown. Her hair is up in pin curls with a net tied over it. "Frenchie Brisson? You mean from Coal Creek? Well, that's Dad's business. I don't see why I..."

"Yeah. He's been drinking ever since God knows when. And your old man said he'd drive him up tonight. Come on, Honey, get dressed."

"What on earth for?" She looks at her watch. " It's after one! I'm not going anywhere." She sits on the couch.

Blackie follows her. "Look, your old man's *broke down*, I said. He needs a push home."

"And why couldn't you help him? Were you too drunk to drive? If you both have to sit in the beer parlour until it closes, I don't see why I should have to get up at this hour and..." She feels in her pocket, takes out a package of cigarettes.

"I'm not that drunk!" He bends over her and takes a cigarette.

"Well, why do you have to come home waking me up?" She strikes a match and they both light up. "*You* can push him."

"No I can't. His goddam car quit in front of the police station. I was following right behind and when I got out to see what was wrong, that bloody bull was there, Sandy, and if I'd even got back in again he'd have nailed me just because I had a few drinks."

"You mean you left the car there?"

"You bet. I would've been in jail by now if I'd touched that wheel. Come on, you gotta get dressed and push him down to his place."

"I'm not going out in this cold. It's more than twenty below. If a bunch of drunks can't look after themselves..."

266

"What drunks?"

"You for one."

"I am not. You think just because I had a few beers..."

"You went out at six-thirty. That's over five hours just sitting in the Roma."

"We weren't in the Roma. You should know your dad's favourite place is the Castle."

"Well, the Castle then. What's the difference? You couldn't sit in either one for half an hour and come out sober."

"I'm not drunk! And neither's your old man."

"He never gets drunk."

"Oh yeah? He sure does."

"I've never seen him drunk."

"You're always saying that. I've told you and told you. He gets as damned pye-eyed as anybody, only he never shows it."

"Well, that's something at least. He doesn't disgrace everyone, like you do."

"Those bloody big guys never show it. He has two to my one all the time."

Blaze butts her cigarette in the ashtray in front of her. "I don't know why he always comes for *you* to go drinking with him. Staggering around, getting into fights. I wish he'd leave you at home."

"Who gets into fights?" He takes off his cap and throws it on the couch beside her.

"You do."

Blackie assumes a menacing stance and shouts, "Goddam you anyway. I do not."

"You've never seen my dad in a fight."

"Oh, for God's sake. No, I haven't seen *DAD* in a fight. But right now he's stuck up there in front of the cops and you just sit here. Come on!" He grabs her arm.

She pushes him away, then stands. "I don't see why I have to get dressed and walk all the way uptown in this cold. I'm going back to bed."

"You can't even help your precious old man. You're always talking about him like he was the only beJesus man that ever lived and then you can't even help him after he sent me home to get you."

"What? That's different." She moves toward the bedroom door. "Why didn't you tell me that in the first place?"

"And he's got Frenchie and all those groceries."

"What groceries?"

"Frenchies's. What he got yesterday."

"You mean he hasn't been home since yesterday?'

"Well, he got to drinking when he hit town..."

"Just a minute." Blaze grabs Blackie by the arm and turns him to face her. " Why didn't Yvonne come to town? She never lets him do the shopping."

"Says she's sick. The kids too. So she had to send him. All the guys have been buying him drinks, it's so long since he's been down."

"And he's been in town since yesterday?" She moves closer to the door.

"Yeah. And of course he missed the train up so your dad promised to take him home." As Blaze exits, he calls after her. "He's afraid some of the stuff'll get frozen sitting in the car."

Blaze enters with a bundle of clothes over her arm. "Why didn't you say so in the first place?" She puts the clothes down on a chair.

"I tried to tell you." Blaze takes off her dressing gown and begins to dress, pulling panties and then slacks on under her nightie. As she begins to remove the nightie, Blackie indicates the bundle on the chair. "You'd better put something warmer than that on. It's a bugger out there." Blaze snatches up the rest of the clothing and exits. "You gotta dress up warm, Mumma." He walks over to the chesterfield, picks up his cap, and puts it on, settling the lugs over his ears.

Blaze enters barefoot pulling a black turtleneck sweater over a plaid shirt. Then she tucks the shirt into the pants. "Why didn't you tell me right away it was Dad's idea?" She crosses right and snatches a pair of socks from the radiator. She puts them on while stepping back left. "Poor Yvonne up there alone. And pay day yesterday. I bet they don't have a thing in the house to eat. And him drinking for two days." She moves into the hallway and steps into a pair of winter boots. "They should have moved out of Coal Creek years ago. It's like a ghost town up there. Those poor kids. We'd better hurry."

Blackie follows her to the hallway, pulling on gloves and patting both pockets. "They'll all be sleeping now but, anyway, you're right Mumma."

Blaze takes a heavy coat off a hook, also a wool scarf, and puts them on, winding the scarf over her hair net and around her neck. "Well, at least we can try to get him home in time for them to have a decent breakfast. Come on."

They exit and the door slams behind them.

SCENE TWO: Tare's house

We can use the same scenario since the actual layout of the place is not important. We still need a livingroom with a view into a kitchen and an entranceway. YOU can dress down the properties to reflect Tare's lifestyle; e.g. remove lamps (bare ceiling bulbs will do) and tables (except for the one visible in the kitchen beyond); throw a worn grey wool blanket over the couch and faded floral covers over the one armchair; replace cushions with ordinary pillows, some without pillow cases; replace drapes with white plastic curtains, and pictures with calendars and plaques depicting game animals. There is a portable record player on a wooden box in front of a large radiator. Draped on the rad is a mixture of wool work socks and greying tea towels. A clothesline is strung across the far wall of the kitchen with a man's khaki workshirt hanging on it and a few handkerchiefs of the same colour. In the hallway, beside heavy coats and a tall black cowboy hat, hangs a rifle by a leather sling, a pair of snowshoes, and an old hackamore (rawhide halter).

There is the sound of a door opening, the stamping of feet. The overhead light switches on. Blackie enters first and walks toward the kitchen. As the others take off their coats in the hall (Tare collects them and hangs them up), they are only partially visible. Blaze is the only one who removes boots, stepping out of them just inside the doorway. Meanwhile, Blackie has opened the fridge, takes bottles from his pockets, one by one, and puts them in.

The other two are still off left. Tare calls out jovially, "Come on there, Frenchie. Let's have your coat. You'll get warmer with it off. Go on in and sit down."

Blackie keeps out the last bottle, takes an opener from a pocket, moves back into the livingroom opening the bottle and drinking from it. "Who's having a beer? Want one Frenchie?" When Frenchie nods he goes back to the fridge for another.

Frenchie collapses onto the couch, holding his head, saying, "Oh Jesus, Jesus." He still has his slouch cap on, his boots are snowy. He is wearing dark pants, a red plaid shirt with a grey sleeveless sweater over it. He looks untidy and not very clean. He takes the beer when Blackie hands it to him but he seems hardly aware of it in his hand. "Oh Jesus."

Blackie sits beside him. "Nothing like a good cold beer to warm a guy up, eh Frenchie?" He offers him a cigarette but, when Frenchie doesn't notice, he takes one himself and lights it.

Tare and Blaze enter. She is hugging herself from the cold. Tare has an arm around her shoulder. He wears dark pants and a solid black Western shirt with pearl buttons, and a black neckerchief with a large silver keeper at the throat. "Well, you got us home, Girl. You sure know how to handle that wheel, even with all the snow. I'm glad it took only the one good push to get me started." He guides her over to the chair by the counter. "You sit right down. I've got something that'll warm you up." She sits huddled in the chair as he goes to the kitchen. "And put on a pair of those socks there. Your feet'll be cold on the linoleum." She reaches forward, takes one sock from the radiator and starts to pull it on.

Blackie raises his half-empty bottle. "Well, we made her, Frenchie. Thanks to the captain there. Sure a good thing I taught her to drive, eh?"

"You did *not* teach me to drive."

"Well, I sure as hell did. In that old Chevy coupe we had."

"You did not. I learned on my uncle's truck before I ever met you. Before I came to Fernie even." She reaches for the other sock.

"Some learning then. That was just farm driving. I had to unlearn you and start all over. And if you think that wasn't a job, Frenchie. It was all she could do to steer."

Frenchie leans forward unsteadily and sets his bottle on the floor. He slumps back into place, shaking his head and blinking his eyes.

"Oh, don't be ridiculous." Blaze has both socks on now. She straightens up. "How many times have I had to go bring you home from the bar because you were too drunk to drive?"

"Well, at least I taught you how to back up. God, Mumma, remember that highway sign you backed into? You tore it right out."

"I did not."

"Then how come I got that letter from the government? Twelve dollars they said. Twelve dollars for one goddam road marker. That's what kind of driver you were."

Tare returns with Blaze's drink. "This girl's one of the best drivers in town, always has been. Here you go, Blaze."

Blaze takes the glass, raises it to her nose. "Oh no, Dad. I really don't want rum. Could I make some coffee?"

"There's some in the pot by the sink if you want to warm it up. I made it fresh for supper."

Blaze gets up with the glass. She looks at Blackie as she passes him. "Are you going to sit with your coat on all night?"

Blackie places bottle between his feet, struggles out of coat without getting up, drops it on floor. Removes cap and drops it on top of coat, takes up bottle again. "Well, here's to your groceries, Frenchie."

Tare sets his glass on top of radiator, sits in Blaze's chair and begins to unlace his boots. "It looks like Frenchie's had it." He calls to Blaze. "With the way my car's acting, maybe we'd better run him up in your car."

Blaze comes out of kitchen, takes cigarettes out of Blackie's shirt pocket, takes one for herself, gives Tare one, lights them both. "Yvonne'll be worried sick, and her sick already. You don't think any of the stuff got frozen?"

"No, I checked it over. I think it's okay. We'll have to change it all over to your car." He sets boots by radiator.

Blackie leans over and shakes Frenchie, who has dozed off. "Come on Frenchie, drink up your beer."

Blaze says, "Oh leave him alone, at least until we decide what to do." She turns to Tare. "Do you want to drive us home and then take him up? We can come over in the morning for the car."

Blackie flings an arm forward. "That car's not going anywhere without me. I'll drive him home myself."

Blaze turns to him. "Don't be so stupid. You couldn't drive around the block, the shape you're in, never mind up that road, at night, in all this snow."

Blackie jumps up. "Whaddya mean? You've never seen me when I couldn't drive."

"Humph, not much." She turns toward kitchen, notices his feet. "Can't you get out of those boots? Look at the mess you're making of Dad's floor, melting all over it."

Blackie lifts feet, looks at floor, begins to pull off boots, muttering "Jesus fucking Christ."

Blaze returns with a cloth. Tare jumps up and grabs it from her. "Never mind, Girl. Give it to me." He bends down and mops floor as Blackie holds feet out of the way, boots now in hand. Tare takes boots from him, places them at end of couch where there is a spread newspaper. On way back, he mops around Frenchie's feet, lifting first one, then the other. Frenchie does not stir. Tare reaches for drink on rad and, making sure Blaze is not looking, hands it to Blackie, winking at him. Then he goes to kitchen, watches as Blaze pours coffee. "Got it hot eh?" He wrings out cloth at sink and hangs it on clothesline. "How about putting on Kathleen Mavourneen for me?"

"Aren't you sick of that yet? You've been playing it steady ever since it came." She moves to the player, setting her coffee on the rad. She crouches on floor looking through records.

"You don't think I'd ever get sick of that, do you? You know how long I was trying to get it." He comes back with drink for himself, sits in chair right, then realizes she is looking for record. "It's on the machine, Girl." He gets up again at once. "Oh Blackie, I didn't get you a drink. Here, you have this one." He hands it to him, goes back to kitchen. Blaze shoots a disapproving glance at Blackie. She starts the record, John McCormack's 'Kathleen Mavourneen,' and stands, sipping at coffee. The music begins. Blackie keeps time with his glass, Tare sings along as he crosses from kitchen to chair right.

Frenchie sits up and opens his eyes. "What the Christ's going on? Oh Blackie, that's you. What am I doing at your place?"

"No, this is Tare's. We're all at Tare's place."

"I thought it was your place." He looks around. "Oh, there you are, Tare." Tare raises his glass to him. "And Blaze too." She gives him a mock wave.

Blackie grabs Frenchie's bottle from the floor and gives it to him. "Hey Frenchie, have a beer!" He downs the last of his own drink and gets up. "Think I'll have one myself." He goes to the fridge.

"Don't you drink any more." Blaze turns to follow him but Tare takes her wrist and pulls her down to the arm of his chair.

"Don't worry so much about him. He's drunk already anyway. I'll see that he gets home."

Frenchie rubs his eyes and takes a swallow of beer. "Turn that damn thing down! Christ!"

Blaze moves toward the player but Tare stops her. "You worry too much about everything, Girl. This is my house and my music and he's too drunk anyway." He raises his voice. "How do you like that for singing, eh Frenchie? Not every day you get to hear McCormack."

Blackie returns with beer, sits in same place. "Hey Dad, why don't you play some Wilf Carter for us? That's what you like, isn't it, Frenchie? Some of that real good yodelling?"

"Yeah." He tries to get up but falls back. "You got any Wilf Carter, Tare? Anything'd be better than that crappy Irish stuff."

"You boys just never mind, and listen. You'll never hear anything better. There isn't another McCormack record in town, maybe not even in the whole country." He puts his arm around Blaze. "My girl ordered it special for me from England."

"Whaddya mean? You don't go ordering goddam Irishmen from England. Isn't that right, Blackie?"

"Never mind asking Blackie. He doesn't know. This here record's from England. That's where they got all the rare ones. And it took over two months to get here."

They sit silently for a few minutes as the record ends, except for Tare who sings along. Blackie leans forward keeping time with feet and head, Frenchie yawns and scratches his stomach, Blaze moves toward player, ready to lift needle.

"Put her on again, Blaze." She looks at him questioningly, he nods vigorously. She starts it again, turns it lower, then crosses left and exits. As soon as she leaves, Tare gets up, turns the volume up again, and fills Blackie's glass and his own. "Guess you'd better keep off the hard stuff, eh Frenchie? If you want to make it home tonight. Come on, Blackie, drink up."

"God, Blaze'll blow her top." He drinks hastily.

"That's the trouble with you, Blackie. You pay too much attention to her. A guy should be able to drink when he feels like it, especially after he's been in the mine all week."

"Oh sure, sure." Blackie gulps down some more.

Tare pours more into his glass. "Come on, enjoy it. Tomorrow's Sunday. You don't have any plans, do you?"

He moves back to kitchen as Blaze enters, retying headscarf at back of neck. "It's nearly two-thirty." She sits in chair left.

"Yeah." Tare comes in from kitchen. "We'll get going right away." He crosses left, places hand on Frenchie's knee as he goes by. "We'll get you home, Frenchie. Right away, old man." He exits left.

Blackie gets up and goes to the player. "I'm gonna turn this bloody thing off, Blaze."

"No, leave it. It's just about finished. Turn it down a bit if you like, but let it finish."

"Him and his goddam Kathleen Mavourneen. I wish he'd stuff it."

"Oh, Blackie. Let him have something. You know how much it means to him."

"Yeah. And you're the one had to go and get it for him. It's all we ever hear." The record ends. "Thank God." He bends low to shut it off, almost falling, but steadies himself with a hand on the floor. He goes back to couch and sits, touches hand to shirt pocket. "Hey, Blaze, where'd you put my cigarettes?"

"In the kitchen, I think." She gets up and goes right.

Frenchie straightens up. "I got cigarettes. Here." They take one each, light up. Blaze returns, lighting one herself, and drops the pack beside Blackie.

"Hey, Frenchie! I wanted to show you the old man's rifle. You've never seen it, have you?" Blackie jumps up, crosses to the hall. He takes down the rifle with both hands, cigarette in mouth.

"No, I've never seen it, but no gun's better than that thirty-ought-six of mine. I got two bucks with her already, right this fall. Yep. Two nice big bucks. Only one of them didn't have any horns." He tries to laugh, but falls forward, then catches himself.

"Look at that, eh? Isn't she a beauty?" Blackie sits, lays rifle across his knees, feels along the stock, then strokes the barrel. "Did you ever see anything like it?"

Frenchie mutters, "A magnum eh? Too much shocking power. It'd blow a deer to pieces."

"Sure. It's the only goddamned three hundred magnum in town. And he just got this scope last week. We're going out with her next weekend. This scope's high power, that's what it is." He puts the butt to his shoulder and sights in on Blaze. "Hi, Mumma."

"I don't know how you can even see me the way you're waving it around." She moves from side to side, laughing.

"Just hold still now and I'll get a bead on you. There you are, one big blur. Hi, Mumma."

Tare enters swiftly, grabs rifle from Blackie. "For God's sake! You bloody fool! Don't you ever let me catch you doing that again!" Blackie picks up his bottle, takes it to kitchen, stands looking at fridge. "And Blaze. You know better than to sit there like that."

"Why? I know you never have it loaded in the house. And I saw him take it down. Anyway, he's always careful with guns."

"Careful, my eye! How can a bloody drunk be careful?"

"Dad!"

"Well, that's what he is and the sooner you realize it the better." He holds rifle with barrel pointing to floor, nods toward it. "You never know what can happen." He turns toward hall.

Frenchie sits forward. "That's quite a rifle you got, Tare. But it's too bloody powerful, isn't it? I was just telling Blackie. Too much shocking power, I said. You take my thirty-ought-six now. It's just right for deer but it's got enough of a jolt for a moose even. You'd blow a deer's guts right out with that thing of yours."

"No. If you get a good clean hit you're okay. The shoulder, or the head. Of course, if you get a belly shot. But that's bad with any gun, even your thirty-ought-six. And it depends on your range too. You don't want to hit anything too close with this."

"But good God, Tare. You can't go choosing your range. You take a bloody big buck comes out of the bush right under your nose. You gonna say 'Stand off aways there you big bastard because I got a gun here that's too high-powered this close'?" He laughs and takes another drink. "That's good eh? Just let him know you don't want his meat buggered up and he'll oblige." He laughs again.

Blaze has been following the conversation with mock interest. Now she settles herself in chair sideways, yawning.

"Yeah, but remember, the closer you are the better chance you have for a good head shot. You're not damaging any meat that way."

Blackie has been following the conversation seriously, reacting to each remark, and can no longer remain quiet. He moves in from kitchen. "You're forgetting about that two-seventy of mine. You talk about wanting shocking power, and wanting distance. Well, you sure got both with a two-seventy. There's enough wham at four hundred yards to drop a bloody grizzly."

Tare turns to him. "You haven't got a scope. You couldn't hit a freight train at four hundred yards."

"I could so." He mimes holding a gun. "I just allow for the trajectory, and I sure know that rifle. How do you think I got that grizzly two years ago? And she shoots clean too. Right through a white-tail without a mark."

Frenchie has turned toward him too. "Whaddaya mean, not a mark? The goddam bullet's gotta make a hole."

"Yeah, but you can hardly see it. Not like your thirty-ought-six or that bloody elephant gun there." He points toward hall where Tare is hanging up the magnum. "You get a hole that big (indicates with both hands about a saucer size) going in, and she blasts one like that (indicates a hole several feet in diameter) coming out the other side."

"Not with mine you don't."

"You get close range, even three hundred yards, and you do. You blast a hole that big." He indicates again.

"Not me!"

As Tare crosses to kitchen, Blaze turns toward them. "Are we going to get Frenchie home or are you going to argue guns all night?"

"Isn't that right, Mumma? Didn't you see me drop that whitetail last fall at about two hundred yards and you could hardly tell there was a mark. Isn't that right, Mumma?" Blaze nods, over-emphasizing her agreement. "See? She knows. She can tell you. If that'd been your thirty-ought-six there'd have been no deer left."

"You're crazy. But anyway, mine's got shocking power at longer range than yours."

"It has not! I told you about that bear. If I can drop a grizzly at over four hundred yards, well, that's shocking power all right."

In the background, Tare takes down hankies and shirt from the line, folds shirt with hankies inside, rolls it all up slowly as he watches and listens.

"You're a goddam liar." Frenchie tries to get up but rolls sideways. "You can't beat that rifle of mine and you know it. You're just praising up the two-seventy because that's what you happen to own."

Blackie turns away. "Oh what a stupid asshole. You're not even worth talking to. You're nothing but a stupid asshole!"

Tare whirls out of the kitchen, catches Blackie's jaw with his fist. Blackie piles over on top of Frenchie. He says, "What the Christ!" and pushes at Blackie. Blaze springs to her feet.

Blackie gets up dazed, shaking his head and holding his face. "What the hell are you trying to pull off?"

Tare stands menacingly. "You can't talk to Frenchie like that!"

"Whaddaya mean? Can't a couple of guys have a friendly little argument?"

"Look, you're not going to talk to a guest of mine like that."

"A what? A guest? You mean Frenchie?"

Frenchie has managed to right himself. "Hell, Tare. I'm no guest. He wasn't doing no harm."

Blaze has been staring at Tare, unbelieving. "What got into you, Dad? I've never seen you..."

"No one is going to come into my house and call my friends names. Not in my place. No sir."

"What did he say that was all that bad? I don't think.... Well, you know what it's like when any of you gets going on rifles."

"No one's going to talk like that to Frenchie in my house." Tare crosses room and exits left.

Blackie sits down and Blaze puts a hand on his shoulder. "Are you all right? Let me have a look."

He shakes her off. "Yeah, I'm all right. Your old man just clobbered me, that's all." He gets up grinning and staggers to the fridge. "I don't know what the hell for, but your old man sure clobbered me." He opens the fridge door. "Hey Frenchie, let's have a beer to get us in shape."

"Yeah. Let's get drunk and be somebody."

The two settle themselves on the couch with the beer. Blaze goes to kitchen, refills coffee cup, returns to chair. After a few sips, she sets the cup down. Absentmindedly she feels tea towels on rad, begins folding them. She rolls socks into pairs.

Blackie holds hand to jaw. "I don't know what's wrong with him. I've never done anything to him."

"Aw hell, he's just drunk." Frenchie settles back, closes his eyes.

Blaze answers immediately. "He is not drunk. You can see by the way he walks, and the way he talks. It's just that he always keeps everything to himself. I guess he can be allowed to lose a little control some time."

"Well, he sure got mad. You gotta admit that, Mumma."

"It's just from being here all alone, never having anybody in the house. I guess when someone does come he just wants it to be right."

"Well, I'm somebody too."

"Sure, but we're not company. Just try not to argue any more. Why don't you go out and get those groceries moved into our car? I sure don't want to be up the whole darn night."

"Okay, Mumma. As soon as I finish this beer."

Frenchie makes an attempt to rise. "Help me up. Come on Blackie, help me up. I gotta go to the can."

"Oh Jesus." Blackie puts down beer, tries to help Frenchie to his feet. They struggle. Finally Frenchie manages to stand with Blackie supporting him. They sway together. Blaze grabs the bottles out of the way. They go off left, staggering together. We hear pounding on door and, "Hey Dad, I gotta get Frenchie in there. Hurry up. Give someone else a turn."

Blaze sinks into chair right, curls up sideways with head in her arms. Tare enters, walks over to her, puts hand on her head. She looks up.

"How can you put up with that bastard?"

"Dad! How can you say that?"

"Why the hell he drinks when he's got you. If you ever want to get away, you could come here."

"No. I've got to work it out myself. Can't we just get Frenchie home so we can all get some sleep? I'm dead tired."

"Yeah, poor girl. We'll get going as soon as they're finished in there. I just want you to know, you have a place here if things get too bad."

"Well, thanks Dad. But even if I decide to leave him, I couldn't come here. I'd want to get right away. Maybe go to the coast.... But I wonder if, well, if you didn't call for him to go out quite so much. Sometimes he'd stay in if you didn't...."

Much noise cuts her off. Blackie and Frenchie stagger back in, holding each other up. They are laughing as they lurch from side to side. "Hey old Frenchie-the-guest, you feel better now, don't you? That was quite a load you had to get rid of in there."

"Don't talk to me like that in this house."

"Well, be *my* guest." Blackie pushes Frenchie to couch. They both collapse onto it, struggling and laughing. Blackie sings loudly: "Kaaaathleeeen Mavoooournin" but he cannot remember any more words, so fills in with "Da da, dah, da, da,dah."

Tare emerges from kitchen with drinks in glasses. "Here you go, Frenchie. Have one last one before we hit the road. You don't get to town very often. Lord knows when we'll see you again." He leans over Blackie. Blaze moves to interfere but doesn't. "And here's one for you, Son." He sits on the arm of the couch next to him, gives him the glass, puts his arm around his neck. "Drink her up lads." He hugs Blackie's head to him and sways back and forth. "That'll fix up your old jaw a bit." Blaze has been watching but now puts her head down wearily.

Blackie drinks, then leans into Tare. "Oh, that was nothing. I can't even feel it." He looks up at Tare. "We'll be going hunting next week, eh Dad? We'll show them how the old magnum can roar."

"Sure, we'll be hunting. Old partners like you and me." He takes the glass from Blackie's hand and holds it to his mouth. "Drink up, Son."

Frenchie holds his glass between his knees and now slumps over to the far side. Blaze appears to be asleep. Tare gets up, sets the glass down, then suddenly brings his fist up hard against Blackie's head, knocking him onto the floor. Blaze jumps up with a startled scream. "Dad! What are you doing to him? What are you doing?"

Tare reaches down and helps Blackie back onto the couch. "Never mind, Girl. You keep outta this." He pushes her back to her chair with one arm.

Blackie tries to stand. He is grinning at Tare. "Sure, we're partners. We'll go hunting together." His eyes keep closing and he opens them with effort. "Dad and me."

Tare reaches across the counter for the liquor bottle. Blaze is crying. "Oh, Dad, don't give him any more. Please don't give him any more."

Tare ignores her. He holds the bottle to Blackie's mouth. "Have another little drink, Son, before we hit the road."

Blackie draws back, coughing, then stands up. Liquor and blood run down his chin. "Good old Dad. Always got a drink for a guy."

He is about to fall but Tare supports him. "Stand up there like a man for once." He lets go of him, hits him hard again, knocking him this time in front of Blaze's chair. He crashes onto the record player. Frenchie sits up blinking.

Blaze yells, "What are you doing to him? What's wrong with you?" She drops to the floor beside Blackie. "You've really hurt him. And look, you've broken the tooth right off his denture." She examines his head and face.

Tare looks into the record player, picks up a piece of broken record and dashes it to the floor. "You little bastard!" He pushes Blaze aside. She falls back by the chair. He rolls Blackie over onto his back, his hands at his throat. "You bloody bastard. You goddam little Indian bastard."

Blaze gets to her feet, screaming, and leaps at Tare. She hits at his back, then at his hands, but she cannot get them free. She looks quickly about her, runs to the hall, returns with the hackamore in her hands. She laces him across the back of the neck with it. He lets go and lunges for it but she jumps back. They stand facing each other, one on each side of Blackie, she with the hackamore poised, he grabbing at his neck. Tare backs to the chesterfield and sits down. Blaze helps Blackie to his feet. He has blood all over his face and he is so groggy that he has to cling to Blaze in order to stand.

He grins and makes a move toward Tare. "Oh, there you are, Dad."

Blaze holds him back. "You keep away from him." She guides him to chair, crosses quickly to kitchen, comes back with a damp cloth.

He turns again to Tare. "Hey there, Dad."

She shouts, "You keep away!"

"Keep away from Dad? We're old partners." He sways forward, almost falls out of chair.

"You keep away from him, do you hear?" She whips the hackamore across his arm. "He just tried to kill you!" He sits back, bleary-eyed and surprised. "Now lean back!" She wipes his face carefully, then pushes his boots over to him. "Put those on." She returns the cloth to the sink and, still carrying the hackamore, picks up Blackie's coat and cap, crosses to him, steadies him while he gets into coat, places cap on his head. She turns and looks at Frenchie. He immediately struggles up, staggers to the hall and gets his coat. She helps him into it, turns and gets Blackie to his feet again. "Now get to the car, both of you!"

The two men exit, holding onto each other. Blaze steps into her boots, and then out of them again immediately. She removes Tare's socks, rolls them up and tosses them on the couch beside him, steps into boots again, puts on coat and begins tying scarf around her head.

Tare gets to his feet. "What about the groceries?"

"I'll manage them. A few groceries are nothing compared to what's gone on here tonight."

Steadying himself, he looks at her directly, for the first time. "There's no coming back after this, you know."

"You bet there's no coming back. I've forgiven you and taken you back before. But this is it! You talk about me leaving Blackie. Well, I'm going to get free of the both of you! NO coming back!" She throws the hackamore down beside the socks.

"You can be goddam fuckin' right there's no coming back!"

She exits. Tare sinks slowly back down onto the chesterfield as the door slams behind her.

PRESS

COMING CLEAN

    YOU have been faithful and responsive readers and, I hope, forgiving. YOU suffered the initial awkwardness of the presentation, the rather forced imagery of the Lotus Flower Game, and then, later, the disappearance of YOUR narrator and the emergence of the narrative, first, by the town, then by the setting, then by the main characters themselves. I appreciate what you went through, believe me, and I must make amends. To do so, I want to use this final section as my own personal "Press," a kind of forum: a place to apologize to YOU, a place to clear up one huge deception.

    In Chapter One when Babe asked Blaze why she couldn't write her own story, Blaze said, "I'm too close to it. Too involved." That is where the deception began. I might as well say it right out:

    I, Blaze, am actually the one who wrote *Big Rock Candy Town*. I admit it was a shoddy thing to do to YOU, thus my apology. Please try to understand; it was the only way I could do it. First of all, it was terribly unfair to ask my young sister to take on the task. She was never even very interested in writing. And second, how could she possibly have enough information to go on to write my story? the town's story? Sure, setting her up with all those books to read may have worked (actually it did work but in another way: she is now writing her own story, the story of a young girl who returned to a Rocky Mountain town and ended up on a honeymoon in Greece), but she needed the substance, the content, as well as the technique.

    The idea actually came from her. I knew I wanted to write about my whole time in Fernie but I couldn't think of any way to handle it. When I said to her that I felt I couldn't get enough distance to do the job, that what I needed was separation, she (in her usual winsome and practical way) said, "Then why don't you pretend you're someone else? Why don't you just pretend it's me writing it?" I hugged her hard for that. I knew immediately that she'd hit it just right.

So I had a sense of the method; what remained was to get the time and the space to write it. But that all worked out too: after the big fight, after all the triviality that I've tried to show building up into a dramatic ending, Blackie saw that I was right to get a separation. His reasons certainly weren't the same as mine, though. He said he was taking Tare's advice that "a guy should be able to drink when he feels like it, especially after he's been in the mine all week." When Tare found out he was quoting him around town to explain our break-up, he got him to move in with him; Blackie became his boarder. I had certainly and irrevocably discovered that there was nothing I could expect of either of them; I separated from both.

Separation. It has its benefits, but it has its costs. Now I must separate from Babe too, the only one left who is really family to me; and from Fernie, the town with its mountains, its river, its rich texture of people and events; and, finally, from YOU (now I dare say it), *my dear readers.*

When this story is published, I will dedicate it, first, to my sister, who made its very existence possible; and second, to my town, which offered itself, with all its complexities, as backdrop.

If there is a fitting way to end, it is simply to say that when it comes down to it, we need separation — in order to begin again — if we are to write our own story.

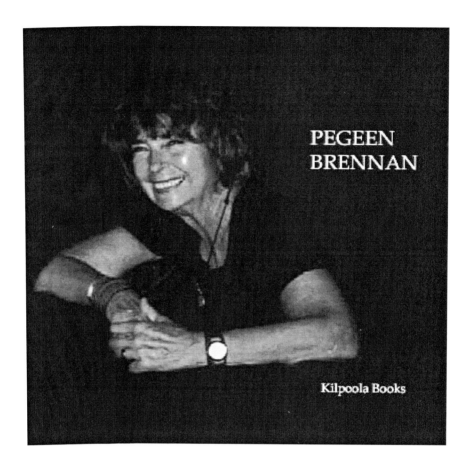

Pegeen Brennan was born in the Cariboo District of British Columbia and spent her childhood years in B.C., Alberta, and Ontario. She moved back to British Columbia in the Fifties.

She was on faculty at the University of British Columbia for over twenty years. Now retired, she lives with her husband, Lee Whitehead, in Kilpoola, B.C. (near Osoyoos.)

Her ficton and poetry have appeared in various literary magazines; she has published one novel: *Zarkeen* (Quadrant Editions, Concordia University, Montreal, 1982), and three books of poetry: *Release, Word Thaw, and Thirteen Curses for Burial.*

ISBN 1-4120-1426-3